WINGS OF WAR

WINGS OF WAR

WAR OF THE ALLIANCE

1

TARA GRAYCE

LCCN: 2024905353

ISBN: 978-1-943442-57-7

DWARVEN MOUNTAINS
AFRISTANI PLAINS
MT. DETMUK
Milnissi River
WESTE
TERMIN

KOSTARIA
OSMANA
PEACE BRIDGE
Gulmorth River
TARENHIEL
LETHOREL
ESTYRA
DANORBIC OCEAN
DAR GORANTH
BRIDGETOWN
FORT LINDER
FORT DEFENSE
Hydalla River
TYNE RIVER
ALDON
FORT CHARIBERT
TREEHAVEN
WHITEHURST MOUNTAINS
LANDRI
ESCARLAND
MONGAVARIAN EMPIRE
Frogg's Hollow
GROYRIA
RN RAIL
NAL
N
W
E
S
THE WORLD OF THE
ALLIANCE KINGDOMS

CHAPTER

ONE

"Keep your guard up, Fieran!"

Fieran Laesornysh scrambled to get his practice swords up, but not soon enough. His father's sword whipped past his head, so close he felt the brush of the breeze and the crackle of his father's magic coating the blade. Fieran stumbled backwards on the slushy dirt, trying to gain space to get his swords up before his father's next strike.

His father, the legendary elven warrior Farrendel Laesornysh, was all crackling magic, flying silver-blond hair, and arcing twin swords.

With a war cry, Fieran's sister Adriana, usually called Adry, leapt forward, her own twin swords flashing and her blue magic—identical to Fieran's and their father's—crackling down her blades and sparking against the ground at her feet. Her strawberry-blonde hair tossed around her face, her blue eyes flashing with the light of battle.

Dacha—elvish for *father*—fended her off easily, and still had enough time to block Fieran's next attack as well.

Adry whirled, swinging her swords even faster. She

1

always had taken to the morning sword and magic practices more than Fieran had. Oh, he didn't mind the swords or training with the powerful elven magic he'd inherited from his dacha. It was the discipline of it that grated on him.

That, and he preferred a gun in his hand more than a sword. Something he'd gotten from his human mother's side of the family. But swords were more useful for learning how to direct the elven magic, which tended to just incinerate bullets.

The magic would have incinerated the practice swords too, if they'd been using wooden practice swords instead of ones forged with dwarven magic that Dacha and Mama had given them when they came into their magic. Even then, Fieran still had to concentrate to keep his magic crackling along the blade instead of devouring it.

Fieran lunged again, his swords coated in magic. Dacha blocked his strike as easily as swatting away a fly.

Not too surprising. Fieran and Adry had been training with Dacha from the moment they had been old enough to hold a pair of wooden training swords, even before they'd come into their magic, but Dacha was the greatest living elven warrior. The stories of his exploits in the wars over seventy years ago were the stuff of myths.

"Fieran, the shield."

Dacha's mild tone made Fieran wince as he hurried to get a better grip on the dome of blue magic he was supposed to be holding in place. The magical shield ensured that the combined force of their magic didn't lash out and destroy the forested parkland in this back corner of their home of Treehaven in Fieran's mother's homeland of Escarland.

Each morning, Fieran and Adry took turns holding the shield to practice fighting with their magic and holding a protective barrier at the same time.

Dacha was big on practice.

Louise, one of Fieran's other sisters, sat cross-legged on a log to keep herself off the muddy ground as she held her magic in a second barrier around Fieran's. Her magic was a lighter blue, almost white, yet she still wielded the magic of the ancient kings that everyone in Fieran's family had, even if it was a milder form of it. While she trained in swords like the rest of them, she preferred to practice her magic in other ways.

She waved her hand and sparked her magic against his, shooting him a look for letting his magic get even that much out of control.

Oops. Fieran settled his grip on the power flooding from him, both into the air, across the ground, and coating his blades.

The whipping of a blade through the air snapped his attention back to Dacha, and Fieran barely ducked in time to avoid Dacha's sword. Fieran scrambled backwards, getting his swords back up. He'd let himself get distracted with the shield and had lost the rhythm of the sword fight before him.

Dacha whirled to parry Adry's swing, his movements fluid, his long elven hair flying around him. Dacha's silver-blue eyes glinted hard, flashing with that warrior's light he always got when wielding his swords and magic. Fieran could only imagine how terrifying his dacha had been when he'd earned the warrior title Laesornysh, meaning "Death on the Wind" in elvish.

It was a warrior name Fieran inherited rather than earned, something most elves would never let him forget, even if they didn't dare say such things around his dacha or his uncle Weylind, the king of the elves of the kingdom of Tarenhiel.

Dacha's sword snagged his, and the next thing Fieran

knew, one of his swords was flying out of his hand to land with a splat in a patch of slush. The flat of Dacha's sword rested across his chest. Across from him, Adry was breathing hard, Dacha's other sword resting on her shoulder.

Fieran sighed and lowered his remaining sword. He mentally grabbed his magic, wrestling with the surging power for a moment before he cut it off, letting the magic in the air fizzle out into a burst of sparks. He swiped his sleeve over his forehead, smearing sweat despite the chill air of the late winter morning. Strands of his short red hair stuck to his forehead. "I know, you don't have to say it. I was distracted this morning."

Adry, too, let her magic dissipate into the air. She grinned at him as she sheathed her swords across her back. "Nothing new for you."

Finally, Dacha lowered his swords and released his magic. A slight sheen glistened on his forehead, but he didn't appear quite as sweat-soaked and grimy as Fieran felt.

It sure would have been nice to inherit a bit more of that elven glow. Instead, Fieran sweated gross, more like a human than an elf.

Dacha sheathed his swords and spoke quietly with Adry, likely telling her she had done well that morning.

Louise pushed to her feet, swiping a strand of her white-blonde hair behind her ear. She glared at Fieran. "You distracted me. I might have burned some of the trees if I lost control."

"Sorry about that." Fieran grinned as he retrieved the sword he'd lost.

At least there wasn't much she could have burned. All the trees around them were spindly and bare, not yet even budding with spring. No undergrowth sprouted yet, leaving the loam a muddy mess beneath their boots.

Louise just rolled her eyes, then brushed off her clothes as Dacha turned to her.

Adry shared a glance with Fieran, then broke into a run, her boots squelching on the forest floor. "Dibs on the zip line!"

"No fair!" Louise took off after Adry, racing toward the tree that held the end of the zip line linking this back corner of Treehaven with the rest of the expansive estate.

Fieran sighed and sheathed his swords. He would have joined the race for the zip line, but Dacha was turning to him, something severe in his gaze this morning.

Dacha's hard warrior mask hadn't faded yet, and his swords rested far more easily across his back than Fieran's did his. "You were particularly undisciplined this morning, sason."

That elven word for *son* showed the warmth to Dacha's words beyond the flint in his eyes. Elves often addressed each other by their familial relationship. More than merely stating the relationship, it was an endearment that signified particular closeness.

"Yes, yes, I know." Fieran shifted, glancing away.

Dacha sighed, crossing his arms. "War is coming, Fieran."

He nodded, though he didn't meet his dacha's eyes. For nearly seventy years, the Alliance Kingdoms of Kostaria, Tarenhiel, and Escarland had been on the brink of war with the increasingly powerful Mongavarian Empire. But recently, reports of Mongavarian soldiers in the ogre kingdom of Groyria to the south of Escarland, increased production of Mongavarian airships, and their navy patrolling international waters off the coast of Kostaria, had all pointed toward war being imminent.

Fieran shrugged and gestured to his dacha. "It won't be

much of a war. The Wall will keep Mongavaria from invading."

The Wall was a magical barrier that Fieran's dacha had created sixty-nine years ago, with help from Fieran's uncles Weylind, king of the elves, and Rharreth, king of the trolls. The Wall had initially stretched between Escarland and Mongavaria, but over the years, it had been expanded to fully surround all three Alliance Kingdoms. As much as the Mongavarian Empire might want to invade, they couldn't get past the Wall.

All they could do was go over it with airships and the newfangled aeroplanes. The Wall was powerful, but it could only extend so far into the sky. Still, airships and aeroplanes couldn't launch much of an invasion all by themselves.

"They will figure out a way eventually. War creates invention." Dacha held Fieran's gaze, his silver-blue eyes especially stern this morning.

Fieran gave a slight shrug at that. He was rather familiar with inventions. Inventing had, after all, defined most of his life.

Over sixty years ago, Dacha, Uncle Iyrinder, and Uncle Lance had started the Alliance Magical Power Company—AMPC—which created magical power cells with Dacha's magic. Those magical power cells fueled Escarland's entire infrastructure, from trains to motorized vehicles to aeroplanes.

Fieran had grown up helping where he could, then he'd gotten a degree in magical engineering so that he was certified to use his magic to fill power cells. His sisters Adry and Louise also worked at AMPC, though Louise was the only one who had inherited Dacha's love of fiddling and inventing. Fieran and Adry just did it because it was something to do with their magic.

Dacha reached out and gripped Fieran's shoulders, tighter than was usual for the elven-style shoulder hug. "When war does come, our family will be expected to take the brunt of the fighting. You will need to be ready, sason."

Fieran tried to nod solemnly, even if his heart was racing more with excitement than fear. Was it bad that he was almost eager for this long-awaited war to *finally* start? War would be his chance to prove he was worthy of carrying the name Laesornysh and wielding the magic of the ancient kings, as the elves called it. "I'll be ready, Dacha. You've trained all of us well."

Dacha's gaze searched his face before he sighed and shook his head with an almost resigned tilt. He released Fieran's shoulders and stepped back. "Go on. Breakfast must be nearly ready."

Fieran grinned, his mouth already watering at the thought of bacon. If he hurried, he might even have time for a quick shower. His family would appreciate it if he didn't reek of body odor at breakfast.

As he spun on his heel to race for the zip line tree, Uncle Iyrinder and Merrik strolled into view, weaving between the trunks of the barren winter trees.

Uncle Iyrinder wasn't really Fieran's uncle, nor was Uncle Lance. But as Dacha's friend, business partner, and one-time guard, Uncle Iyrinder and Aunt Patience were pretty much always there during Fieran's childhood. They owned a house here on the Treehaven estate, and they lived in a house on the forest floor near where Fieran's parents lived in Tarenhiel. Calling them aunt and uncle had come naturally.

Merrik, Uncle Iyrinder's and Aunt Patience's oldest, was only two years younger than Fieran, and the two of them had basically grown up like brothers. With hair that was shades of red—though Fieran's was bright red and Merrik's was a darker brown-orange chestnut—they were often mistaken for brothers.

While Merrik had inherited a bit more of the elven mannerisms from his elven father, including wearing his hair long, Fieran had always had a bit too much human in him. Too loud. Too boisterous. Too unconcerned with dirt and grime. Even his hair was just annoying the times he'd tried to wear it long. Despite using the magical elven shampoo and conditioner Aunt Illyna made, Fieran's hair still lacked that little extra something that elven hair had.

Another way Fieran just couldn't measure up to his dacha.

As Uncle Iyrinder joined Dacha, Fieran strode to Merrik's side and bumped his shoulder. "Done communing with the trees this morning?"

Merrik rolled his eyes. "Done causing explosions?"

"Not a chance." Fieran grinned and reached for the bottom rung of the ladder formed of living roots and branches that stretched down from the tree. "The latest shipment of engines for testing should be arriving today. You know how I love blowing a few of those up."

Merrik sent another look heavenward. "You have a problem, you know that? No one should love explosions that much."

"Explosions are a natural part of invention. Just ask Uncle Lance." Fieran scrambled up the ladder, then onto the higher of the two platforms grown from the tree using elven plant magic. A stainless-steel cable disappeared into the distance among the forest of Treehaven.

"There is a difference between an accidental explosion in the name of invention and relishing destruction." Merrik climbed up the ladder after him, resting his elbows on the edge of the platform as he waited for Fieran to get out of the way.

"But blowing stuff up is so much fun." Shooting Merrik one last grin, Fieran grabbed the handle that hung down from a pulley, then launched himself off the platform with a whoop. He was supposed to use the safety harness, but he and his siblings rarely bothered to take the time.

Merrik followed, also not bothering with the safety harness. He might protest Fieran's recklessness, but he was secretly just as bad.

Fieran whipped between the trees. The cold air slapped his face, smelling of that particular late winter mix of wet earth and fresh air that hinted of the coming spring. The pulley hissed against the cable until Fieran slowed as he reached another platform. This one formed a hub of lines, going off in various directions.

From this platform, Fieran could see the estate's original brick manor house, which had been claimed by Uncle Lance and Aunt Illyna. To one side of that, a large barn had been expanded and converted into a workshop that Uncle Lance, Uncle Iyrinder, and Dacha used when tinkering with inventions they weren't ready to unveil just yet. Their main inventions and power company was based in nearby Aldon, the capital city of Escarland.

Fieran's family's home, a large wooden manor house, was set to the other side of the broad lane from the brick manor, though they were shielded from each other with thick stands of trees. Uncle Iyrinder's and Aunt Patience's smaller house was tucked farther back in the woods.

With one last glance at Merrik, Fieran grabbed the handle for the zip line toward his parents' manor house and flung himself off the platform again. He zipped through the trees, the line lowering until his feet touched the ground.

The line dumped him out at the base of the tiered garden that ringed the balcony at the back of the turreted manor house perched on a small hill. A brick staircase wound up the terraces with iron handrails bordering each side.

Fieran launched himself up the stairs. Only a few steps up, something rolled beneath his foot, and he nearly tripped. He grabbed one of the iron handrails before he could face-plant into the bricks.

"Fieran!" His brother's voice rang from somewhere farther up the stairs.

Fieran froze, glancing down. He'd stepped on a row of toy soldiers, knocking them over and breaking one of them.

The stairs above him also had row upon row of soldiers, meticulously lined up. The soldiers were humans, elves, and trolls, all painted in bright colors and wielding a variety of weapons.

"Sorry!" Fieran shifted his feet, trying to find a safe spot. He fumbled to re-align the soldiers, but he couldn't get them as neat as they had been before.

"You are just making it worse." His brother Tryndar sounded even more indignant.

He glanced up to find Tryndar—his only brother and youngest sibling—with his bare feet braced against one handrail, his toes gripping the spindles, and one hand on the other rail in complete disregard for the cold winter morning. With his free hand, he was arranging soldiers on a step. His silver-blond hair tumbled around his face and shoulders, long and flowing like an elf child's.

While Tryndar was ten years old, he aged slower than a human but faster than a full elf. That put him more like five years old in human years.

That made quite the age gap between him and Fieran. At 68 in half-elf years, Fieran was about 136 for an elf, 21 to 23 for a human. The whole slow aging thing wasn't so bad, except for the fact that his parents only looked like they were 35 or so in human years since their aging had slowed so much. It got a little awkward when his parents looked more like his siblings than his actual siblings did.

"Sorry, sorry." Fieran stopped messing with the toy soldiers. Instead, he straddled the railing and shimmied up it so that he didn't knock over any more of his brother's carefully arranged warriors.

When he reached where Tryndar was braced across the stairs, Fieran rolled off the railing onto a step clear of toys. Before his brother had a chance to move, Fieran swept Tryndar up, then dangled him upside down. "Hey, monkey."

Tryndar gave a laughing shriek, wiggling and swinging in Fieran's grip. "I am not a monkey! I am an elf!"

"Really?" Fieran grinned at the running joke between him and Tryndar, ever since they'd visited the Aldon Zoological Park and Tryndar spent a full hour just watching the monkeys. "You shriek like a monkey. And wiggle like a monkey. And climb like a monkey. I think you must be a monkey."

"No!" Tryndar giggled harder, swinging around to put himself almost right side up. Once Fieran set him on his feet, Tryndar gestured at himself. "See. I am an elf."

"Hmm. Yes. You're right. You're an elf." Fieran squeezed his brother's shoulder, then turned his attention to the epic battle Tryndar had arranged. "Who's winning?"

"The Alliance, of course." Sitting cross-legged on the step, Tryndar rolled his eyes, as if that much should be glaringly obvious.

"Ah, of course." Fieran pointed at one of the elven warriors, this one with long blond hair and wielding two swords. It was hard to tell on the small figurine, but the face was a decent facsimile. "Is that Dacha?"

"Yes." Tryndar waved his hands and made a noise, as if trying to imitate the crackle that Dacha's magic made.

Fieran grinned and called up a hint of his magic, then let it crackle down the stairs, spreading out around the figurine of their dacha.

Tryndar sighed, his silver-blond hair lying so magically tamed and flowing around his shoulders. He swung bright green eyes up at Fieran. "I cannot wait until I get magic."

"I know it's hard to wait, but you'll come into your magic eventually. We all did." Fieran tapped Tryndar's forehead with a magic-laced finger.

"I suppose." Tryndar heaved a sigh. Then he wrinkled his nose. "You smell."

Fieran sniffed at his shirt. A bit ripe. A shower was definitely in order.

"There the two of you are." Mama strode down the steps. Her hair—red as Fieran's—draped in its customary braid down her back. She wore a simple, Escarlish-style brown skirt and light blue shirt. "It's time to come in and wash up for breakfast."

"Aw, Mama." Tryndar hopped to his feet. "Do I have to?"

"You can leave everything set up and come back after breakfast. But you can't eat bacon with grubby fingers." Mama turned Tryndar's hands over, showing off the black, sooty marks from rubbing against the iron handrails.

"Bacon is eaten with a fork, not fingers." Tryndar's nose wrinkled in that very elven way of showing disgust that he'd inherited from Dacha. Along with his propensity to use a fork for bacon rather than getting his fingers greasy.

But the sight of his dirty hands was enough to send him scampering toward the house.

Mama swept her gaze from Tryndar to Fieran, her eyebrows raising. "You need to wash up before breakfast even more than Tryndar."

Fieran peered down at himself. The rail had left a dirty streak down the center of his clothes, smeared into the darker spots where sweat had soaked through his shirt. Not that more dirt mattered at this point when added to all the sweat and grime from training.

"Don't want to smell me while eating?" Fieran grinned and gave her a quick good morning hug. Because what else was he going to do but distribute hugs when he was this gross and sweaty?

CHAPTER
TWO

After his shower, Fieran followed the raucous sounds of laughter to the dining room.

Most of the family was already gathered there. Adry lunged past Elliana, Fieran's youngest sister, to reach for the plate of bacon. Her red hair in a braid similar to Mama's, Ellie lifted her book out of the way and stuck out her tongue at Adry. Louise smothered her pancakes with syrup while Tryndar bounced in his seat as he valiantly tried to keep his syrup from drooling into his eggs.

Mama sat at one end of the table, her green eyes bright as she listened to the cacophony. Tryndar was telling her about his soldiers. Adry chattered about practice that morning.

Fieran plunked into his seat and took the plate of bacon from Adry. "Telling Mama all about my embarrassing sword practice this morning?"

"Nope." Adry gave him a far too innocent expression in return.

"Of course you didn't." Fieran piled bacon and eggs on his plate.

The door opened, and Dacha strode inside, his hair wet

down his back. He took his seat at the head of the table, though he didn't add anything to the general hubbub. The elven moss earplugs tucked into his ears kept the noise level from becoming too overwhelming for him.

Fieran claimed one of the daily newspapers that had been tossed into the center of the table and flicked through it. The headlines were filled with speculations about the possibilities of war alongside another scandal from the Escarlish royal family. Fieran didn't know that set of cousins —well, cousins several times removed—but they were forever getting up to some scandal or another, much to his ninety-seven-year-old uncle Averett's chagrin.

After flipping to the second page, Fieran stilled, taking in the column. Both the Tarenhieli and Escarlish Flying Corps were actively recruiting new pilots. For the past year, the Flying Corps had been recruiting *trained* pilots. But they were now ready to take on new recruits with the intent to begin joint operations between the two Corps in the near future.

Flying. The rush of air. The whoosh of the breeze beneath the wings of his aeroplane. Something inside Fieran soared.

Better yet, Dacha had never fought in a flyer. He was a warrior of swords and hand-to-hand combat. If Fieran fought the coming war in the infantry, he would always be the second-best warrior, after his dacha.

But he could make his own legends in the sky.

Not that he resented his dacha. But always carrying the burden of those legends grew wearisome, especially when he could never measure up.

Fieran shoveled the last of his eggs into his mouth, grabbed both his plate and the newspaper, and hopped to his feet. "Adry, Weezer, I'll meet you at the carriage house to drive into Aldon."

Louise rolled her eyes at the childhood nickname. Adry just flapped a hand at him, still locked in conversation with Elliana, who was sneaking glances at her book.

If Fieran were to guess, all Ellie wanted was for Adry to stop talking so she could disappear back into her book, which appeared to be the latest Star Forest novel, a very fictional, highly inaccurate adventure romance story about an elf warrior falling in love with a human princess in the bygone days when the elven empire ruled the continent. The novels had recently been turned into a moving picture sensation sweeping across both Tarenhiel and Escarland.

Sticking the newspaper under his arm, Fieran hurriedly washed his plate and fork. Then he dashed out the back door, slid down the iron railings to avoid Tryndar's toy warriors, and raced down the path.

Uncle Iyrinder and Aunt Patience's house was tucked into a glade in the forested parkland. While the two-story house was built in the square, box-like Escarlish style, it had live trees at each corner with a roof formed of interlaced branches. Several neat gables peeked through the branches, adding more light for the upstairs. The front porch had pillars formed of living trees.

Skidding to a halt, Fieran knocked on the door, hardly able to stand still on the back step.

The door opened, and Aunt Patience stood there with a crisp white apron over her blue floral print dress, her blonde hair in a neat bun at the back of her head. "Fieran. Is anything wrong?"

"No, nothing's wrong. Everyone's fine. Is Merrik done eating yet?" Fieran rocked back and forth from heels to toes, barely restraining himself from rushing inside and grabbing Merrik by the arm like he used to when they were both boys. He'd dragged Merrik away from many a meal, filled with ideas for a new game or a new fort or some other grand scheme.

Merrik appeared behind his mother, still holding his plate of pancakes. "So eager to start blowing up test engines?"

"Yes, but it isn't that." Fieran clenched and unclenched his fingers so he didn't just haul Merrik outside.

Merrik sighed, shoved the rest of his pancake in his mouth, and handed his plate to Aunt Patience. He eased past her, shutting the door behind him on the way out. "Well, what is it?"

At least, that was what Fieran thought he said past his mouthful of pancakes.

Fieran unfurled the paper and jabbed his finger at the column. "Look. The Flying Corps is actively looking to recruit *new* pilots. For training."

Merrik swallowed, then took the paper from Fieran, scanning the news story quickly. Finally, he lifted his gaze and eyed Fieran. "You want to enlist."

"Yes! I'm sure your dacha has been pushing you as hard in training as my dacha has. War is coming. If we wait to join up, then we'll spend the first months of the war in training and miss everything." Fieran gestured, trying to put into words all the desperate hunger in his chest. "This way, we can choose our own path instead of being drafted into the infantry. We can *fly*, Merrik. Thanks to the Wall, that's where the real war will be. In the air."

"You want to join the Flying Corps." Merrik huffed it out as a statement, all but rolling his eyes. "What about joining the navy? Everyone knows the war will be fought with airships rather than flyers."

"You know I've wanted to fly from the first time I saw that aeroplane show a few years ago." Fieran jabbed a finger at the paper. "If we enlist in the navy, there's no guarantee we'd even be stationed on an airship. Even if we were, we'd just be two ensigns among many. If we are in the army's Flying Corps, we'll be officers in charge of our own aeroplanes. With the lack of trained pilots, we might find ourselves in command of our own squadrons within a few months."

"I do not think it will be that simple." Merrik shook his head with that long-suffering look he often wore around Fieran.

"Maybe not, but our odds of quick promotion are pretty high." Fieran grinned, already imagining a sharp uniform and a few officer braids adorning his sleeves.

Their odds of a quick death would be pretty high too. Aeroplane pilots had a tendency to crash and die frequently.

But they'd be in less danger of that than most. Everyone knew that the superior elven reflexes made them superior pilots, and elven flyer pilots died less frequently than human ones. Fieran and Merrik were half-elves. They'd be fine.

"You would last longer giving commands than taking them," Merrik muttered, half under his breath.

Fieran just waved that away. "This is our chance to finally *do* something. Something great. Not just twiddle our thumbs testing engines and following orders in our dachas' factory. We can be warriors, like our dachas were."

Merrik grimaced. "You are not going to let this go, are you? You will just enlist whether I do or not."

"Nope, and yep." Fieran probably should've felt bad that he was dragging Merrik along, as he always did. But this was far too exciting to hesitate.

Merrik heaved a sigh. "Escarlish or Tarenhieli Flying Corps?"

Thanks to having parents from Escarland and Tarenhiel,

both Merrik and Fieran were dual citizens and could join either army, if they wished.

"If we join the Tarenhieli Flying Corps, we'll just be seen as less than, never able to measure up to our dachas." Fieran frowned and shook his head. "I don't really want to be up there flying with a bunch of snooty elves who never let me forget that I'm only half the elf my dacha is. Of course, we'll end up in the sky with elves eventually since the Flying Corps intends to operate as one Allied unit, but at least we would answer to Escarlish commanders instead of elven ones, for the most part."

Merrik, too, frowned. "Many elves in the army have never forgotten that my dacha gave up the noble duty of guarding the king to follow your dacha to Escarland."

Not that Merrik's dacha had done anything wrong, but elves could be particular about certain things. There was also the little matter that long ago Fieran's dacha had been born an illegitimate prince. The elves never forgot that either, despite the legends.

"The EFC it is." Fieran would much rather join the Escarlish army, where he would be a famed elf who was physically stronger than those around him, than join the Tarenhieli army where he would be considered weaker.

"Yes." Merrik's jaw tightened, far more somber about this than Fieran was. "Fine. When do you want to sign up?"

"As soon as possible. Today, even. We're going to Aldon anyway. We can sign up during our lunch break."

"Today." Merrik crossed his arms, eyeing him. "Should we not think this through a little longer than that? Maybe talk it over with our dachas?"

The thought of telling his dacha was a weight thumping Fieran back to the ground. His dacha wouldn't be happy about this, even if he knew Fieran was going to have to fight, eventually.

"More time isn't going to change my mind. And…maybe we can hold off on telling our dachas until after we've done it?" If only there was a way Fieran could just avoid telling his dacha entirely. He wasn't looking forward to seeing the look on his face.

Merrik glanced over his shoulder at the closed door, something flicking through his eyes. Perhaps he had similar thoughts when it came to telling his own family because, after a moment, he nodded. "Fine."

Fieran held out his palm. "It's a deal."

"No, do not—"

Fieran spat onto his palm, then held out his hand to Merrik.

"Do we have to? It is rather childish." Merrik grimaced, not reaching for Fieran's hand.

"Come on. One last time. A sign of our enduring brother-hood as we go into battle together." Fieran wiggled his fingers, his hot spit sliding down his palm.

He and Merrik had sealed their deals with spit from the time they had been young and read a fiction series about an elf and a human who had become friends and like brothers during a time when the elves and humans had been at war with each other. The stories caught their imaginations, and they had pretended to be those two friends in many of their games, with Merrik as the elf and Fieran as the human.

"This is highly unsanitary and immature." Merrik spat onto his palm, then shook Fieran's hand, their spit squishing between them.

Merrik grimaced; Fieran grinned.

This was going to be a grand adventure. Fieran was finally going to fly.

THREE

Enlisting in the army was almost laughably simple. A stop at the military recruitment office in Aldon, a few pieces of paper, a few signatures, and Fieran had signed his life away. Merrik, too.

At least Fieran could easily pledge loyalty to Escarland's current king. His uncle Averett was ninety-seven years old, but he didn't look a day over seventy, thanks to being an elf friend with Fieran's uncle Weylind. The extra years given to a human who was an elf friend weren't quite like those given in a heart bond, which was what Fieran's mother shared with his dacha. Mama would live hundreds of years beyond what a normal human would. Uncle Averett would only gain a few extra decades.

Fieran and Merrik stepped from the recruiting office and into the bustle of Aldon's streets only a few blocks from Winstead Palace. A crush of people—from brawny, gray-skinned trolls in workers' worn garb to human women in neat shirtwaists and bustled skirts to newsies with grimy faces—milled along the sidewalks and spilled into the cobbled streets. The streets themselves were clogged with horse-drawn carriages and magically powered vehicles, the drivers of each shouting at each other.

Fieran checked that his slouch cap was pulled low over his distinct red hair and the elven points of his ears while the collar of his coat was turned up against the brisk, late winter wind. He would rather not be recognized today.

Merrik still got a few second glances due to the elven style of his long hair cascading down his back. While trolls had become a common sight in Aldon, elves didn't usually take to the bustle and lack of trees in the large city.

Technically, the trolls were a form of elf as well—mountain elves rather than forest elves. But long animosity between the forest elves and mountain elves had led to the gray-skinned, generally white-haired mountain elves becoming their own culture and identity. They had embraced the formerly derogatory term "troll" for themselves, even though the tall, athletic mountain elves were far from the hulking, disgusting figures implied in the word "troll."

There was some talk about coming up with a different term that didn't have its root as an insult, but the trolls didn't want to go back to calling themselves mountain elves and no other term had caught on just yet.

After a brief stop at a soda parlor to purchase four bottles, Fieran and Merrik fought their way through the crowd to the nearest entrance to the Underground, the network of magically powered trains that ran beneath Aldon. Fieran and Merrik paid the fare, then climbed onto one of the train carriages, gripping one of the poles instead of bothering with seats.

The magically powered train clacked over the iron rails,

the cars vibrating slightly. The smooth walls of the troll-made tunnel closed around them, but the darkness was broken by white lights fueled by the magical power grid.

Fieran and Merrik hopped off only three stops later, climbing up the stairs and back out onto Aldon's streets.

Here, large factories filled whole blocks. A few still wafted plumes of smoke, but the days of a smoke haze were long gone now that most industry had switched to running on magic rather than coal.

The bustle had calmed as most people in this district of Aldon were occupied within the buildings at this time of day. Only those making deliveries or running errands hurried along these streets.

After only a short stroll, they reached the complex of eight massive buildings that comprised the AMPC, Uncle Lance's invention warehouse, and affiliated factories.

Fieran turned off the walk, entering beneath an arched sign for the Alliance Magical Power Company. He showed his badge to the security guards standing in the alley, though the guards—one troll and one human—were already waving him through. It wasn't like the guards couldn't easily recognize him.

To Fieran's left, the factory rang with the tings and screeches of metal as the workers constructed the empty magical power cells. On a walk overhead, a troll pushed a cart loaded with finished power cells from the building on the left to the warehouse on Fieran's right.

Fieran opened the door to the warehouse on the right and stepped inside. There, the well-lit space crackled with the taste of magic. To one side of the space, Adry stood behind a protective, tempered glass barrier next to one of the machines that filled the magical power cells. She touched her magic-laced fingers to a wire overhead. The magic leapt along the wire, over the barrier, and down into the magical power cell.

In front of the barrier, Louise wore a set of goggles as she flipped the switches and pushed the buttons that ran the machine, all while monitoring the dials that tracked power levels.

To one side, racks upon racks of filled power cells lined up on carts, waiting to be hauled to the next warehouse over, where they would await distribution to the various companies and people who purchased the magical power cells from the AMPC. Some of the power cells glowed with Adry's bright blue magic, but most of them flashed with Louise's more blue-white magic.

Something dinged, and Louise flipped a switch. The machine whirred down, and Adry cut off her magic.

As Merrik stepped inside behind Fieran and closed the door, Louise turned to the two of them. "What took you two so long? That was a rather generous lunch break."

"I fetched sodas." Fieran strolled across the warehouse, reached into the deep pockets of his coat, and presented each of his sisters with their favorites, the carbonated beverages sparkling inside glass bottles. The newfangled sodas were all the rage in Escarland.

Louise took the bottles from him, still eyeing him suspiciously. "Getting sodas still wouldn't have taken you this long."

Fieran just shrugged. He wasn't about to explain about signing up for the Flying Corps. He'd tell the whole family over supper. If he could work up the courage. His stomach twisted in knots every time he thought about telling Dacha what he and Merrik had just done.

Popping off the metal cap of his own soda, Fieran headed

for the other side of the warehouse, separated from the magical power cell filling machine by a thick stone wall reinforced with both troll stone magic and Dacha's magic.

On the other side of the protective wall, Merrik was already shrugging into padded coveralls made from thick canvas material. After placing his soda and coat on a table to one side, Fieran claimed his own set of coveralls, though his magic would likely provide more protection in the event of an explosion. But procedure was procedure.

He could follow rules and regulations when he put his mind to it. Joining the army wouldn't be that bad. Right?

Once Fieran had buttoned up the coveralls and wiggled his safety goggles into place, he strode to the line of magically powered engines waiting for testing. The company had sent over a randomly selected batch of ten engines for AMPC to test their compatibility and hardiness when the magical power cells were installed. Only after AMPC had certified that the engines were safe for their power cells could the company go into full-scale production of the new engines.

Merrik took up his post behind yet another protective barrier. He set his soda on the desk there, shoved the elven-made moss earplugs into his ears, then picked up a clipboard. He pointed with a pencil, his voice raised to compensate for his muffled ears. "We are up to engine six."

"Right." Fieran shoved his own earplugs into his ears and made his way to engine six.

That morning, the first five engines had held up decently well. None had exploded, so far. The only problem they had come across was that one of the power wires had a tendency to burn out when the engine was under particular strain. Not an uncommon problem when it came to dealing with the magic of the ancient kings.

Fieran wheeled engine six onto the testing floor and slid one of the cylindrical magical power cells into the space in the engine, locking it tight. "Starting test one of twenty."

"Test one. Check." Merrik made a note on his clipboard.

Together, Fieran and Merrik tested the rest of the engines. None of them exploded, sadly. The wire problem persisted, but that was manageable.

More manageable than telling his family what he'd done during his lunch break.

FIERAN COULDN'T KEEP his knees from bouncing as he sat at the dining table with his family. At least the table hid his nerves, as long as he refrained from bumping the table and rattling the dishes.

Adry and Louise chattered about how many magical power cells they filled that day. Mama and Ellie described the event they attended to announce the new collection of books translated from elvish now available at Aldon's largest library. Tryndar babbled about whatever he observed while spending the day with Dacha, though it was hard to understand exactly what Dacha and Uncle Lance had been working on in their top-secret invention workshop. Dacha didn't clarify.

Mama swallowed her bite of roast. "Fieran, you've been quiet."

Everyone else around the table paused their conversations, turning to him as they realized he hadn't been adding to the boisterous banter like he usually did.

Fieran drew in a deep, steadying breath, the roast he'd eaten sinking like a stone in his stomach. Time for his announcement. "During our lunch break today, Merrik and I enlisted in the Escarlish Flying Corps."

For a heartbeat, Fieran's entire family just gaped at him.

The book that Ellie had been not-so-secretly reading below the table hit the floor with a thump.

"What?" Louise dropped her fork into her roast.

"*That's* what you were doing?" Adry waved her fork, flinging bits of gravy into the air.

Tryndar blinked, as if he couldn't quite process what was going on.

Fieran shrugged and risked a glance at Dacha, his breath tight and aching in his chest. Of everyone, he was most nervous about Dacha's reaction.

Dacha had gone hard as stone, his jaw set, his gaze on his plate. After a strained moment, he shoved away from the table, spun on his heel, and marched from the room, the door swinging shut with a clunk behind him.

Fieran sagged in his chair, his stomach twisting into even more painful knots. All he wanted was for Dacha to be proud of him. Instead, it seemed Dacha was angry.

When Fieran managed to drag his eyes up from his plate again, he met Mama's gaze.

She was smiling that sad smile she wore as a mask even when it didn't fully reach her green eyes. "When do you leave for basic training?"

"A month from now." Fieran's throat was squeezing closed. He didn't think he could handle it if his mother gave him that disappointed look as well. "So I'll still be here for your birthday party next week."

As his mother was turning ninety years old—a prestigious age for any human, but one rarely reached while still looking as young as his mother did thanks to her elven heart bond with Dacha—the entire family, including some of his aunts and uncles, had a large celebration planned.

"I wasn't worried about that." The sad tilt to his mother's mouth remained. "How long will you be gone?"

"It's an accelerated training, so it will be basic training, flight school, and officer training all in one." Fieran shrugged. "And after that…"

He had no idea. He'd go wherever he was stationed. And when war broke out, well, who knew what would happen then.

Mama's shoulders heaved with a long breath, her voice burdened but steady. "With the war coming, it was inevitable that you'd enlist. All of us will be called upon to serve in one way or another once war breaks out."

Mama glanced around the table, her gaze lingering on Adry and Louise before she turned back to Fieran.

Something squeezed in Fieran's chest at the thought of his sisters getting dragged into the war. Adry would be fine. She fought better than he did most days, and she had that same fire in her that was driving him to enlist.

But Louise was quiet, her mind always spinning with mechanics and new inventions. She wouldn't do well, if asked to fight in a war.

At least Ellie and Tryndar would be spared from fighting, even if they'd still feel the effects of a war. At thirteen and five in human years, they were far too young and wouldn't come into their magic for many years yet.

Fieran would just have to contribute enough that none of the kingdoms thought to ask more from his sisters than they were willing to give.

Then again, Dacha would never let the Tarenhieli or Escarlish army call up Adry or Louise if they weren't willing. Neither would Uncle Weylind nor Uncle Averett. Adry and Louise would be fine.

Supper was finished in near silence, then Mama pushed to her feet. "Adry, Tryndar, it's your turn for the dishes. Louise, Ellie, you can help clear the table."

As Fieran's siblings jumped to obey, Mama tipped her head toward the door in a subtle command. Fieran followed her from the dining room and across the hall into the smaller of their two parlors.

Mama sat on the couch, shooing Munchkins, one of their orange tabby cats, out of the way.

Fieran sank onto the seat on the far side of the couch. "I know it's sudden, and I probably should have talked to you and Dacha first. But I…"

He wasn't sure what to tell his mama or how to describe that feeling inside him driving him toward this. Or admit that he hadn't dared tell them beforehand.

"You wanted a grand adventure. I understand." Mama leaned forward, running a hand down the cat's back as Munchkins huffily curled up next to her. A hint of her usual smile returned to her face. "I decided to marry your dacha after meeting him mere minutes before because an arranged marriage with an elf sounded like a grand adventure. I'm not angry. Neither is your dacha."

Fieran released a long breath. Thanks to the elven heart bond, his mama had a pretty good idea what Dacha was thinking at the moment. A heart bond didn't give them telepathy, but there was a certain awareness of each other and their emotions. At least, that was what Fieran had heard. "I'm sorry it's a shock."

"Not exactly a shock." Mama shook her head, a wry twist to her smile. "I was expecting something, though I wasn't sure what or when. You've been restless."

Fieran shifted, glancing away. He hadn't realized his mama had noticed the way his current life had begun to feel a little...small.

Mama trailed her fingers over the cat as Munchkins purred even louder. "Your dacha will adjust. He feels the weight of the coming war and our part in it very keenly."

"I noticed." Fieran leaned his elbows on his knees, rubbing a thumb against his palm. His palms still ached from sword training that morning.

Mama sighed, her gaze going unfocused as she stared out the window into the forested parkland. "Seventy years ago, we chose to avoid war and buy ourselves decades of peace to raise you children. The consequence of that choice is that we will have to watch you go to war. This war is of our making, but it will be yours to fight. That's not an easy thing for your dacha to come to terms with."

Fieran braced his hands on his knees to keep them from bouncing. At least talking about this with her was easier than with Dacha, who had the scars and the memories of torture in his eyes. "I'll be fine, Mama."

She looked up, blinking as if remembering he was there. She shook her head, a hint of a smile returning, though the smile didn't banish the sadness in her eyes. "I can see my words are making little difference. You can't hide your eagerness."

"I'm not eager, exactly. Just..." He wasn't quite sure how to describe it. He knew war was terrible. And he wasn't exactly hoping for war.

But if war was inevitable, then what was the harm of hoping he'd get his chance for glory and great deeds once it came?

Mama nodded, as if she understood what he wasn't saying. "Give your dacha time. He will come around.

Though I'll warn you, your morning training won't be easy for the next month. Your dacha was sent off to war unprepared and far too young. He doesn't want that for you."

"I know." Fieran grimaced, rubbing harder at the calluses on his palms. Mornings were majorly going to hurt from now on.

FIERAN FOUND his Dacha leaning against the railing of the patio balcony. A slight breeze toyed with his dacha's long elven hair while he stared unseeing into the nighttime forest.

Fieran rested his elbows against the railing. It took some doing, but he swallowed back his words and didn't immediately speak.

After long moments of silence, Dacha's shoulders hunched as he dropped his gaze from the distance. "You enlisted."

Fieran suspected his dacha wouldn't be pleased with his logic that they should join up now so they didn't miss any of the war. "Yes."

Dacha's shoulders slumped further, his head hanging. More long moments of silence stretched between them.

"I'm going to be all right, Dacha. I'll have Merrik to guard my back, and you've trained me well." Fieran shrugged, unable to keep the excited note from his voice.

"I have trained you to fight, but I have not trained you to kill. There is a difference." Dacha lifted his head, though he still did not look at Fieran. His voice held a raw, weighty note. "I mourn what I know you will lose."

Fieran swallowed. He wasn't sure what to say to that. While his dacha did not talk about the wars often, Fieran had seen the scars that traced thin lines over his dacha's wrists, arms, torso, and even his ankles. His dacha had been thrown into war when he was barely grown, far younger than Fieran was now. Dacha had been captured twice...and tortured twice.

"But, sason." Dacha turned to him and gripped Fieran's shoulders in the elven way of hugging. "I am proud of who you are now, and I will be proud of who you will become."

Great. His dacha so rarely said such heartfelt things. For once, Fieran was at a loss for words.

He returned his dacha's elven shoulder-hug and cleared his throat. "Linshi, Dacha."

The elvish *thank you* rolled easily from his tongue. Fieran had grown up speaking both elvish and Escarlish as his family spent half their time in Tarenhiel in the royal elven palace and half their time at their Escarlish estate.

Dacha released Fieran, and they both stepped back to lean against the railing again.

Fieran turned his face to the forest as the icy breeze brushed his face and ruffled his short red hair. Soon, that breeze would be the cold winds of the sky as he piloted his very own flyer.

After long minutes of quiet, Dacha abruptly gave a soft snort of a laugh and shook his head.

"What was that laugh for?" Fieran eyed his dacha. He hadn't expected laughter in the wake of his enlistment.

"Did you make your bed this morning?" Dacha raised his eyebrows.

"Uh, maybe? I don't remember."

"And your room? When was the last time you picked up your clothes?"

"Um..." Fieran winced, thinking about the clothes he'd left tossed on a chair and on the floor.

Dacha was smirking now, a knowing glint in his eyes.

"The discipline of the Escarlish military will be quite the shock for you, sason."

Fieran couldn't argue with that. Of course he would have to get used to making his bed and being neat and tidy with his clothing. But he could handle a little discipline.

And once he was in the air…nothing else would matter.

FOUR

Pippak Detmuk-Inawenys wiggled on her back underneath the train car, checking each of the devices that automatically applied grease to the bearings while the train was in motion. As she went, she looked for any loose or worn parts.

Dust rained down on her every time she brushed the underside of the carriage or gripped an axle. She scrubbed a sleeve over her protective goggles, but that just smeared the film of dust around.

So much dust. The trains and the cars picked it up as they rumbled back and forth across the Afristani prairies that separated the western edge of Escarland and Tarenhiel from the dwarven mountain kingdoms. If it wasn't dust, then it was mud. Lots and lots of mud and slush dripping onto her head.

Pip shuffled to the next wheel, then grimaced at the grease device, which was all gummed up with dirt and grime. She reached for her low cart of tools and pulled it closer, fishing around until she found her blue, elven light. Closer inspection with the light revealed that the bottom side of the wheel was ground slightly flatter than the rest, flakes of metal curling around the edges.

Well, that would explain the loud squealing the conductor had complained about. With the grease plugged up, the bearing had seized and the wheel no longer turned. It had probably been grinding most of the way on the return trip from the mountains. The linkages between this wheel and the others had warped and snapped, leaving the rest free to turn while this one skidded.

Pip picked up the right-sized wrench and put it on the nut of the center hub over the bearing. She called up her magic, sending it through the wrench into the nut. With her magic, she loosened the nut even as she turned with the wrench.

Having the ability to bend and move metal with her magic sure came in handy. Especially since her magic was rare. Perhaps even unique to only her.

Most dwarves had some kind of stone- or metal-working magic. But the magic operated differently than elven magic. Their magic needed a rhythm, and it was wrought alongside their picks or hammers in a different way than the trolls wielded their similar, but elven, stone magic.

Pip's metal magic came from her dwarf mother, but it operated like her father's elven magic, flowing out of her directly into whatever metal she wanted to work. Her magic was so strong that she could even create a solid barrier of pure magic with it, something only the strongest of the elves could do, whether that pure magic was plant or ice or stone.

While Pip's mother could work metal with her magic, she used her magic differently, not melding the metal as directly as Pip did. Muka's magic was more crafted, and she could do much that Pip couldn't do.

Once Pip removed the nut, she disassembled the seized

bearing, fixing what she could with her magic, replacing what she couldn't. After repacking the bearing and thoroughly greasing it, she reassembled everything, including replacing the broken linkages.

Finally, she rested her palm on the wheel and sent her magic into the metal, molding it so that it was no longer ground into a flat spot on the bottom. She had to thin the metal from other places around the wheel, but it wasn't enough to weaken it. Another mechanic would have had to regrind the wheel into shape.

After cleaning out the grease device, she topped off the grease before moving on to the next wheel.

The rest of the wheels needed nothing besides a bit of cleaning and a top off for the grease. She was just putting her tools back onto her cart when footsteps crunched in the gravel alongside the siding.

"Hey, Pipsqueak, are you finished with the inspection yet?" Mak, Pip's older brother, knelt as he peered beneath the train car.

"Just finished. One of the bearings seized, but I set it to rights." Pip gestured with one grease-stained hand at the problem wheel.

"Rather handy, your magic. I'll get this car moved back to the others." Mak slapped the wheel. "There's an elf official here asking for you. I left him in the front office."

"And you didn't lead with that?" Pip rolled onto her hands and knees, then crawled out from under the train car. As she stood, she dusted off her green coveralls, though the effort did little good beyond shaking off the worst of the dust. Grease smeared her hands, the sleeves of her coat, and probably her face.

She pulled the goggles onto her forehead, then checked that most of her hair was still up in a messy bun at the top of her head. Several strands had fallen out, but she wouldn't be able to fix it without a mirror.

Mak smirked and leaned his elbow on her shoulder. At over a foot taller than her, Mak had to bend over to do so. "If he's asking for you, then he should expect to find you a bit grimy."

From her position underneath his arm, Pip nudged Mak in the stomach with her elbow, making him step back with a laugh.

At only five feet tall, Pip had inherited their dwarven mother's diminutive height. While she wasn't stout like a dwarven woman, Pip carried a few more curves than an elven woman. At least she hadn't inherited dwarven facial hair, though her eyebrows were on the thick side. Her hair was sleeker like her father's but with a curl to it like her mother's while her skin was lighter than Muka's but darker than her elven father's pale, silver skin tone.

Mak had their elven father's height, though he was broader in the chest and shoulders and sported a thick brown beard unlike anything an elf male could normally grow. His brown eyes sparkled as he grinned down at her.

Pip swiped her hands on the front of her coveralls. Mak had a point. There wasn't much she could do about her appearance without a full shower and a change of clothes. "What does the official want?"

"He didn't say, but he had an official-looking document with the king's seal." Mak shrugged. "Dacha is waiting with him."

Pip nodded, her stomach sinking as she turned toward the railroad hub's main office. What could the king possibly want with her? She was just a half-dwarf, half-elf mechanic living on the far western edge of Tarenhiel, a place the elves who lived deeper in Tarenhiel's forests considered rustic in the extreme.

The railyard sprawled between the trunks of a stand of poplar trees. At this time of spring, the branches overhead were bare, lacking the pleasant canopy they'd provide in a few months. A few storage sheds were grown from the trees while open-sided roofed areas provided a place to park trains out of the weather. Train tracks wound between the trees, branching out from a turntable in a cleared space between trees.

The railyard bustled with activity, from elves using a crane to transfer cargo from one train onto a train that would take the goods deeper into Tarenhiel, to a human operating a small train engine to push cars from one siding onto another. Even a few half-humans and half-trolls mingled with the other workers, finding a haven here at the fringe of the kingdom away from the snooty society that looked down on those of mixed blood.

Many of the workers paused what they were doing to wave at Pip as she strolled by. As the boss's daughter, she could have been disliked. But everyone here knew that her family worked just as hard as everyone else, from her mother who was the chief mechanic to her father who handled the mountains of paperwork a railroad hub generated.

Pip set out through the maze toward the longest building at the far side of the yard. Oak trees grew in two neat rows that formed the two long sides of the building, their branches arching and intertwining to form a roof. The main maintenance facility also housed the office in a smaller building tucked to one side.

Here the trees weren't as massive and lofty as the trees found in the heart of Tarenhiel. While these trees would be considered large and old by the standards of most humans, they were normal-sized. Many of the elves in western Tarenhiel lived on the ground or in treehouses close to the ground, unlike the dwellings high in the trees found in other places of Tarenhiel. Strong winds often howled across the plains and battered this side of Tarenhiel, making tall trees and high homes impractical.

As she neared the building, sunlight sparkled off the broad Milnissi River that ran along one side of the railyard and formed the border between Tarenhiel and the Afristani Plains, a land populated by nomadic human tribes that formed a coalition. On the other side, a few spindly trees and scrub brush lined the river while rolling hills of grassland disappeared into the hazy distance.

A metal trestle bridge crossed the river, the dark line of railroad stark against the hills on the far side. Even as she watched, a train rumbled across, headed farther west. It would likely be carrying goods from all three of the Alliance Kingdoms for the markets of both Afristan and the dwarf kingdoms. Once empty, that train would return filled with dwarven-mined refined metals, which would be used all over the Alliance Kingdoms for everything from railroads to guns to dreadnought battleships in the Kostarian shipyards.

Halting before the door to the office, Pip took a moment to wash her hands in the slop sink just outside of the door, using the pumice stone scrub to scour as much grease as she could off her skin. She scrubbed her hands on her coveralls to dry them, though all she succeeded in doing was coating her hands with dust. Oh, well. The dust was better than grease.

Straightening her shoulders and standing as tall as she could manage, she opened the door and strolled into the office vestibule.

The walls were formed of living branches, a few twigs formed into coat hooks on the inside wall while a root formed a long bench along one side.

The elf official wasn't waiting on the bench. He stood in the center of the room with his arms crossed, his nose in the air, and a curl to his lip as his sharp gaze darted between her dacha and her muka.

Her dacha was a tall, lithe elf with an angular face, long brown hair braided along the sides in the style of the elves of western Tarenhiel, hazel-brown eyes, and skin so silver pale it was somewhere between porcelain and moonlight. As with many elves, he was handsome to the point of almost beautiful while his life behind a desk hadn't given him the muscles of the warrior elves.

Next to him, the top of her mother's head barely reached above his elbow. Muka—dwarven for mama—had a well-endowed figure that was all bosom and hips with no waist in between while her arms were well muscled. Her dark brown hair spiraled around her head in thick curls while her neat, feminine beard was curled and braided. Her skin was a bronze-brown with wrinkle lines around her dark brown eyes.

They were an odd pair. To the elves of Tarenhiel, Pip's mother was far from what was considered feminine beauty. Then again, to the dwarves of the mountains, Pip's dacha was far from the pinnacle of male strength.

As Pip stepped inside and closed the door behind her, the official elf gracefully turned to her. The curl to his mouth deepened as he swept a glance over her, as if assessing her from the dirt-smeared goggles in her messy hair to her dust-covered hands, and finally to her grease-begrimed coveralls.

Typical arrogant attitude from an elf from the capital,

Estyra. He, clearly, wasn't the type to get dirt underneath his prissy-clean fingernails.

In general, elves tended to have a superiority complex, and the elves in the central forests especially so. While dwarves weren't hated like the trolls had been nor were they seen as utterly inferior the way humans had been, dwarves were disdained as filthy and uncouth. Thanks to the Alliance, attitudes toward the trolls had drastically changed and even humans were seen with a little more tolerance. At least, the humans of Escarland were generally well-regarded.

But attitudes toward dwarves hadn't changed all that much.

Then again, dwarves didn't exactly like elves in return either, so it wasn't like elves had a monopoly on bad attitudes. The ability to be prejudiced was one thing that didn't discriminate.

"Are you Pippak Detmuk-Inawenys?" The elf official stumbled over her dwarven-sounding first name and the first part of her family name before he hit the final, elven half. Her parents' decision to combine their dwarf and elf family names created a mouthful.

He probably wouldn't appreciate it if she offered for him to call her just Pippa, which she'd found was easier for elves and less exotic for humans. She'd gone by Pippa for years while she had been away from home, studying magical engineering.

Though she wasn't going to offer her nickname of Pip. He didn't deserve that.

"Yes, I'm Pippak." Pip glanced from the official to her parents. Their somber expressions didn't give any more indication of what was going on than the official's did. "What's this about?"

"You attended Escarland's Hanford University and have

a degree in magical engineering." The official said it somewhere between a question and a statement, that curl to his mouth both doubtful and disdainful.

"Yes." Pip wasn't sure if he was looking for confirmation, but she gave it anyway, holding the elf official's gaze while she did.

The prestigious Escarlish university had become *the* place to study magical engineering after Tarenhiel's Prince Farrendel Laesornysh—Pip had to bite back the instinctual squeal—attended there for a magical engineering degree.

Pip had been a young half-dwarf, half-elf child when Tarenhiel and Escarland signed their peace treaty and Prince Farrendel of Tarenhiel married Princess Elspeth of Escarland.

And Pip had become obsessed. There was something romantic about the king's own brother in a mixed elf-human marriage. Until then, Pip's parents had seemed like the only ones. Sure, there were others scattered all along the borders of Tarenhiel, mostly troll-elf pairs or human-elf pairs. But they kept their heads down, staying away from the public eye.

When the news broke that Prince Farrendel was attending Hanford University to get a magical engineering degree, his status as Pip's childhood hero was cemented into place. From that moment on, Pip had dreamed of attending Hanford University herself. She'd even had a poster of Prince Farrendel on her wall while she'd been saving up to go.

Traveling across Tarenhiel and Escarland had been quite the experience, as had living in Escarland for four years among humans. While humans still had prejudices, mixed marriages were more common in Aldon. For the first time in her life, Pip hadn't felt like as much of an oddity as she did when among the elves of her home village or the dwarves when visiting her mother's family.

At the end of those four years, she'd returned to her backwater home at the edge of Tarenhiel and continued to help her family keep the trains running as if her little jaunt to Aldon had never happened.

"Hmm." The elf official didn't look entirely convinced, though he lifted the sealed envelope he had been holding. The green wax seal glittered with edges of gold and was pressed with the oak tree symbol of the king. "As preparation for a likely war between the Alliance Kingdoms and the Mongavarian Empire, the Flying Corps of both Escarland and Tarenhiel are recruiting mechanics to form an auxiliary mechanic unit to repair the aeroplanes, flyers, and all assorted flying vehicles of the joint operations of the Alliance Flying Corps."

Her heart squeezing in a strange way in her chest, Pip took the letter, holding it in her grimy hands for a moment. Was she supposed to break the seal and read it in front of the official? Or wait until he left? Did he need an answer right away?

Before she could do more than awkwardly stand there for a long moment, the official straightened and nodded to Dacha. "Thank you for your hospitality. I will take my leave. I will await a response in Morne."

He named the local village, which boasted a single boarding house to accommodate the occasional visitor they got all the way out here.

With that, the official swept from the office. Through the window, she caught sight of him climbing onto his bicycle, then pedaling off along the forest path that wound from the railyard to the village.

"Well, that was something." Muka rested her hands on

her hips just above her tool belt, which held everything from a hammer to her favorite wrench to a tin of grease.

Dacha made a noncommittal murmur of agreement, his gaze fixed on the letter. He would be the most interested in the official paperwork side of things. "What does the king have to say?"

Pip wedged her grease-stained finger beneath the pristine white flap of the envelope and peeled up the seal. Once open, she dug out the thick piece of paper and unfolded it, quickly scanning it. "It basically repeats what that official said, though it adds that if I agree, I'm to report to Aerodrome D at Fort Linder outside of Bridgetown in a month to begin training with the latest aeroplanes with the Escarlish Flying Corps. Since I know Escarlish, I'll be training with the EFC, though I'll technically be on loan from the TFC. Once trained, I would be sent wherever I was needed at any of the aerodromes across all three Alliance Kingdoms."

The letter also listed her accommodations and pay. The pay was comparable to what she was making now, though living in military barracks would be a downgrade.

Why was she even considering this enough to compare living quarters? She had no reason to even think about taking up this offer.

It wasn't like she had any strong feelings one way or another about the possible war with Mongavaria. Here at the far western side of Tarenhiel, the Mongavarian Empire seemed so far away. Even if war broke out, it would change their life here very little, except that demand for dwarven iron would go up and a few of their workers might leave to volunteer.

Dacha nodded, his mouth still in a grave line. "I see. I do not think we can dismiss this lightly."

Muka gave a harrumph. "The offer might have come

from the king, but you are under no obligation to agree. In the event of war, our railyard will be more important than ever. A war will demand iron from the dwarven mountains at a prodigious rate. All our workers will be exempt."

"Perhaps, but I am not sure Pippa will be included in that number." Dacha's gaze settled on her in a way that held an added weight. "Certified mechanics are rare. Especially ones with magic like hers who also have a degree from Hanford University. The king or his officials might deem Pippa to be more useful elsewhere. A mechanic without her degree could do her job here just as well."

"I could find myself drafted into a war effort regardless of what I choose now?" Pip swallowed and stared down at the letter in her hands. The king had always seemed so far away. It seemed unthinkable that he had such power over her life that she could find herself drafted into the war against her will.

At least if she went willingly now, the Mechanics Auxiliary was currently considered a civilian contractor unit. She wouldn't be officially in the army, even if she would be more in the army than a regular civilian.

"Perhaps. I do not know if it will come to that. We may not even go to war, as likely as a war looks at the moment." Dacha's gaze dropped to the letter in her hand rather than continuing to meet her eyes.

"Nor does that mean you have to go now." Muka tapped her fingers against her hammer. "*If* there is a war and *if* you're drafted into these auxiliary mechanics, then we can worry about it."

Pip nodded, folded the letter, and tucked it into one of the large pockets of her coveralls. "You're right. No reason to leave now."

Then why did her heart sink at that?

Pip nestled into a crook of the branches that formed the roof of her family's home on one side of the western rail terminal. At this time of night, a cold breeze wafted up from the Milnissi River, stirring her hair and bringing with it the thick, wet scents of mud and algae. A liquid sheen of moonlight skimmed across the water's surface, while in the distance, a train's whistle carried on the breeze.

She tugged a blanket tighter around her shoulders. Her hair remained slightly damp after her shower, and the temperatures were rapidly falling as the night deepened. At least her clean coat and coveralls kept most of her protected from the cold and the jabbing sticks of the roof.

With a grunt, Mak clambered up the last few feet of the wall and leveraged himself into the nook beside her. "Thought I'd find you up here, Pipsqueak."

Pip rolled her eyes and elbowed him. The childhood nickname—both a play on her name and a reference to her stature—was somehow both endearing and annoying. It would be nice if her brother stopped, but she also didn't know what she'd do if he did. "I'm just getting a bit of fresh air. That official sure was something today, wasn't he? All pompously expecting I'd leap at the chance to get out of here. But I'm not going to go. Don't worry."

Mak nodded, drawing up one of his long legs and resting his arm on his knee. "Actually, I think you should go."

"What?" Pip swiveled to better face him. "Why?"

"Your magic is too great to be wasted out here." Mak shrugged, pulling out a piece of wood and one of his carving knives. "That's why you went all the way to Hanford University, after all. I've never seen you quite as happy as when you were studying there."

"I'm happy here. This is home." Pip gestured at the railyard.

"Oh, sure. It will always be home. Doesn't mean you have to stay forever." Mak tapped his knife against the piece of wood, starting a rhythm. "After all, Muka left home for Dacha. You are free to pursue your magic or mechanics or whatever you wish. We'll be sad to see you go, but we also want what's best for you."

"But I can't leave you short-handed. And do you really want me volunteering to be part of a war, if war does come?" Pip scrubbed her hands on the front of her coveralls.

"Well, I don't really like the idea of you caught in a war. You're my little sister, after all." Mak grinned and leaned his elbow on her shoulder. "Emphasis on *little*."

Pip groaned and shoved his arm off her. "Mak."

His grin dropped. "But Dacha was right. You might not be given much of a choice. I might not either. Trained mechanics will be scarce, and if there's a war, the officials might not care about leaving this particular railyard short-handed if young and trained mechanics are needed elsewhere."

Pip swallowed, her heart aching at the thought that both her and her brother could be drafted into the war.

If the war came. It was all the rumors in the papers, but that didn't mean it would actually happen. The papers were known to hype up the smallest thing.

"But even beyond the war, I have another reason for thinking you should go." Mak gestured from her to their perch. "*You* want to go. You wouldn't be up here so torn if you didn't. You would have flat-out refused. You're as stubborn as Muka."

"So are you." Pip poked him in the ribs. "You're more stubborn than me."

Mak grinned, picked up his wood and knife, and started the tapping rhythm once again.

The two of them lapsed into silence. Well, not exactly silence since Mak murmured in dwarvish under his breath, a rhythm to the words. He changed his tapping to long, cutting strokes with his knife, peeling curls of wood. Yet even his shaving motions were timed with the rhythm he'd established.

Pip could sense his magic gathering around the piece of wood, even if it was only the faintest green, not nearly as bright as their dacha's plant magic. While Mak might have inherited elven plant magic, he worked it as a dwarf would, crafting the magic in time with knife and hands, song and rhythm.

In Mak's hand, the wood transformed, and Pip couldn't have said what part was magic and what part was the knife. There was no separating the two, not really. That was the power of dwarven magic that melded the skill of hands and tools with the power of magic.

Within moments, Mak stopped his carving and low guttural chanting. He held out a tiny, miniature train. It was detailed down to wheels that spun, connected by delicate coupling rods. "Wherever you go, Pip, you'll never forget us. But you can do so much more with your magic. Don't hold yourself back out here."

Pip took the tiny train, turning it over in her hands before she looked up at Mak. "Your magic is special, too, Mak. The same goes for you. You might not have studied at Hanford University, but you could be doing so much more with your magic too."

Mak just shrugged, though he didn't meet her gaze. "Maybe. But you know how the full elves are. They don't see a lot of use in plant magic that is wielded like a dwarf."

"Who knows? They might if war breaks out." Pip wasn't sure why she was making war sound like it would be a good thing.

But oddly, it would bring new opportunities for both of them. They would become important. Necessary. Barriers would be broken for them because of their unique skills and the demands of war.

It wasn't easy to be divided in halves, always torn between cultures and kingdoms. Perhaps a war would be the only thing that would help them find a place where they truly belonged.

FIVE

Fieran hugged his mama as they stood on the platform at Princess Station in Aldon. All around them, other young men with bags and packs were saying farewells to families. Other new army recruits, gathering to take the designated train car to Bridgetown.

To one side, Merrik hugged his younger sister, his parents clustered around them.

"Do you have to go?" Tryndar swiped at his face, his hand gripped in Mama's.

Mama released Fieran, giving him that sad but calm smile of hers.

Fieran knelt in front of Tryndar, then gave him a squeezing hug. His brother normally wasn't big on touch, so hugs were rare. "I'll write lots of letters, and I'll be depending on you to write to tell me everything you've been up to."

Tryndar squirmed in Fieran's hug. "You are squishing me."

Fieran released him. He moved on to hugs with Ellie, Louise, and Adry. They all murmured farewells and stay safes and teasing *Don't get thrown out of the army on your first day.*

Then Fieran was facing his dacha, struggling to meet that silver-blue gaze that held far too much. Fieran's throat closed, and he couldn't think of anything to say.

Perhaps that was just it. There was nothing left to say at this point.

Dacha reached out and gripped Fieran's shoulders in an elven hug. When he spoke, it was only a single, strained word, as if Dacha, too, didn't know what else to say. "Sason."

The weight of that one elven word—the meaning behind Dacha calling Fieran *son* with that elven emphasis—just choked up Fieran even more.

An elven hug just wasn't enough. He stepped forward and hugged Dacha, even though Dacha, like Tryndar, wasn't big on physical shows of affection like human hugs.

For a moment, Dacha froze, his arms still awkwardly hovering in the air. Then he gave Fieran one perfunctory thump on the back in an attempt at the manly hugs that Fieran's human uncles exchanged.

Fieran thumped Dacha's back in return, then stepped from the embrace. If this farewell lasted too much longer, he was going to disgrace his dignity by doing something like crying. Tryndar was already crying, his face pressed against Mama's coat as she rested a hand on his hair.

Fieran slung his small pack of belongings over his shoulder. It didn't weigh much. He knew the army wouldn't let him keep much anyway, and there was no reason to take a bunch of stuff just to have it sit in a cupboard for months.

With one last nod to his family, Fieran strode toward the waiting train. Moments later, Merrik fell into step with him, his own small pack of belongings over a shoulder.

Fieran lightly leapt up the steps and entered the train car. Row upon row of forward facing wooden benches greeted him, most of the benches already filled with young men. Fieran navigated his way down the aisle, avoiding packs and elbows that protruded into the narrow aisle until he found an empty bench.

He slid onto the bench until he was next to the window, a draft of cold air tickling his neck from the places where the windowpane rattled in the frame. The frayed fabric on the bench seat barely counted as a cushion while a layer of grime skimmed the floor and the windows.

Merrik eased onto the seat beside him, his arms and legs tight to his body as if he were trying his best not to touch anything.

Fieran gingerly settled against the back of the seat. He was more cavalier about dirt than Merrik was, but the general stickiness of the place was disconcerting.

He'd traveled on the cheap seats of the train occasionally, but only for short trips. Even then, he usually paid for at least second class, if not first class. It wasn't like more expensive tickets were a financial hardship. For longer trips, he was usually traveling with his parents in their personal train, powered by Dacha's magic and designed to travel on both the steel rails of Escarland and the forest root rails of Tarenhiel so that it didn't need to stop all the way from Aldon to Estyra.

The train gave a whistle—using compressed air rather than steam—then the wheels ground forward. As the train crawled into motion, Fieran peered out the window one last time.

Mama, Fieran's sisters, and Aunt Patience were talking with a man and woman wearing work-worn clothing, the man's coverall's patched and the woman's dress an indeterminate color of greige.

Dacha had retreated to put his back to the wall of the train station away from the bustle, gripping Tryndar's hand. Tryndar shrank against Dacha's leg and plugged his ears as best he could with one hand and a shoulder as the train gave another shrill whistle. Uncle Iyrinder had taken up a spot a few feet away from Dacha, his gaze darting between Dacha and the others, his posture that of a guard on duty.

Then the train was gaining speed, and the station disappeared from Fieran's view, replaced with Aldon's brick buildings crowding all the way up to the train tracks.

A lanky young man with straw-blond hair sticking out in all directions and wearing a set of coveralls swiveled in his seat on the bench in front of Fieran and Merrik. He gaped around, his blue eyes wide as goggles, his mouth hanging open.

His gaze drifted over them, then snapped back to Merrik. He turned all the way around in his seat. "Are you elves?"

Merrik hunched in his seat, but it did little to hide his long chestnut hair and pointed ears.

"Half-elves." Fieran stuck out a hand. "I'm Fieran. He's Merrik."

"Elijah, but most people call me Lije." The young man grinned, showing off a gap in his front teeth. He had a slight accent that Fieran couldn't place. "Where are you from? I'm from the south of Escarland near the border with Groyria. Never been farther north than Mount Husken until I joined up. Had quite the train ride to get to Aldon. Whoo-whee, but Aldon is a sight! Never seen so many people and buildings in one place! You could lose all of Frogg's Hollow in Aldon and never miss it."

Fieran eyed Lije. And everyone thought Fieran was talkative. This young man from the southern hills of Escarland could put him to shame. "Aldon is something. Merrik and I grew up just outside of Aldon."

"Have you ever visited Estyra? I hear the elves have trees as big as mountains." Lije was on his knees now, the better to peer over the back of his bench at them.

"Yes. The trees of Estyra are impressive." Fieran wasn't going to mention that when he wasn't in Aldon, he lived in a room at the elven palace of Ellonahshinel itself. Everyone in the unit was likely to find out Fieran was a prince with far too many useless titles to his name sooner or later. He would just rather it be later.

Lije didn't seem the bad sort. He didn't seem prejudicial about Fieran and Merrik's heritage. That was a mark in his favor.

"Are you brothers?" Lije pointed between them.

"Kind of." Fieran shrugged, even as Merrik sank further on the bench. "Our parents have been friends for a long time, so we're like brothers."

Lije nodded, as if that wasn't too surprising of a scenario. "Could have fooled me with that hair. Though yours is a lot redder than his. Never seen hair that red."

Fieran suppressed his sigh. He didn't mind his red hair. Not really. But everyone always insisted on commenting on it.

"So you're half-elves, huh? Are your papas the elves or your mamas?" Lije leaned his elbows on the back of the bench, even as the train shuddered into motion. "I've met a few ogres and half-ogres in Frogg's Hollow—they occasionally cross the border to trade in our town—but never any elves before."

"Our fathers are elves; our mothers are humans." Fieran stretched out his legs beneath the bench in front of him. With the lanky young man kneeling on the seat, he wasn't using the leg room. Fieran might as well take advantage of it.

"My parents are both human as human comes. Though family legend on my mama's side says there's ogre in the blood from some grandpappy or other." Lije settled more comfortably where he was, kneeling on his bench and leaning over to speak with them. "People say such awful things about ogres, but they aren't disgusting swamp creatures or anything like that. They're people too, you know. Just a little extra green. Not as green as the cartoons you see going around. They're more a kind of mottled green-brown."

Elves were generally well regarded and didn't engender some of the prejudices that the trolls or ogres experienced. But the elves still sneered at Fieran's human side and the humans mocked his stuck-up elf side. He simply couldn't win sometimes.

"I'd like to meet an ogre someday." Fieran sank even lower on the bench to attempt to lounge more comfortably. The lack of padding wasn't helping anything. His rear end was going to be asleep by the time they reached Fort Linder. "Are things between Groyria and Mongavaria as bad as the papers say?"

"Hard to tell." Lije shrugged. "But I'll say this, I haven't seen any ogres visiting in months now. They've just disappeared."

That wasn't good. At least if one was hoping there wouldn't be a war. From what Fieran had heard, ogres were reclusive. But not *that* reclusive.

His parents probably knew more of what was going on. Uncle Edmund, head of Escarland's Intelligence Office—as in, Escarland's top spy—certainly knew more.

The train was really picking up speed now, farm fields and tiny villages flashing by outside the windows.

Beside Fieran, Merrik dragged in a breath, his shoulders relaxing, in that sure sign that he had warmed up to Lije enough to finally join the conversation.

That was Fieran's cue to stop talking long enough for Merrik to get a word in edgewise. It often took Merrik a few extra moments to get comfortable with new people, and Fieran was more than happy to do all the talking until that point.

Merrik's tone was low, barely carrying over the clacking of the train wheels on the tracks. "I hope for the ogres' sakes that the papers are simply fear-mongering. The Mongavarian Empire is not known for treating races other than human very well. They don't even treat all human races that well, if the rumors about their march through the king-doms south of Groyria are to be believed."

Fieran squirmed on the grimy, ill-padded bench. He probably should be thinking more about the consequences of war rather than his own eagerness to take to the skies and prove himself in battle.

It wasn't like his attitude was rare. The Kostarian papers were just as filled with calls for war as the Escarlish ones were. The trolls had never forgotten how, sixty-nine years ago, Mongavaria had sent poisoned grain into that kingdom, killing many men, women, and children before the poison was discovered. With how long-lived trolls were, most of those who had lived through that poisoning were still alive and young enough to go into battle to avenge those they lost all those years ago.

If Mongavaria invaded Groyria, they would not treat the ogres any better than they'd treated the trolls all those years ago.

"Yeah, me too. The ogres keep to themselves, but they're good folks." Lije's somber expression was swept away with a grin. "But if the Mongavarians do invade Groyria, we'll be ready, and we'll beat the stuffing out of them."

Fieran smirked, resting his head against the hard top of the bench and resisting the urge to let his magic play over his fingers. "Yes, we will."

SIX

After eight hours, Fieran was ready to climb onto the top of the train to get some fresh air and stretch his legs.

But that was something he could only do on his parents' private train. Public train conductors got a little nervous when their passengers wandered about on the roof.

At last, the train sped toward the city of Bridgetown as the setting sun cast long, orange beams across the rippling water of the Hydalla River, which formed the border between Escarland and Tarenhiel.

On the Escarlish side of the river, the nearly flat, open plains gave way to tall brick buildings clustered in the tight, neat grid of a city that had only sprung into existence in the past seventy years.

On the northern side of the river, the dense Tarenhieli forest grew right up to the water's edge for as far as anyone could see. Directly across the Hydalla, the elven city of Calafaren—which meant Bridgetown in elvish—was grown into the trees. Unlike most elven cities, this city was designed with human tourists in mind, so everything had handrails and was kept far closer to the ground.

Between these two sister cities, the graceful stone arches of the Alliance Bridge spanned the Hydalla River, as it had for the past sixty-nine years, a monument to the close friendship between the three kingdoms.

When it had been built, the Alliance Bridge had been intended for train traffic. It had served that purpose for forty years before it was converted into lanes for automobile traffic, with one lane set aside for pedestrians and bicyclists.

The trains, both cargo and passenger, had been diverted to the eastern side of Bridgetown where tunnels beneath the Hydalla River took the trains north into Tarenhiel.

As the train swept past the outer edge of Bridgetown, Fieran all but pressed his face against the glass of the window.

In Bridgetown, everything was new and vibrant, from the fresh paint on the street signs to the pristine tarmac of the asphalt roads. Automobiles with shining chrome, sweeping fenders, and open carriages zipped up and down the streets, honking as they dodged around the few horse-drawn carriages that dared venture into Bridgetown. Red-and-white-striped awnings covered little patios where groups of people chatted as they sipped sodas and enjoyed the first pleasant day of early spring.

Trolls, elves, and humans strolled along the sidewalks or poured out of a cinema, mingling in a way that they did in no other city in any of the three kingdoms. Human women in bustled and puffed-sleeved dresses strolled through the many green spaces and parks inside of Bridgetown, passing elves in traditional silken tunics and trousers. Human men wearing bowlers paused to talk with trolls wearing trousers and shirts in the human style along with more traditional troll leather vests.

Fieran loved Bridgetown in a way that he did few other places in all three kingdoms. Estyra was stuffy and slow to change. Aldon was old and dirty.

But Bridgetown was the future, its streets paved in the peace of this golden age, its very design a testament to a modern era.

And sure, there were just a few too many monuments to his parents for Fieran's liking. One couldn't turn a street corner in Bridgetown or Calafaren without smacking into some memorial, monument, or museum dedicated to the Alliance. But Fieran was willing to overlook that one flaw in his favorite city. It came with the territory of having rather famous parents.

The train whistled and shuddered slightly as the air brakes engaged. The wheels squealed as the train slowed, finally coming to rest with a hiss of air and clang of metal at the station in Bridgetown.

No sooner had the train squealed to a rolling halt than the train's door slammed open and a well-built man wearing a drab green uniform hopped into the car. His short hair stuck straight up, and his eyes flashed with such fire that the front rows of young men quailed even before the man began shouting at a volume that rang in Fieran's ears. Fieran couldn't even make out what the man was saying besides a general impression of *loud*.

Next to Fieran, Merrik flinched, his hands twitching like he wanted to plug his ears.

"Move! Move! Move!" The drill sergeant—for the man yelling could only be the infamous drill sergeant Fieran had been warned to expect—stalked down the aisle as the young men on the train stumbled to their feet and rushed to bail out. "Move, you lazy slugs!"

Then Merrik, Fieran, and Lije were on their feet and hustling off the train. No steps had been lowered, so Fieran had to jump to the platform. He landed lightly, as did Merrik. But Lije nearly fell, and Fieran grabbed his arm and hauled him to his feet.

On the platform, another drill sergeant was shouting and herding the recruits into straight lines while the passengers from the other cars gawked. A cordon of soldiers in uniform kept this section of the platform clear.

Fieran, Merrik, and Lije hurried to step into line, staring straight ahead lest the drill sergeant notice their straying gazes and come back to yell at them.

Once everyone from their train car had disembarked, they marched from the platform to the street, where a line of green army trucks waited. Each truck had a small cab with only enough room for a driver and passenger. Then the back bed had a canvas top and benches on either side.

Fieran, Lije, and Merrik managed to climb into one of the trucks together, and Fieran found himself smushed between Merrik and the back wall of the cab.

As the truck lurched into motion, Fieran peered between the cab and the flapping end of the tarpaulin. As the truck rumbled forward, the towering buildings gave way to rolling hills, fields, and stands of forests, the trees still stark and bare at this time of year.

Then a tall, wire fence came into view as the truck slowed. Two Escarlish soldiers barred the way, and one stepped up to the truck's cab to briefly exchange a few words and papers before he waved them through.

Fieran's knees bounced as he swiveled as much as he could on the bench to take in Fort Linder. A collection of both wooden and cement buildings were laid out in a grid even more precise than that of Bridgetown. Fifty years ago, the old, outdated outpost on the hill in what was now Bridgetown had been closed and turned into a museum. Fort Linder had been founded east of the growing town, situated along the river with the intent to provide protection for the vital rail and communication hub between Escarland and the two Alliance Kingdoms to the north.

Three flagpoles stood at the center of the military base with Escarland's red and white flag in the center and slightly higher than Kostaria's gray and white banner and Taren-hiel's green and silver flag on either side.

On the western side of the base, a field had been mown short, the dead winter grass plastered close to the earth. The stretch of shorter grass ran in a long, straight line, almost like a road.

Not a road. An airstrip. A biplane with its wood frame and canvas-stretched wings was lowering from the sky before it touched its wheels onto the ground, bumping along before the rear of the aeroplane fell onto the wooden tailskid. The tailskid dug into the earth, slowing the aeroplane.

Soon, that would be Fieran, coming in for a landing. Climbing out of the cockpit with that little extra swagger that pilots had.

Fieran's bouncing knees grew worse, so much so that Merrik nudged him with an elbow. Even then, Fieran didn't quite manage to stop his jitters. How could he when they were finally here? In a few weeks, they would take to the sky at last.

The trucks slowed, then parked in the central square beside the flagpoles.

The yelling began again, and all of them bailed out of the trucks onto the cement-paved parade ground, standing in front of a large, cement building with a rusted metal roof. All around them, more cement buildings with metal roofs spread out in neat rows in all directions. The sides of the buildings were labeled with letter and number combinations.

They were instructed to line up, then yelled at some more until they lined up to the drill sergeant's satisfaction.

Then they were left there, standing in their stiff, neat rows, their bags and packs of belongings at their feet. A cold wind swept between the concrete buildings and straight through the thin coat Fieran had worn. He hadn't bothered to dress any warmer. He hadn't realized he would be left standing outside in the early spring cold for hours, unable to do more than watch the sun set while the night breeze blew with a chill swept up from the nearby river.

After they had been standing in the cold for nearly three hours, darkness having fully descended, the drill sergeants, who had been pacing and yelling at anyone who broke into noticeable shivering, marched them into the large building and assigned numbers. Each of them was issued a clipboard with a few sheets of paper on it.

From there they were herded into a room where they were told to write down their last will and testament, along with *If I Die* letters for their families.

Fieran stared at the blank pieces of paper, not sure what to write. Oddly enough, he didn't have much of his own to will to anyone. If he died, his stake in the AMPC would be absorbed back into the company. Any of the estates and titles he would inherit from his parents would go to his siblings. All there was left to do was designate his savings and personal funds to one of his parents' charities, and that was that.

The *If I Die* letter was harder. He'd spent far more time

contemplating glory and grand battles than the possibility of death.

But maybe that was the point of having all the recruits sit down to write a letter like this, right before starting their training.

Finally, Fieran wrote something cheesy about loving all of them and hoping they wouldn't mourn forever since he died doing what he loved.

It wasn't like he was in much danger of dying, even if he was sent into war. Sure, flying was a bit more dangerous even for those with magic, thanks to the propensity of aeroplanes to crash.

But Fieran wielded the magic of the ancient kings. He was about as invincible as it was possible to get.

Once the recruits were done with their wills and letters, they handed the items over to a secretary, who recorded their numbers and how many letters and so forth they had.

Once done, they were herded into the next room and ordered to strip to their undershorts. All their civilian clothes —civvies—and any items they weren't allowed to have were bundled into a wooden locker, not to be seen again until they were finished with basic training. Each item in the locker was, of course, inventoried and recorded.

Standing in their undershorts, they were sent through a series of stations for the various medical examinations, certifying that they were healthy. Then came a round of vaccines, each one meticulously checked off on the clipboard.

Fieran approached the next nurse in line. After the first few stations, he'd quickly gotten over the awkwardness of walking around in nothing but his undershorts in front of a bunch of female nurses, doctors, and even an elven healer. Behind him in line, Merrik's ears were permanently red with embarrassment.

Fieran handed the nurse his clipboard. "Sixty-six."

The nurse set his clipboard aside, reaching for the next prepared hypodermic needle. This one held some kind of brown, sludgy substance, and that needle looked suspiciously larger than those of the previous vaccines that had been jammed into Fieran's arms. In a nasally monotone, the nurse gestured to him. "Turn around, drop your shorts, and bend over."

"Pardon?" Fieran froze as he tried to process the order. Was she telling him what he thought she was saying?

The nurse eyed him with utter boredom. "By order of all three kings of the Alliance, all soldiers, warriors, and civilian contractors stationed on base are to receive vaccinations so that in the case of war the elven healers can focus on healing wounds rather than staving off disease. You are not exempt even as an elf."

Fieran could only imagine the resistance there must have been among the elven warriors for this particular vaccine, if it involved getting the shot in the rear end rather than the arm. "I know, and I'm only—"

"The vaccines have been tested and certified by a team of elven healers." The nurse spoke as if she'd said the same speech multiple times.

This was what he'd signed up for. All bodily autonomy went out the window the moment he signed that enlistment paper. The army owned him—body and vaccines and all—until his enlistment was up.

One of the drill sergeants was headed in their direction. Fieran hurriedly turned his back to the nurse, dropped his shorts, and presented his rear end to her.

A moment later, the needle the size of a sword stabbed into his butt cheek with such force it seemed the nurse was trying to jab all the way to his hip bone. The viscous substance hurt as it pushed into him, and Fieran gritted his teeth against the pain.

Finally, the nurse withdrew the needle. Fieran yanked up his shorts, telling himself that he was *not* going to rub his butt no matter how much his stab wound hurt.

The nurse initialed the clipboard, then handed it back to him. "Next."

Merrik had gone white, though his ears were burning red. He handed over his clipboard, mumbled "Sixty-Seven", turned around, dropped his shorts, and bent over as if he had to get it over with before he could chicken out.

Fieran didn't see Merrik actually get jabbed as he stepped into a hallway. He waited in a short line before he was ushered into another room where three chairs stood, barbers with clippers waiting behind each.

He sat in the first chair, and the barber set to work on his red hair. As Fieran already kept his hair short, it wouldn't take much to get it to regulation buzz cut length.

Merrik stepped into the room, and somehow his face paled further. He straightened his shoulders, marched to the chair next to Fieran's, and sat down rigidly, his long, elven style hair flowing over his bare shoulders and back.

Fieran tried to tilt his head and catch Merrik's eye, but the barber grabbed the top of his head and forced him to look forward.

Out of the corner of his eye, Fieran could only watch as Merrik gripped the armrests of the chair with white knuckles, his jaw set, and stared straight ahead as, snip by snip, the barber cut off the warrior-long hair Merrik had worn all his life.

Fieran couldn't quite swallow back the sour taste rising in his throat. This struck home far harder even than writing that *If I Die* letter. Flying was his dream, but Merrik was the one sacrificing for it.

It was far too late for Fieran to tell Merrik not to follow him, not this time. It had been selfish of him to leap into this, just expecting Merrik to follow, without even stopping to think of the cost Merrik would pay to do so.

The barber working on Fieran's hair finished far faster than the one hacking away at Merrik's hair, so Fieran was rousted from his chair, told to brush off, then sent on to the next room long before Merrik was finished.

In the next room, Fieran joined a cluster of some of the other recruits. There, he was issued his uniforms and could finally dress. He was given two sets of uniform fatigues, matching drab green undershirts and undershorts, socks, and two pairs of boots.

The sergeant had him unlace one pair of boots, put a knot in the middle of the laces, then re-lace so that the knot was visible. Fieran was to wear the Knot Boots and the Not-Knot Boots every other day so that the other pair would have a chance to dry out. The sergeant would be checking that they wore the correct pair of boots on the right day.

Fieran packed his rucksack with the gear he'd been issued, following the barked instructions.

No sooner had he finished packing than the drill sergeant grabbed the rucksack and dumped it out, yelling out orders to repack the rucksack in between profanities that Fieran would have been squirming to hear, if he hadn't been so busy scrambling to repack the bag.

Fieran stumbled as the man next to him bumped him in his scramble to stuff his items back into his bag. Dodging the others, Fieran repacked his rucksack, only to have the drill sergeant dump it all out again amid yelled curses and insults.

Merrik joined him, and soon the two of them were packing and re-packing their rucksacks until the drill sergeant was finally satisfied.

Sweating and prickling with pieces of hair still stuck to him, Fieran lugged his rucksack down the hall, Merrik just behind him.

At the end of the hall, a sergeant barked orders, directing everyone without magic to the left and those with magic to the right. A recruit who must have been half-troll entered the room, followed by one human who must be some kind of magician.

Inside the room, part of the room was walled off by protective glass. Inside the protective bubble sat a complicated apparatus of wires and machinery. In front of the bubble, a technician stood before an array of dials, buttons, levers, and flashing lights.

Fieran grimaced, recognizing the device. Uncle Lance developed it as a way to measure a person's magic level. Uncle Lance had been obsessed with coming up with a way to quantify Dacha's otherwise unquantifiable magic, and he'd finally figured out a magical scale that was exponential rather than linear. That scale—the Marion Scale—became the universal way to judge magical power levels in the three Alliance Kingdoms.

The problem was that the device before him wasn't designed to test magic as powerful as Fieran's.

It wouldn't have to be, normally. Most human magicians rated only a 1 to 5 at the highest. Even less powerful elves or trolls were 6 to 10. The more powerful elves and trolls were often up to 13. Only trolls or elves like Fieran's uncles Rharreth and Weylind could get up to a 15. Anything beyond that was a range only shared by Fieran, his dacha, and his siblings. Oh, and one of his cousins.

The half-troll stepped into the protective bubble. When the technician nodded, the half-troll called up his white ice magic that swirled around his hands before spreading along the wires. Some of the lights flashed, beeps sounded, and something whirred. The technician made a few notes before he gestured to the half-troll and shut down the magical sensor.

A clerk by the door handed the human recruit's clipboard back to him, then turned to Fieran. "Number?"

"Sixty-six." Fieran handed over his clipboard. "I—"

"Type of magic?" The clerk wasn't even looking up at him.

"Magic of the ancient kings."

The clerk's gaze snapped up to Fieran, even as he scowled. "That is not listed as an option. Please give your correct magical designation."

"Magic of the ancient kings. It's what the elves call it."

"Hmm." The clerk checked the box listed as *Other*. He waved Fieran into the room as the technician was finishing the test for the human. "Proceed."

"I can't. That testing device isn't rated for my power level." Fieran gestured to the device.

The clerk rolled his eyes. "There's no need to lie to avoid having your magic tested. There's no embarrassment in having a low level of power."

"I'm not lying. I'm telling you, I will destroy the device if you try to test my magic." Fieran jabbed a finger at the machine. "That magical testing device isn't built to accommodate my type of magic, much less my level of power."

"You are required to submit to having your magic tested." The clerk was speaking through his teeth now. "Are you refusing an order?"

"No, I'm not. I'll go blow up your machine if you want

me to." Fieran couldn't help the note of frustration in his voice.

"Is there a problem here?" The sergeant's voice boomed from behind Fieran.

The clerk pointed at Fieran. "This recruit is refusing to submit to the magical testing."

"No, I'm not, Drill Sergeant. I'm just—"

"Did I give you permission to speak, knucklehead?" The sergeant marched over to Fieran, yelling into his face. Or as much as he could since he stood several inches shorter than Fieran.

"No, Drill Sergeant." Fieran kept his eyes focused above the sergeant's head.

"Drop and give me fifty."

"Drill Sergeant?"

"Are you hard of hearing, elf? I said fifty. Push-ups, Red, push-ups. Better make that a hundred, you dunderheaded elf. Do you want me to make it two hundred?"

"No, Drill Sergeant." Fieran dropped to his hands and feet. It took several tries before he had his back, toes, and hands all positioned to the sergeant's satisfaction. Only then could Fieran begin his count of a hundred.

When he sneaked a peek, he found Merrik standing just inside the doorway, unable to hide a smirk.

The sergeant must have caught Fieran's glance because he whipped around to face Merrik.

Merrik didn't wipe the smirk off his face fast enough.

The sergeant jabbed a finger at him. "You. Fifty."

"Yes, Drill Sergeant." Merrik dropped to the ground and began his own set of push-ups. He must have been paying attention when the sergeant was yelling at Fieran because he got his hands, toes, and back in proper posture almost right away.

"Drill Sergeant?" The technician was holding a clipboard, glancing from it to the clerk, then to Fieran.

"What?" The sergeant glared at the technician.

The technician quailed, clearing his throat. But he didn't step back. "He's correct. Our testing device is not rated for his power level."

"Then get your hands on one that is rated for him."

"I'm afraid that isn't possible. The only one rated that high is a permanent installation at the Alliance Magical Power Company in Aldon. It can't be moved."

Fieran had to work hard to keep his face blank. The last thing he wanted to do was smile in vindication, only to find himself doing another hundred push-ups.

A hundred push-ups wasn't anything too strenuous for him. His half-elf blood and training with his dacha every morning saw to that. But two hundred might be a stretch.

For a moment, the sergeant just glared at the technician, as if he wasn't sure how to handle this situation. Then he spun back to Fieran. "Red, what is your magical power level?"

"Nineteen, Drill Sergeant." Fieran didn't pause in his push-ups.

The clerk's eyes bugged at that. After all, the scale only went up to twenty—a power level reserved solely for Fieran's dacha.

But the technician quickly scribbled that down, as if to get it recorded before either the clerk or the sergeant came up with any objections. "I can verify that is correct. As part of the training for certification in magical testing, we visited the AMPC and used their magical testing device. I didn't personally test Fieran Laesornysh's magic, but I was present. I tested his sister's, and she is also rated at 19 on the Marion Scale."

Fieran's stomach dropped. Up until this point, he had just been a number on a clipboard. Once everyone put it together who he was...

The sergeant crossed his arms with a grunt, his brows lowering as something in his eyes flashed with understanding. He glared down at Fieran. "Make that a hundred and fifty."

"Yes, Drill Sergeant," Fieran said between counting out his push-ups. He would be a target for the drill sergeants as word spread that he was *special* because of his famous parents and family.

Merrik finished his push-ups first, meekly handed over his clipboard to the technician, and stepped into the testing bubble. It was a familiar routine, and Merrik probably could have just told the technician his rating as well. But he didn't have Fieran's excuse and wouldn't want to risk another round of push-ups.

Fieran finished his hundred and fifty push-ups as Merrik stepped from the testing bubble, his magic rating a 9.2. It wasn't hugely powerful by elf standards, but he wasn't incredibly weak either. A perfectly average amount of plant growing magic.

The technician held out Fieran's clipboard with a slight nod.

Fieran didn't recognize him, but AMPC had visitors all the time for various reasons, from internships for magical engineering to the certifications for the magical testing devices. He had helped run the magical testing simulations several times so that the trainees could get a taste of what testing powerful magic was like—important so that they knew the warning signs if the machine was about to be overpowered by the magic they were testing and, hopefully, they could shut it down before anything exploded.

As Fieran retrieved his clipboard, he glanced down at it. Underneath the checkmark for *Other*, the technician had written: *Magic of the Ancient Kings*.

At least Fieran's magical designation was now accurate. Not sure if it had been worth a hundred and fifty push-ups, but oh, well. It wasn't like he'd had much of a choice about protesting. He would have blown up their machine if he'd obeyed the order, and he probably would have gotten even more push-ups for that.

Or, perhaps, that had been the point. He was supposed to blindly follow orders, even if it led to a bad outcome. Like blowing up a highly expensive magical testing device.

Fieran and Merrik stepped into the next room, joining the end of the rather long line. For a moment, they were far enough back to avoid the drill sergeants.

Merrik elbowed Fieran, though he kept his voice low. "Not even through processing yet, and you already got us extra physical training."

Fieran shrugged, stretching out his arm muscles before they tightened up after all that exercise. "I'm beginning to understand why my dacha laughed when I told him I joined the army. What did your dacha do?"

"Warned me that my friendship with you was going to be hazardous to my health," Merrik muttered as the line shuffled forward.

Fieran didn't have a chance to respond since a drill sergeant was patrolling the line, and he and Merrik had to go back to blank-faced silence.

SEVEN

Fieran levered himself onto the top bunk and collapsed onto the hard, flat mattress, too tired to care if it wasn't nearly as soft as what he was used to back home. After the day of travel and the long night of processing into the army, his eyes were gritty, his body sagging with the urge to sleep.

But his butt cheek still throbbed from that shot, as did both of his arms from those vaccines and push-ups.

At least with the last names of Laesornysh and Loiatir, he and Merrik had gotten top bunks side by side in the barracks. It turned out their new friend Lije's last name was Lake, so he was assigned the bed below Fieran's.

"Would anyone like some ice?"

At the high-pitched tenor, Fieran rolled onto an elbow to peer across the barracks.

A troll stood almost directly across the barracks from Fieran's bunk. He was unusually short for a troll, his head barely level with the bunk next to him, yet he retained the broad shoulders and brawny arms, making him look a little bit like a bulldog. Despite his huge chest, he had the highest pitched tenor voice Fieran had heard, a surprising sound coming from such a well-built troll.

But as he held up his hand, white magic laced his fingers. With his other hand, he poured a stream of water from a canteen onto his palm. The water froze as soon as it came into contact with his magic. He shaped the water into flat circles.

A few of the others made their way around the center "sergeant's zone" where the recruits weren't allowed to step. Reaching the troll, they claimed a handful of ice, pressing it to whatever butt cheek received the stab.

Fieran hopped down from his bunk as Lije shoved to his feet. Merrik joined them, and the three of them strode around the perimeter of the room to join the line.

As Fieran reached the troll, the troll started to hold out the ice, only to pause, his eyes lifting as he took in Fieran. "You're an elf."

"Half-elf." Fieran waved to him. "Troll?"

"Half-troll." His high-pitched tenor was even more out of place this close. He grinned and held out a hand. "Donkyn Sairdror, but I go by Tiny. My da helped build the Alliance Bridge before he moved to Aldon and married my ma."

Fieran returned the handshake, grinning, even as he internally braced himself. "Fieran Laesornysh. My parents are the reason there is a bridge."

Tiny's bushy white eyebrows shot up. "Son of Prince Farrendel Laesornysh?"

"Yeah." Fieran shrugged, as if the Laesornysh name wasn't that big of a deal.

Tiny just grinned wider, showing off his white teeth, and handed over the chunk of ice. "Won't Da and Ma be surprised? Serving in the same squadron as Laesornysh's son."

Fieran really needed to change the topic before this turned into more of a discussion of his famous parents.

Not to mention, the ice chunk was rather cold in his hands. He pressed the ice to his butt cheek. "Well, you're a life saver."

Lije reached past Fieran, claimed an ice chunk, and held it to his own rear end, heaving a sigh. "Don't you mean butt saver?"

A few of the others around them devolved into ever more crude versions of butt-saving.

Tiny rolled his eyes and handed off a piece of ice to Merrik.

As Fieran and Merrik made their way around the perimeter of the room once again, avoiding the lines that denoted the sergeant's zone at the center of the room, a short, scrawny young man knelt before a footlocker, a box made of shabby, cheap wood and painted an even shabbier green. He was arranging everything from toilet paper to extra toothbrushes in the space allotted to him.

"How did you manage to get all that stuff in past processing?" Fieran halted next to him, still holding the ice to his rear. At least the troll magic was keeping the ice from melting as rapidly as it normally would, though it burned his fingers with cold.

"I have my ways." The scrawny young man grinned up at Fieran with a smile that was missing a few teeth. "I have toothbrushes, toothpaste, foot powder. You name it, I got it. Toilet paper sold by the square or by the roll."

The young man named a price that was about ten times the normal price of toilet paper.

"That's highway robbery!" The young man on the bunk above snorted.

"When the army food starts hitting and the latrines run

out of toilet paper, you'll change your tune." The young man closed the lid of his footlocker. "Plus I got the good stuff. None of that scratch-your-skin-off stuff the army uses."

"How do you even know what army food is like?" Fieran leaned a shoulder against the bunk.

The young man lounged on his closed footlocker. "My brothers warned me that army food is even worse than prison food. And they should know. I'm the youngest of six brothers, and all five of my older brothers are—or were—in prison. The oldest one was hung a while back. Anyway, one of us had to stay out of the joint and take care of our mama, so when the judge gave me the choice of prison or army, I picked army."

Fieran opened his mouth, then shut it. What was he supposed to say to something like that? He wasn't sure if he'd ever met a criminal before. Well, Uncle Edmund had a bit of the criminal about him, but he was a spy so it was okay. More or less.

The young criminal went on without waiting for Fieran to respond. "At least I could pick the Flying Corps. They're so desperate for pilots they'll take anyone, even someone like me, as long as I can pass all the tests and stuff. Parking my rear in a flyer sounds better than marching on the ground, and I'd never make officer rank in the regular army. The officer's pay will be rather nice to send to my mama."

Fieran cleared his throat and managed a few words at last. "I'm sure she'll appreciate it."

"She will. She might even be able to afford to take the train to visit my brothers now and then. She misses them something fierce." The young delinquent held out a hand. "I'm Stickyfingers Smith."

"Fieran." Fieran shook Stickyfingers' hand, glad to find

that the moniker wasn't literal. He gestured to the others. "This is Merrik and Lije."

Stickyfingers waved to each of them. "Nice to meet you."

Merrik gave a stilted, subtle elven wave in return, as if he, too, wasn't sure if associating with a criminal was wise.

Lije grinned and shook Stickyfingers' hand. "Are any of your brothers in Endow Prison? I got a couple of distant cousins in there."

"No." Stickyfingers rattled off a list of the prisons where his brothers were at.

Fieran nodded along, then gave another deeper nod before he and Merrik meandered away, leaving Lije still talking with Sticky.

Back at their bunks, a young man with dark brown hair was settling into the bunk below Merrik's. He had the kind of chiseled features Fieran's sisters assured him was handsome, and the droop to his eyelids and languid pose suggested he knew it. He held a small hand mirror and was inspecting the lighter patches on his face that must have been covered by a fashionable mustache and small beard before the army barber got a hold of him.

The young man's eyes remained on the mirror as they approached. "Do you think the ladies will mind the new look?"

"I don't think we'll be seeing many ladies around here." Fieran leaned against the back of the bunk.

"I spied a few cute secretaries, and then there's the ladies who serve in the mess. Not to mention we'll eventually get leave to go into Bridgetown." The young man smoothed a hand over his recently shaved cheek, then finally lowered the mirror. As his gaze landed first on Fieran, then on Merrik, he swung upright with a groan. "Oh, come on! Elves! Here I joined the army hoping to pick up dames—you know how the ladies love a man in uniform—but I can't compete with a couple of elves. Not fair."

"Half-elves. Our mothers are humans." Fieran gestured from himself to Merrik. "And you can have the ladies' fawning."

He'd dealt with it his whole life, and it only got worse once the young women realized he was a prince.

At least having the ladies flirt with him wasn't as bad as when they flirted with his dacha. Dacha never flirted back, of course. He was utterly devoted to Mama. But it was just awkward watching ladies throw themselves at Dacha because he was an elf with a pretty face, not seeming to care that he was married with five children.

Then there was that awkward poster that had gotten around years ago that featured a sketch of Dacha lounging about in a shirtless, sexy pose. Dacha had never posed for such a thing, and the artist had only gotten away with it because he'd marketed it as a poster of a generic elf rather than one of Dacha.

But it had clearly been Dacha. Dacha had been mortified.

Fieran was mortified whenever that poster made its rounds again.

"Even half as pretty as a full elf, you're still half an elf too handsome." The young man grumbled, sighed, then tucked the mirror into a pocket. "I suppose I will just have to settle for being the third most handsome specimen in the unit."

"Such a hardship, I'm sure." Fieran shook his head and climbed back onto his bunk. It was beyond time to get some shut-eye before morning muster.

EIGHT

Pip clutched her small bag of essential belongings to her chest as she sat on the cushy bench seat in the train's passenger car. The curved silver sides were filled with windows all down the car's length, providing plenty of views of the Tarenhieli forest for the elves inside.

Craning her neck, Pip located her parents and brother where they stood on the platform in Morne. She waved, not sure if they'd be able to see her through the glare on the windows.

Dacha's wave was the smaller, graceful elven tilt of a hand. Her muka gave that wide smile of hers that nearly disappeared into her beard as she waved back so exuberantly she nearly whacked a passing elf in the arm. Mak, too, was waving wildly enough to make the other elves on the platform give Pip's family a wide berth.

As the last passenger settled into a seat in the train car, the train eased into motion, soundlessly gliding forward on the root rail system, propelled by magic.

Only a few other elves currently filled the train car. They'd likely pick up more as the train wound its way from the far western edge of Tarenhiel and into the deeper forests of the elven heartland until they reached Estyra.

Most of Pip's belongings were stowed in the cargo train car. As she had purchased the cheapest through-ticket, she had an assigned bunk in the sleeping compartment. The bunks were stacked three high with only about two feet of headroom and little curtains to provide privacy from the neighbors. As she was small and short, the space was almost roomy for her, though she could only imagine how squashed her brother Mak would have been.

Mak. Muka. Dacha. She swallowed back the lump in her throat as she stared out the window, not really seeing the trees as they flashed by.

Was she doing the right thing in leaving home? She wasn't particularly patriotic or driven toward the lure of glory and adventure.

She just wanted…more. She couldn't even define what that *more* might be. It wasn't like she had been discontent at home. She loved working on the trains. She was just indefinably restless, much as she had been before she'd gone to study at Hanford University.

Perhaps that restlessness had never fully left, even after she'd returned.

She pulled out one of the manuals she'd kept from her university days. This one focused on the workings of magical power devices. She might as well use the time to brush up before she arrived. There would be additional training for the Mechanics Auxiliary, but she wasn't sure how much would be review and how much would focus specifically on aeroplanes and their engines. She didn't want to look ignorant compared to everyone else.

The closer they got to the center of Tarenhiel, the larger the trees became. Buildings had been grown into the branches, connected with branch pathways and swinging wooden bridges. On the ground, pathways meandered between the tree trunks. Elves either walked or bicycled as they went about their business. While elves had yet to take to the motorized vehicles that were growing in popularity in Escarland, the bicycle had quickly become ubiquitous even in the most far-flung elven village.

At supper time, an elf pushed a cart down the center aisle, and Pip paid for a sandwich.

After eating and making her way from the passenger car to her bunk, she wedged herself inside, shut the curtain, and slept the rest of the way to Estyra.

When the train pulled into Estyra the next morning, Pip had four hours to spend before her next train left south for Escarland. She stowed her luggage in a wooden locker provided in a tree near the train station, then joined the bustle of the elven capital city.

Towering trees rose so high into the sky that she couldn't even see the tops beyond the network of branches, empty of leaves as winter verged into a tentative spring. Without the leaves, the tiers of elven homes and shops grown into the trees were even more visible than in the summer, with elves strolling along branches between homes that were dizzying heights in the air.

At ground level, elves walked on either side of the meandering pathways while bicycling elves filled the center. The occasional elf on horseback rode by, but as bicycles were cheaper and required less maintenance than horses, many elves had switched in recent years.

To one side of the station, a massive airship hovered among the trees, a wooden gangway connecting it to a platform several stories in the air. A few humans strolled from the airship, heading into Estyra for sightseeing on this stop of their airship cruise.

A signboard at the train station showed a map of Estyra with important points marked in both Escarlish and the elvish language that was shared by the elves and trolls. It denoted the locations of Estyra's various inns, places to eat, and, of course, the elven palace of Ellonahshinel, the great oak tree that dominated one side of Estyra. Its name meant *Heart of the Forest* in elvish, and the tree itself was held in reverence.

Since she wouldn't be there long enough to need a place to stay, Pip wandered down the main street—well, grass-covered pathway—stopping at a few of the shops. She ate at a small café, then wandered east, heading in the direction of Ellonahshinel.

As she neared, the forest cleared slightly, giving her an unobstructed view of the oak tree that was so gargantuan that it made the already massive trees surrounding it look skinny. While Ellonahshinel wasn't the tallest tree, it was thick and sprawling, its branches holding the many grand rooms of the elven royal palace.

While Pip didn't have the full elven depth of veneration for trees, she halted at the end of the pathway, taking in the wonder that was Ellonahshinel, and something inside her stirred in a way that made her think she might have a bit of her dacha in her after all.

A thin fence formed of interlocking saplings demarcated the public roadway and the space beneath Ellonahshinel that was off-limits for regular citizens or tourists. A few elven guards, dressed in full elven armor regalia from shining helmets to metal and leather breastplates strolled back and forth across the open gateway to Ellonahshinel, looking for all the world as if they had stepped out of a different era. One where elves had ruled an empire and the great warriors of old fought with a strength of magic only a few living elves could match.

Pip stepped off the road, standing at the fringe of a cluster of humans who were also gaping at Ellonahshinel. The men wore fine bowlers, trim jackets, and polished shoes while the women trailed long skirts over generous bustles in the back with pristine, frilled blouses. One man was in the process of setting up photography equipment, proclaiming in Escarlish about the light in between trying to cajole one of the elven guards to take a step to the right so that he would be perfectly in the frame next to Ellonahshinel.

Pip stood on her tiptoes to better peer over the sapling fence, which must have been designed with elven height in mind rather than a short half-dwarf.

"This is even more magnificent on the ground than it was from the airship." One of the ladies waved toward Ellonahshinel.

"It was quite the experience as the airship drifted down to the dock and the trees closed over us, wasn't it?" Another lady frantically fanned herself, as if she hadn't quite recovered her nerves. "It was like the forest was swallowing us whole."

A movement on the long sweeping staircase that spiraled down the side of Ellonahshinel's trunk caught Pip's eye.

Two male elves strode down the steps, their bearing tall and regal. The one on the left wore a thin crown on his black hair, his tunic a dark green emblazoned with a silver oak tree. He could only be King Weylind of the elves.

The elf on the right, though…Pip's heart beat in her ears, and she had to press her hands over her mouth to stop her squeal. It was Prince Farrendel Laesornysh. *The* Prince Farrendel Laesornysh. Co-inventor of the magical power cell and a hundred different devices that were powered with his magic. Her childhood hero—well, he was still her hero—was *right over there.*

"Oh, I say. Is that the elf king?" One of the men pointed in that direction.

The women burst into a flurry of murmuring and squeals as they crowded the fence, trying to get a glimpse. The man with the camera yelped, barking at them to move out of his shot even as he dove beneath the hood and fiddled to focus his lens.

All the commotion drew the elf king's gaze in their direction. He lifted his hand in a single, regal wave before he continued his conversation with his brother.

Prince Farrendel glanced in their direction, just the briefest flash of movement, before he ducked his head. Moments later, he and the king turned a corner of the staircase and were hidden from sight.

"Oh, and they're gone. Bother." The lady fluttered her fan before her face despite the early spring chill. "Tell me you at least got a picture, Gerald."

"I'm not sure how it will turn out since all of you kept crowding my shot." The man, Gerald, disentangled himself from the hood of his camera and glared at the rest of the tourists.

One of the other men glanced in Pip's direction, his brow furrowing. "Miss, are you all right?"

The women turned to Pip, and the fan lady bustled closer and waved her fan vigorously in front of Pip's face. "Dear me, you look like you are about to faint. Are you feeling quite the thing?"

Another reached into her reticule. "I have smelling salts."

"Gerald, fetch that bench for the poor girl." Another of the women flapped her hand at Gerald.

Pip's entire body was petrified with hero-worship over-load, her breath seizing in her chest, her joints cramping.

Gerald placed a wooden bench behind her. The fan lady firmly pressed on Pip's shoulders, shoving her to sit on the bench.

With a great effort, Pip blinked, then shook herself. Her breath whooshed out, then she gasped in a breath of the fresh, forest-scented air.

"There, there." The fan lady returned to setting up a breeze. "That was quite the spell that came over you."

Pip flushed, her face burning. She wasn't about to explain that she had hero-worshipped herself into shock. "That was my first time seeing Weylind Daresheni."

While that was technically true, it wasn't the reason for her temporary paralysis. But saying it was far less embar-rassing than explaining the truth.

The lady perked up, likely catching Pip's use of the king's elven title. "Oh, you're an elf? I should have guessed. You have the pointed ears. But I have never seen an elf so…"

"So vertically challenged?" Pip gave a wry laugh and pushed herself to her feet, stepping out of fanning range. "I'm half elf and half dwarf."

"Ooh, I've never met a dwarf before! Much less a half-dwarf!" The woman beckoned to her. "Come. We simply *must* have a picture with you. Please? Gerald, get back behind your camera."

As Gerald scurried to return to his camera, the ladies herded Pip into the center of their cluster.

Pip didn't try to resist, still in a bit of shock over the glimpse of Prince Farrendel. Not to mention that she'd never had anyone ask to take her picture, as if she was someone famous instead of a nobody half-dwarf from the far edge of Tarenhiel.

Once the shutter clicked, and they held their pose for the required amount of time, Pip extracted herself from the huddle and said her farewells to the tourists. They wished her well and gave her a whole list of shops, stores, cafés, and soda parlors to check out in Bridgetown while she was there.

Pip returned to the train station with plenty of time to collect her things from the locker, see them loaded onto the baggage car, and board the passenger car, settling down for the trip to Bridgetown.

THE TRAIN NEARED Bridgetown in late evening, the lights of the sprawling city reflecting on the rippling waters of the Hydalla River.

Pip twisted in her seat, all but pressing her face to the glass to catch a glimpse of the city ahead. Lights twinkled along either side of the Alliance Bridge. The train swerved around the bulk of Calafaren, heading a hint west before turning south again.

The train glided to a halt next to the moss-covered, tree-shaded platform at the far side of Calafaren. Most of the elves stood, making their way to the doors to disembark.

Pip remained where she was, peering through the reflection on the windows to take in what she could of Calafaren's quiet pathways. Perhaps she'd have the chance to better explore Calafaren and Bridgetown if those in the Mechanics Auxiliaries were allowed to leave the base.

Once the others had left, a trickle of new passengers climbed on board. One elf took a seat at the far end of the car while a troll family—their gray skin and white hair a contrast to the other passengers—found seats across from

Pip. She smiled at the family and nodded her head to a little girl, who shyly tucked her face against her mother.

A few humans wearily clambered on board as well, talking in voices that punctuated the quiet that had filled the train car for most of the trip.

As the doors shut once again, the train car shuddered, a clunking, grinding noise coming from outside.

"What is that?" The little troll girl tucked herself closer to her mother.

"They are lowering the iron wheels for the trip under the river into Escarland." The troll mother patted her daughter's head.

This was one of the few trains in Tarenhiel designed like this, to run on both Escarlish iron and Tarenhieli root rails. Pip had heard all three kings had private trains that could travel over both systems, as did Prince Farrendel and his family.

With a final clunk and screech, the whole train car lifted slightly, settling onto the iron rails instead of the root rails. When the train eased into motion again, it was with the familiar clack of iron wheels on iron rails that Pip had grown up hearing as a constant background to her life at the far western rail hub.

As the train picked up speed, it swerved away from the lights of Calafaren before it straightened out to face the river once again.

There was a dropping feeling in the pit of Pip's stomach, then darkness swallowed them as the train plunged underground.

The few elves in the passenger car around Pip stiffened. One even rubbed at his temples. Being underground was difficult on an elf. Many of them even had physical symptoms, such as headaches, if they were surrounded by too much stone, like the stone tunnel that currently provided passage for their train beneath the Hydalla River.

It was that sensitivity to being underground and surrounded by stone that prompted her mother to move to Tarenhiel when she fell in love with Dacha rather than Dacha move to the dwarven mountains. While her mother was often scorned by some among the elves, she wasn't in physical pain living among the trees. Dacha would have withered and died if he'd been the one to move.

Unlike the elves around her, Pip peered out the windows, trying to take in as much of the tunnel as she could as it flashed past the windows. A few blue elven lights were spaced along the sides, providing some illumination for the rock walls.

If she could have, Pip would have asked the train conductor to stop so she could get out and inspect the troll workmanship that went into carving the tunnel into bedrock beneath the river. A few glints of the troll magic still remained, glittering gray in the walls. It would have been fascinating to compare it to the dwarven stone construction she was familiar with from visits with her grandparents.

Across the way, the troll girl was peering through the windows with a similar wonder.

Then the train rose again, bursting into evening daylight on the other side of the Hydalla River and into a bustling city that was a sharp contrast from the peaceful, tourist retreat on the northern side.

Here, brick and stone buildings rose into the sky alongside the blocks of straight, asphalt or stone paved streets. Even more newfangled automobiles rumbled back and forth along the roads than there had been the last time she had visited Escarland, their shiny chrome fenders reflecting the streetlights. Horse-drawn carriages clogged the streets between the automobiles while bicyclists wove in and out of the traffic, nearly running over the pedestrians that choked the walks on either side even at this time of night.

Pip pressed her face to the glass, but she couldn't spot the Outpost Museum between the other buildings. Too bad she didn't have time to tour the museum tonight or before she reported to Fort Linder in the morning. Visiting that museum was on the top of her list of things she wanted to see if she had the chance. She, sadly, hadn't spent enough time in Bridgetown during her days at Hanford University to visit back then.

The train's air brakes hissed while the wheels squealed against the rails. With a few jolting shudders, the train ground to a halt at the station in Bridgetown.

Pip gathered her things, but she waited for the other passengers to disembark first. At her diminutive height, she'd just end up taking an elbow or two to the face. Unless she had someone taller and larger to shove a path, it just wasn't worth it.

Once the car had nearly cleared out, she headed for the door and climbed down the two stairs onto the wooden platform. A wooden porch roof strung with lights sheltered the platform while the building beyond held ticket offices, a communications hub, and waiting rooms.

Pip strode the length of the platform toward the baggage car. She had to duck one man's elbow and dodge out of a troll's way. The troll hadn't even been looking down, and he would have plowed her over if she hadn't moved.

Once she reached the baggage car, she waited in the line until it was her turn to present her carved wooden token to the attendant. She pointed out her bag, and the attendant went to fetch it. As soon as he picked it up, he grunted at the weight. After checking that the leather tag matched the token, he unclipped the tag to reuse both it and the token before he handed the bag over. "Can you carry this, miss? It's heavy. A porter can help you transport it to your destination."

Pip resisted the urge to roll her eyes. Just because she was a pipsqueak didn't mean she wasn't strong.

"It's not that heavy." She hefted the bag easily enough. Sure, it was on the heavy side. She didn't know what kind of tools the army would provide the mechanics, and she'd rather have her own tools anyway. She didn't go anywhere without her favorite wrench.

Bag in one hand and her smaller pack on her back, Pip drew in a deep breath and joined the flow of people from the train station onto the streets of Bridgetown, which were busy even at this time of night.

Just past the train station, she had to worm her way through a crowd pouring out of a cinema. The posters on the front of the building proclaimed showings of the hit multi-reel film *Star Forest and the Castle of Doom*, complete with images of Tenian Daefiel, the elf who played Star Forest, giving that come hither smolder while his shirt seemed to lack any kind of buttons or laces. His leading lady draped in a swoon in his arms.

Neither the books nor the films were as questionable as the marketing posters made them appear, though the film version had reduced the leading lady to a swooning, too-silly-to-survive-more-than-two-seconds-on-her-own maiden who only existed for the elf hero to save her. The books were, of course, far superior.

As the streets were so well lit and busy, Pip felt perfectly safe, even as a tiny woman all alone in a strange city. She still kept her eyes peeled and her bag close.

Not that she had to fear much. She could shield herself

with her magic, and the wrench in her bag also made a good defensive weapon if she needed it.

Well, she was here. All she needed to do now was find a room for the night, then report to Fort Linder in the morning.

Yet a strange emptiness filled her, despite the lively bustle surrounding her.

It was the same hollowness that had filled her when she'd put her things in the tiny room of the boarding house in Aldon her first year at Hanford University. At least then, she'd had the burning desire of her dreams to fuel her through the loneliness and long nights.

What was she doing here? There was still a burning inside her, but she didn't have a dream to direct it toward just yet.

Hopefully this experience would give her direction. Otherwise, this had all been a huge mistake.

NINE

Fieran stood at attention in the crisp row of recruits. It took all his concentration not to bounce on his toes like he was a little kid with a handful of his favorite candy.

They were lined up to one side of the large hangar that sheltered the base's flyers. The biplanes were constructed of a wooden fuselage, the wings formed of a frame of wood and stretched with canvas. A layer of paint coated all surfaces while the wings were emblazoned with the red, gray, and green circle that was the symbol of the joint Alliance Flying Corps. Each of those aeroplanes was fueled by a magical power cell containing either Dacha's, Fieran's, Adry's, or Louise's magic.

But it wasn't the flyers—or only the flyers—that had him struggling to keep the grin off his face that would earn another round of physical training or PT.

It was the man striding back and forth before the lines of recruits, his hair threaded with a few strands of gray while deep lines on his face gave him the appearance of being an older man than he was. While he was only in his mid-forties, he was one of the few pilots from the early days of flight who had lived to even see his fortieth birthday. Most had crashed and died long before then. Still, he was muscular and had that dashing hero look of a pilot with a leather jacket, silk scarf, and goggles perched on his forehead.

Of course he looked the part of a dashing hero. He was Joe Arfeld, an early Escarlish pioneer of flight. A true legend. It was all Fieran could do to stay where he was and not march over there and beg to shake his hand.

Though Joe Arfeld was now a captain in the army's Flying Corps. Fieran could settle for saluting him instead.

Capt. Arfeld swept his sharp blue gaze over the line of recruits. "Over the next weeks, you will study aeroplanes, the physics of flight, air navigation, weather patterns, and much more. This is not just busywork. Once we are in the air, there is no room for error. You will die. I will die. And I have no intention of dying anytime soon. So you will learn well, or you won't be allowed to so much as sit in a cockpit."

Fieran swallowed. The last thing he wanted to do was kill off one of his heroes. Odds were, Fieran would probably survive a mild crash, thanks to his magic and being half elf. But Capt. Arfeld was human and thus far more breakable.

To one side of the large hangar, a large man in green coveralls was leading around a group of men, also dressed in coveralls.

Except that one of the men was tiny…and definitely *not* a man. Fieran couldn't get a good look at the girl out of the corner of his eye, and he couldn't turn his head without the nearby sergeant noticing.

Moments later, the group disappeared behind one of the rows of flyers.

"Red, are you listening?" The sergeant was suddenly there, right in Fieran's face. "Drop and give me fifty."

So much for the sergeant not noticing. Fieran bit back a sigh, dropped to the floor, and started in on the fifty push-ups. At least fifty wasn't too many compared to the amount Fieran normally had to do.

Capt. Arfeld cleared his throat, then continued with his speech about the various flyers and engines housed here in the aerodrome at Fort Linder.

Once Fieran was finished, he joined the rest of his unit as they marched into a small room off to the side.

A lieutenant stood at the head of the room and began a lecture on the basics of flight.

Fieran settled into the desk, his legs scrunched to fit, his knees hitting a bar at the front. Time to dust off his old university habits. It had taken some practice to sit still and pay attention in classes, even if he was smart enough that tests weren't hard, if he devoted some focus during class.

But the daily class times to learn about flight were going to be far harder than all the physical training, drills, push-ups, and whatever else the army would throw at him.

Pip pushed one of the rolling ladders up to the fuselage of one of the T-05 Soarwing biplane flyers that were a favorite among the Escarlish pilots. After climbing the ladder, she opened the hatch to the engine, lifting it up and out of the way.

A male mechanic with longer arms would've had no trouble reaching into the engine compartment from the ladder. But she had to basically stick her whole upper torso inside to reach some of the parts of the engine to inspect it, her feet losing contact with the ladder in a way that left her rear end sticking up into the air.

She was sure to get a few wolf whistles, mostly from the pilots-in-training who spent a chunk of every afternoon in the hangar. At least her fellow mechanics no longer pulled such shenanigans around her. She'd proven herself over the previous two weeks at Fort Linder.

The head mechanic here believed in hands-on learning, so after only a week in the classroom with schematics, he'd turned them loose in the hangar, though he checked their work before the aeroplanes took to the sky.

While Pip had proven her skills—the switch from trains to aeroplanes hadn't been all that difficult—she wasn't particularly close with her fellow mechanics here at Fort Linder. She recognized a few of them from her Hanford University days, but that was about it. She'd been the odd one out at Hanford—the only female mechanic, the only half-dwarf. And she was just as odd here.

Reaching into the engine, Pip checked each of the parts, from the magical power cell to the propeller shaft.

As she suspected. It was the wiring harness that tended to burn out under the force of the magic of the ancient kings. An easy fix, at least.

She pulled out her three eights inch drive socket wrench, then worked her hand under the buttoned flap of one of her cargo pockets, searching through her sockets by feel. With her magic, she had marked each socket so she could find the correct one by feel instead of manually checking the numbers etched on each one.

When she found the correct one, she wiggled her hand out of her pocket. Clicking the socket into place, she removed the four bolts on each of the corners of the hatch on the side of the engine housing. For most mechanics, they would've had to take off the magical power cell housing to get at the last bolt, but with her small hands and thin wrists, she could wiggle her hands into the space and do it without the extra work.

As she removed the final bolt, footsteps clunked closer, then halted beside the aeroplane.

Must be one of the pilots-in-training. One of her fellow mechanics would have called out to her.

She suppressed a sigh. She might as well head off the wolf whistle or lewd comment. "You had better not be gawking at my rear end."

"Of course not. My parents taught me to keep my hands, eyes, and inappropriate comments to myself." The baritone male voice held a note of easy, congenial laughter. He spoke in Escarlish—as she did—though his voice didn't have the elvish accent that hers did.

"You have rare parents." Pip ratcheted the wrench with small movements. "Not everyone teaches their children such basic manners."

"My parents are more rare than you know." His voice had a droll tone, as if in some joke, though she wasn't sure what it was. When he spoke again, some of the laughter faded into something almost sheepish. "Though, um, I have to confess I looked. Just now. Sorry."

Apologies instead of whistles? That was a new one. She wiggled her hand free of its tight confines, going carefully so that she didn't drop the bolt or the cover for the terminal. "At least you're an honest flyboy."

"How do you know I'm one of the flyboys? You're still head-down in an engine." That baritone voice was back to light-hearted again.

"You sound slightly arrogant." After setting the bolt and the terminal cover on top of the engine housing, she wiggled her hand into the tight space again to disconnect the end of the wiring harness that connected the terminal on the engine housing with the magical power cell. "All flyboys are slightly arrogant. It's just a fact."

He laughed. A genuine, open-hearted kind of laugh. "Very true. Yes, you're correct. I'm a flyboy. And based on how much extra PT I've received, the drill sergeants are very convinced I'm arrogant."

She laughed as she disconnected the wiring harness from the magical power cell housing. Her laughter quickly died. She hadn't grabbed new wires before climbing up here. She'd have to wiggle her way down, always nerve-wracking since right now she couldn't see if the ladder was still directly beneath her feet.

Setting aside her socket wrench, she gripped the side of the fuselage and began to squirm, reaching with her toes for the ladder.

The flyboy's voice drew closer. "Can I fetch something for you?"

She paused. He was a flyboy. He wouldn't know what she needed. But what was the harm in seeing if he could figure it out? "Probably not. Unless you can tell the difference between gauges of wire?"

"Ah, I see." The flyboy almost sounded like he did, indeed, understand. "That flyer has the latest Dymman engine. The wiring harness burned out, didn't it?"

Pip froze, her middle aching from hanging over the fuselage at her waist. "How would you know that? I didn't think the flyboys learned more about the engines than what gauges to watch in the cockpit."

"Let's just say I've had more experience with a variety of engines than most." The flyboy gave that easy laugh again. Despite her calling him arrogant earlier, he said this last bit almost self-consciously instead of arrogantly. "Wait there a moment, and I'll fetch a new wiring harness for you."

While she waited, Pip checked a few of the other pieces of the engine. Calling up her magic, she reinforced the metal.

The footsteps returned, quicker and lighter than she would have expected. "I'm coming up the ladder behind you, just so you know."

A creak of wood came from the ladder, then she could sense the warmth of someone at her back. An arm clad in basic army green reached into her view, holding out a bundle of wires in long, slim fingers.

"Thanks." She took the wire from him, comparing it with the wires she'd taken off. Not only was it formed of the right gauges, but it was correctly bundled together and so close to the right length that this flyboy must have worked with Dymman engines before.

"Here. I wasn't sure if you'd have the right pliers in your belt." The hand came into view again, this time holding the large combo pliers and wire cutter.

She did, but it was all the way on the wrong side of her belt in a place that she'd have to squirm around awkwardly to try to reach.

"Thanks again." Pip took the pliers from him. "Could you fetch—"

"A torque wrench for the bolts?" he finished for her. Strangely, the interruption didn't feel rude. Instead, it felt like he was too eager to help and couldn't stop himself from interrupting. The kind of interruption experienced between friends or family who were comfortable with each other.

"Yes, that would be great." She set to work with the pliers, swapping the connecting ends from the old wiring harness to the new one. While she was at it, she called up her iron magic and sent it over the wires to reinforce them.

By the time she had the wiring harness in place, the flyboy had returned and was holding out the correct torque wrench to her. The thin wire and dial on the bottom of the wrench measured the amount of pressure she put on the bolts.

As the flyboy retreated to the ground, she torqued the bolts holding the wiring harness into place, then replaced the terminal covers and wrenched the bolts down.

As she finished, she gathered her tools and stowed them back in her toolbelt and pocket. After one last check that she hadn't left anything undone or any tools in the engine, she squirmed again to lower herself out of the engine, feeling with her toes for the ladder.

The ladder creaked again, then the flyboy's voice came from beside the aeroplane. "The ladder is about three inches directly below your feet. I'm holding it steady."

"Thanks." She shook her head, even as she was glad for the extra reassurance that the ladder was beneath her. "I've done this loads of times before. You get good at scrambling over stuff when you're as short as I am."

Once free of the fuselage, Pip straightened, her head whirling slightly. Her feet tingled as blood flowed better into her toes once again.

Now that she stood on the semi-solid though wiggling step, the flyboy let go of the ladder, stepping back before she caught a glimpse of more of him than his short-cropped, red hair.

Within moments, Pip had the hatch in the fuselage latched back in place, and she quickly climbed down the ladder.

As her feet hit the ground, she turned around and got her first good look at the mechanically inclined flyboy.

He was at least a foot taller than her with that rangy, slim build often found among elves. He even had pointed ears, hinting at some kind of elven heritage despite his presence here on an Escarlish aerodrome. He had the most brilliant red hair she'd ever seen, and the red of his hair only seemed to highlight his bright blue eyes. A hint of a smirk played around the corners of his mouth.

Aw, man. She had *such* a thing for tall, skinny guys. She didn't know why. Perhaps it was her elven heritage. Or maybe, she was just a short girl with a thing for guys who were tall enough to get items off the top shelf.

Even worse, this handsome, red-haired elf with laughing eyes and chiseled features had a hint of freckles across his nose, stark against his pale skin. Freckles! How could she not get a little flutter at the freckles?

FIERAN FACED the tiny female mechanic he'd been slightly flirting with for the past few minutes. He'd seen her at a distance several times over the last two weeks. But she was far cuter up close. Her dark brown hair was currently knotted up in something of a messy bun, but the tendrils that fell free spiraled in curls. Her skin was a warm light bronze while her eyes were the kind of dark chocolate that made a man want to lose himself in her gaze. The points of her ears were just visible through her hair, so she wasn't a human. Perhaps half-human since Fieran had never seen an elf that short.

Even with grease smeared across her cheeks and wearing coveralls—or perhaps because of the grease and coveralls— she was adorable.

As he swept a glance over her, a smile pursed her mouth as she took him in. She stuck out a hand. "I'm Pippak Detmuk-Inawenys. But that's a mouthful, so most people just call me Pip."

Pip. An adorable little name for an adorable little mechanic.

Fieran shook her hand, impressed at the way her grip was strong and firm. Nothing shirking or retiring about her, despite her size.

Yet as he opened his mouth, his stomach sank. Proud as he was to be his dacha's son, he hated watching the reactions in people's eyes when he introduced himself.

"I'm Fieran." He swallowed. As much as he wished he could, he couldn't leave off his last name. She'd find out eventually. "Laesornysh."

"Laesornysh?" Her eyes lit, and her voice went up. "The son of Prince Farrendel Laesornysh?"

Ugh. She'd said his dacha's name in *that* way. The octave higher, voice-squeaking way that suggested she was one breath away from breaking into a squeal.

Great. It was even worse than he'd feared.

Bracing himself, Fieran forced out the word. "Yes."

This time, she gave a slight squeal, her hands over her mouth. She spoke rapidly behind her fingers, as if the words were popping out without her permission. "I have his poster on my wall at home!" Her hands clapped harder over her mouth, as if she couldn't believe she'd just said that.

Oh. Oh, no. It was much, much worse. This adorable mechanic had one of *those* posters on her wall. One with his shirtless dacha lounging in a sexy way.

Well, so much for flirting with her. He would never flirt with anyone who had a pin up poster of his dacha.

Fieran's ears burned. He edged backwards. "Um, well, I probably should…"

Pip's face flushed, and she flapped her hands as if she didn't know what to do with them. "I didn't mean to say that. It isn't as weird as it sounds. I dreamed of going to

Hanford University just like he did, and he was the first elf to do so, and I put up that recruiting poster as motivation and..." She dropped her face into her hands. "Ugh. I sound like a stalker. I promise, I'm not stalking your dacha."

Fieran released a breath, some of the urge to run fading. She didn't have one of *those* posters. She was talking about one of the Hanford University recruitment posters. Dacha had posed for one of those decades ago—fully clothed, thank you very much—with goggles on his forehead, magic lacing around one hand, and a textbook in the other hand. The result had been an unusually high number of elven university students—and female students—in the next few years after that marketing campaign.

"I don't think that...well, for a moment..." Fieran shook his head and forced a smile back onto his face. "He's my dacha, you know? He's just normal to me. But he's not normal to everyone else, and that's...weird."

"Sorry." Pip's smile was lopsided. "If you hadn't guessed, he's my childhood hero."

"Understandable. He's a hero to a lot of people." Fieran nodded, working to keep his smile in place. As cute as she was, he probably wouldn't flirt with her again.

But he could be friendly with her. If he ignored everyone who looked up to his dacha as a hero, then Merrik would be his only friend in the world. And Merrik only didn't see Dacha as his hero because he saw him as an adopted uncle.

Come to think of it, Merrik *had* been his only friend until he'd met Lije and the others in the barracks. The whole famous parents thing made finding genuine friends rather difficult.

Her eyes cleared a bit from the hero-worship haze. "Oh, that's why you knew so much about the engine."

A slight topic shift. He could work with that. Fieran

gestured around them. "I work—well, worked—for AMPC, so I've done a lot of testing on all kinds of engines, including these most recent Dymman models. Not to mention that my magic is in the power cells in about a third of the flyers around us." Fieran pointed to the aeroplane she had been working on. "Not that one. My dacha's power is in that one. But mine is in that one. And that one." He waved to two of the nearby aeroplanes.

He wasn't boasting. Well, okay. Maybe he was boasting a little bit. But she was a mechanic who dreamed about going to Hanford University so much that she tacked a poster of his dacha on the wall as motivation. She'd find the fact that he could tell whose magic was in which aeroplanes fascinating.

As he'd expected, her eyes took on a gleam as she glanced around at the aeroplanes. "That's really interesting." She turned back to him, cocking her head as if she was now studying a piece of machinery instead of a man. "I've always just worked with the magical power cells. It makes it easy to forget there's actual people's magic in there."

Fieran raised his hand, then let a tendril of his magic loose from that tight control he always kept on it. After two weeks of holding his magic in check without the daily release of morning practice with his dacha, his magic flared bright and blue, crackling as it twined around his fingers and up his arm. Something almost like relief flowed through him, as if he'd been in pain and hadn't even realized it from holding his magic back for so long.

Pip's eyes widened, her mouth falling open. "Oh, wow. That's…so neat. I never expected to see the magic of the ancient kings in person. Does it feel different than normal magic when you wield it?"

"I wouldn't know. It's my magic, so it just feels normal to

me." Fieran let his magic play around his hand and arm before he, reluctantly, suppressed his magic again, locking it once again into the iron control his dacha had drilled into him over years and years of practice.

"I guess that makes sense." Pip held out her hand. A shimmer of some kind of silvery magic glowed around her fingers. But it didn't look like the gray stone magic Aunt Vriska wielded. Or any other stone magic he'd seen over the years. Pip glanced up, meeting his gaze and smiling. "I have an unusual form of iron magic. It just feels normal to me too."

"Iron magic? I've never heard of an elf with iron magic." Fieran crossed his arms, wishing there was a wall nearby so he could lounge nonchalantly.

"Half-elf. And half-dwarf." She gestured to herself, her smile tipping as if she knew exactly what he was thinking.

She probably did. Being half-dwarf explained her height and her magic. "I was guessing you were half-human like me. You have a good grasp of Escarlish."

"I had to learn it to go to Hanford University." Pip fiddled with one of the wrenches tucked in her tool belt. "Not to mention that Escarlish has become the language of trade among many of the human kingdoms. My family runs the far western rail terminal in Tarenhiel, so we interact with some of the Afristani tribes on the other side of the river. Many of them have begun learning some Escarlish since that's easier than elvish."

Fieran opened his mouth, but tromping boots behind him had him straightening.

"Red, are you bothering this mechanic?" the sergeant's voice barked from behind him.

"No, Drill Sergeant." Fieran kept his gaze straight ahead.

"He really isn't bothering me," Pip added, stepping closer.

Her defense didn't matter. The sergeant shouted, "Put your face to the floor and give me a hundred."

More push-ups. He was going to have the arms of a gorilla at this rate.

At least with Pip standing there, Fieran could take the opportunity to show off a bit. He might not want to flirt with her more than that, but showing off was still always acceptable.

TEN

Fieran waited in line in the mess hall, counting those ahead of him in line, then the seats left at the next table. Four people in front of him in line. Five seats left on one side of the table.

That meant he would be the last person to sit down, and he'd have the least amount of time to eat. As soon as the first person who sat down was done eating, the whole side of the table had to be done, no matter how much or little they'd eaten.

At least they only had one more day of this. After tomorrow, they would get five minutes to eat.

Five whole minutes. Such luxury.

At the moment, Merrik was in that first spot. He'd slopped some of the tough mystery meat onto his tray, and he was gamely chewing the leathery stuff, buying the others as much time as he could without getting yelled at by the drill sergeants for obviously delaying.

As the line moved forward, Fieran grabbed two slices of bread and scanned the offered food.

Ah, good. Spaghetti and meatballs. Lots of good carbs and proteins there.

He slopped the spaghetti and meatballs onto one of his slices of bread, flopped the other bread on top, and hurried to the table.

The fastest way to eat anything was as a sandwich. If there was mac and cheese? Put it between bread and it was a mac-and-cheese sandwich. Spaghetti? Spaghetti sandwich. Even soup was poured onto bread and eaten as a sandwich.

Fieran plunked his rear into the last seat on the bench, picked up his spaghetti sandwich, and wolfed down a huge bite. He spared only a brief nod for Stickyfingers sitting next to him.

Next to Stickyfingers, Tiny hunched to take up less space on the bench, his elbows tucked as close to his body as he could, given his brawny arms.

Lije squashed onto the seat on the other side of Tiny, and he dug into his own spaghetti sandwich as if it was his favorite meal.

Across the way, more recruits began filling up the table. The self-obsessed handsome man who had the bunk below Merrik sat across from Fieran. Everyone called him "Pretty Face." Pretty Face had turned out to be the seventh son of an earl who was more prolific at producing children than was fiscally wise, given his penchant for gambling. As Pretty Face had become a bit of a wastrel himself, his only way to dodge both his and his father's creditors had been to join the army.

At the far side of the mess hall, a group of mechanics sat at a long table, sequestered away from the army recruits. Pip sat at the far end of the table, the table coming up higher on her than on the others.

She glanced up, and Fieran caught her eye. He grinned, and she smiled back.

Merrik glanced down their bench, gave them all an apologetic wince, and popped his last bite into his mouth.

As a sergeant was already patrolling in their direction, Merrik grabbed his tray and stood.

On cue, the rest of them slid to their feet. Even though Fieran's mouth was already full, he shoved the rest of his sandwich in anyway, struggling to chew so much food. But he had to eat every calorie he could get.

He'd thought himself fit before, but after two weeks with the army, he'd dropped so much weight he had to cinch his belt to the last hole to keep his pants up. He'd need the next size down if he kept losing so much weight.

After filing out of the mess hall, Fieran, Merrik, and the others lined up on the parade ground before their barracks, standing at attention while they waited for the rest of their unit to finish eating.

A light drizzle misted the air while dark clouds piling in the west threatened more rain. Their slickers shed most of the rain, but some dribbled down Fieran's collar onto his neck.

Fieran worked a bit of gristle from between his teeth with his tongue, careful to keep his expression blank and his jaw from moving. If the sergeant caught so much as a hint of movement in his face, he'd be down in the mud doing push-ups or sit-ups in a heartbeat, especially if one particular drill sergeant happened to look his way.

Several of the drill sergeants seemed to have it out for him and Merrik because they were half-elves and, worse, they had famous parents. If the rest of the unit had to run two miles, Fieran and Merrik had to run four. If the rest of the unit had to do the obstacle course in under a minute,

Fieran and Merrik were expected to do it in less than half a minute. Sure, they could usually pass the extra duties, given their elven agility. But it still rankled, and Fieran had gotten extra PT more times than he could count in the past weeks.

At least he had no trouble with the actual training part. He'd easily won hand-to-hand combat sessions with everyone but the most experienced drill sergeants or if he was paired with Tiny, who had the immovability of a boulder. He was top in their class at the gun range with both pistol and rifle, though he shared that top spot with Merrik.

As the last of their unit joined them, the drill sergeant swept his hard, assessing glance down the line. "Kit up."

Under the drill sergeant's orders, they marched into their barracks and over to their bunks, where they were ordered to pack their rucksacks.

There was, of course, a special way everything had to be folded and an order in which it had to be packed. Fieran checked everything as he packed, from the rolls of his spare underwear to the placement of his Not-Knot boots. Today was a Knot boot day, so those were on his feet.

Once he was fully kitted out from his helmet on his head to his rifle resting on his shoulder, Fieran stood at attention next to the end of his bunk for inspection, his toes right at the line that marked the sergeant's zone in the center of the room but not crossing over.

The drill sergeant paced in front of them, his gaze taking in their uniforms, searching for any flaw.

One recruit's rifle wasn't clean enough. Another was wearing his Not-Knot Boots instead of his Knot Boots.

Fieran held his shoulders straight, his eyes straight ahead, as the sergeant halted in front of him. Surely there was nothing wrong this time.

"Is that what you call a well-made bunk, Red?" the drill sergeant yelled in his face.

Fieran couldn't turn his head to look. What was wrong with his bunk now? He'd made sure the sheet and blanket were perfectly tucked and taut this morning.

What was he supposed to say? He settled on, "No, Drill Sergeant." It seemed like the less insubordinate option.

The sergeant stalked past him. Fieran caught a glimpse of his blankets tugged askew—he must have caught it with his rifle or pack when mustering—before the drill sergeant flipped Fieran's mattress off the bed, tumbling blankets all over the floor. Among a slew of insults and curses, the drill sergeant barked, "One minute, knucklehead!"

After properly setting down his rifle—he'd get even more PT if he treated his weapon less than carefully—Fieran rushed to heave the mattress back onto his top bunk. He tucked in all his blankets, keeping them tight in proper military fashion. While lower bunks were favored because they were easier to make, especially quickly, Fieran's height helped negate the difficulties of a top bunk.

He grabbed his rifle and toed the line just before his minute was up, though he was breathing hard and trying not to show it.

As the sergeant finished his inspection, he swept a glance over all of them. "Due to the sloppiness of your bunkmates, your two-mile ruck march is now a five-mile march. Move it! Left, right, left, right."

Fieran fell into line behind Lije and before Pretty Face, Merrik marching behind him.

The drizzle had turned into a cold rain that slanted on a breeze seemingly determined to drive the water through any gaps in their slickers. The muddy ground slipped beneath the treads of their boots even as the mud spattered up their boots and onto their clothes.

Just as bad as the chill rain, his spaghetti sandwich sat like a rock in the pit of his stomach. His joints and shoulder muscles felt the weight of the sixty pounds of gear the longer he marched. It would have been easier and lighter to carry his little brother Tryndar on his back than his pack.

By the time they finished, he was more than ready for the two-minute shower that was all he was allowed.

They were lined up before their bunks for one last inspection. As the sergeant finished, the corporal stepped up, a bag at his side and holding a stack of letters. "Mail call."

Fieran stayed where he was until his name was called. He walked the perimeter of the room, staying out of the sergeant's zone, and claimed the stack of letters. As he returned to his bunk, he passed Lije on his way to claim a package.

Reaching his bunk, Fieran climbed up and sat on the hard mattress cross-legged, paging through the letters. Three from his mother and one each from Adry, Louise, and Ellie. If Tryndar included anything, it would be in one of the letters from Mama. Same with anything from Dacha.

The final letter appeared to be some kind of official letter. Fieran set aside the other ones and tore open that letter first. He scanned it, then laughed, waving it at Merrik, who sat across the way on his bunk. "The Flying Corps is trying to recruit me into the Mechanics Auxiliaries because of my magical engineering degree. Joke's on them. I'd rather fly the aeroplanes than fix them."

Though if he was one of the mechanics, he'd have the chance to flirt with Pip far more than just smile at her across the mess hall.

Not that he was flirting with her. Nope. Not flirting.

Merrik huffed, sorted through his letters, then held out an identical letter of his own. "Looks like they sent me one too."

The way he looked at it made something in Fieran twist. Had he made a mistake in dragging Merrik along with him as he always did? Was Merrik having second thoughts about taking the more dangerous choice?

After a moment, the look cleared, and Merrik raised his eyebrows at Fieran. "At least we'll have a backup plan for when the army kicks us out due to your insubordination."

"Hey, now. I'm a model recruit." Fieran flapped a hand at his bed. Which he had somehow managed to muss up even more than Merrik had, even though all he was doing was sitting on it.

"The amount of extra PT we have had to do because of you would say otherwise." Merrik rolled his eyes and set aside the recruitment letter. "The only reason you have not been kicked out yet is that you easily pass every drill and test."

"Yeah, that's the reason." Fieran muttered this last bit under his breath, tossing his Mechanics Auxiliaries recruitment letter aside.

It wasn't like the sergeants would have a downright difficult time kicking him out. Despite all of Uncle Julien's changes to the army, names and reputations still carried weight. And no one would want to be the person who kicked the son of Farrendel Laesornysh out of the army. Not to mention the nephew of the great General Julien Ardon, Spymaster Edmund Ispamir, King Averett of Escarland, King Weylind of Tarenhiel, and King Rharreth of Kostaria.

Come to think of it, Fieran was probably every commanding officer's worst nightmare.

But he didn't want to be there because of whom he was

related to. He wanted to prove himself. Prove that he was worthy to carry the name and legacy he bore.

No matter what he did, people would assume that he only got where he was because of his father and mother. Or because of his highly connected aunts and uncles. What no one realized was that he had to work twice as hard as anyone else for his accomplishments to be taken seriously.

He shook off those thoughts. Nothing he could do about that. Right now, he just had to survive training. Only then could he get his butt in a flyer, take to the sky, and chase a few legends of his own.

Fieran opened all the letters from his family, checked the dates on the top, and arranged them in order.

The bunk creaked as Lije plunked onto his mattress below Fieran. The sound of crinkling paper came from below, then Lije's excited, "Yes!"

Fieran peered around the end of the bunk, but he couldn't see much more than Lije's knees and feet. "Got something good?"

"A care package of my ma's best soap." Lije leaned out and showed off the box. Inside nestled a row of cream-colored bricks of soap. "Nothing takes off grime like my ma's goatmilk lye soap."

On the lower bunk across the way, Stickyfingers snorted. "Don't tell me you'll smell like roses or flowers or something. You'll be duded up worse than Pretty Face."

Lije sniffed the box. "Nope. Oatmeal and honey. Nothing fancy."

On the bunk below Merrik, Pretty Face reached across the aisle and made a grab for one of the bars of soap. "You're going to share, right?"

Lije yanked the box out of reach before Pretty Face could snag any of the soap. "Not a chance. Just because you're missing your high-class perfumes doesn't mean I'm going to share my ma's soap."

"Cologne, not perfume." Pretty Face huffed as he flopped back onto his bunk. He waved his stack of letters. "Perfume is what ladies use on their letters to me. See?" He sniffed one. "Ah, Lorelei." He sniffed another one. "And sweet, sweet Marianne."

Lije made a disgusted noise in the back of his throat and turned his attention back to his soap and accompanying letter.

Fieran raised his voice to be heard across the way. "You get any mail, Sticky?"

"One from Mama." Stickyfingers held up the single sheet of yellow, cheap paper filled with a rough scrawl. "My brother Kevin is back in solitary so he won't be able to get a letter out for a while. But she's hoping to visit Jack and Ron soon so I might hear from them. She's hoping they'll be able to get their transfers to Saltan Prison soon so they'll be closer to home."

"That's...good news." Fieran wasn't sure what else to say to that. Sticky might have grown up in Aldon like Fieran had, but his life experiences and family were vastly different.

Once everyone else was absorbed in their letters, Fieran finally took the time to read his.

His mama's letters had all come from Estyra. She, Dacha, Tryndar, and Ellie were there at the moment, while Dacha trained with the elven warriors and discussed plans with Uncle Weylind about the possibility of war.

Aunt Jalissa was currently also in Estyra while Uncle Edmund was off somewhere doing something that no one could talk about, especially in a letter. Nor was there any mention of Fieran's cousin Jayna, Uncle Edmund's and Aunt Jalissa's daughter. Fieran hadn't seen hide nor hair of Jayna in over two years, and he highly suspected that wherever she was, it was classified.

Tryndar had included a picture he'd drawn and colored of their cat Munchkins sitting on the workbench in Dacha's inventing workshop in Estyra.

Dacha had added a small postscript to two of Mama's letters. Just a few short, stilted lines. But that wasn't unexpected. Dacha wasn't all that great with words.

Ellie's letter was mostly filled with a recap of the recently released Star Forest novel she'd read. Which was convenient for Fieran. He could save all the work of reading the book himself if Ellie was just going to tell him the whole story in a nice, shortened version.

Adry's and Louise's letters were filled with news from Aldon. They'd stayed behind at Treehaven while they created a stockpile of magical power cells. The newspapers were filled with stories of Mongavarian aggression toward the ogre kingdom of Groyria.

As the Alliance Kingdoms didn't have an official alliance with Groyria, nor had Groyria reached out to Escarland asking for aid, there was nothing Uncle Averett or any of Fieran's other uncles could do. Their hands were tied, politically.

Yet the calls for war were building. Articles declared that war was just around the corner while Parliament members pushing for war were making speeches decrying Mongavarian aggression.

"Your parents are in Estyra too, I take it?" Fieran glanced across the way at Merrik.

"Yes." Merrik folded his letter and neatly slid it back into the envelope. He met Fieran's gaze, something in his brown eyes even more serious than usual. "I suspect we will see our dachas as the warriors they once were rather than the inventors and businessmen they have become, before the year is out."

Fieran nodded, dropping his gaze to his letters. For seventy years, his and Merrik's dachas had been Prince Farrendel and Iyrinder Loiatir, partners in the AMPC and the wealthy inventors of much of Escarland's infrastructure.

But they'd once been the warrior Laesornysh and his faithful bodyguard. Sure, Fieran caught glimpses of the warrior of stories in those morning practices with his dacha.

Yet the warriors of the legends were greater, more deadly, than anything Fieran had ever witnessed. His dacha was just...his dacha. It was hard to picture him with so much blood on his hands no one was even sure just how high his body count in the previous wars was.

If war came, Fieran's dacha would have to become the warrior Laesornysh once again.

And Fieran wasn't sure if he was prepared to see it.

CHAPTER
ELEVEN

Standing next to her bunk, Pip tied back the upper part of her long wavy curls, leaving the rest down. For once, she wore a nice set of trousers and shirt in the elven style, though the cut of the shirt was more fitted in a human style.

While the shutters on the lower halves of the windows were kept permanently closed to give the women in this barracks privacy, morning sunlight poured through the upper half. The miniature train that Mak had carved for Pip rested on the top of the shutters of the window next to her bunk, casting a train-shaped shadow on the floor. The sight sent a stab of homesickness through her, and she worked to swallow it down.

While the Escarlish Army didn't allow women—yet—both the elven and troll armies did. In the past seventy years, all Escarlish Army bases had been forced to accommodate visiting female elf and troll warriors for war games. Once the accommodations were made, Escarland had begun employing more and more female civilians on the bases for various roles. It was likely a matter of time before certain branches—like the Flying Corps—opened to Escarlish women. The coming war might even make Escarland desperate enough to lift that restriction.

Currently, this bunk room held several secretaries, a few nurses, two telephone operators, and Pip, the only female mechanic.

Pip checked that her hair had been sufficiently tamed as best as she could by feel. "Are you sure there will be enough room for me?"

"Oh, yes, the more the merrier!" One of the nurses leaned closer to the one mirror the group of them had scrounged up as she applied bright red lipstick. "That unit of flyboys got a pass today too, so Todd requisitioned a truck. It might be tight in the back, but we'll fit all of us."

"I don't mind snuggling up with a few of those flyboys." Chelsea, one of the other nurses, fluttered her lashes in an exaggerated manner.

"As long as they take the time to clean up." The final nurse in the group gave a shudder. "One of them had to stop by the hospital for a pulled muscle after a ruck march the other day, and, ugh, he was gross."

"Must not have been one of the elves." One of the secretaries stepped closer to the mirror, straightening her neat shirtwaist and skirt. "Everyone knows elves even sweat pretty."

Pip clamped her mouth shut and didn't mention that she'd met one of those elves—half elves, actually—the other day. These girls would be sure to go into a peal of giggles if they realized one of those elves was a prince.

Not that Pip blamed them. She had totally gone into hero-worship breathiness over Fieran's dacha right in front of him. That had been *embarrassing*. What a way to make an impression.

Pip nudged the nurse out of the way long enough so she could peek at herself in the mirror. Her hair was actually behaving today, lying in gentle waves just past her shoulders.

Then she returned to her bunk, grabbed her bag, and looped the strap over her head so that it crossed her body and rested at her side. It weighed heavier than most would expect, considering it had a wrench tucked in there. It was always best to be prepared, whether to fix a truck or bash a too handsy guy over the head.

Pip, the three nurses, and the two secretaries made their way from their barracks, across the main square of Fort Linder, and found the truck parked to one side of the drive, pointed toward the distant smudge that was Bridgetown.

As she and the other girls approached, Fieran and a whole bunch of other young men wearing uniforms that were nicer than the fatigues they normally wore approached the truck from the other side.

Fieran met her gaze, and his resting smile brightened into something wider, sparkling in his eyes.

Ugh. Did her heart have to give that little flutter at seeing him? She didn't even know Fieran beyond that one conversation. He just happened to be the son of her childhood hero. And the kind of guy she had a physical attraction for, in general.

Though, why her flutters weren't as strong for the second elf—or half-elf, most likely, considering he'd joined the Escarlish Army—with short-cropped chestnut hair that walked at Fieran's side, she couldn't say. Perhaps she just needed to talk with that half-elf, and she'd find herself infatuated with him as well.

A rather handsome human man bowed to Pip's companions and held out a hand, waggling an eyebrow in a sugges-tive way. "Would you like a hand up into the truck, ladies?"

Chelsea, the most flirtatious of the nurses, flicked her hand at him. "Yes, but not from you." She turned to one of the other young men standing by. "You'll help me up, won't you?"

The young man stammered something, then finally held out his hand. The nurse winked at him, then used his hand to steady herself as she stepped up into the truck.

The nurse dating Todd rolled her eyes and rounded the truck, presumably to join her boyfriend in the square, enclosed cab.

Fieran held out his hand to Pip. "Would you like a hand up?"

She eyed his hand, then the back of the truck. The metal step below the bed was so high up that she'd have to lift her knee to her nose to reach it. The other ladies were barely managing it, even with their over half a foot height on her.

It would have been easier if Fieran had left her to get into the truck by herself. She would have boosted herself up with her palms, gotten a knee up, then scrambled inside. It wouldn't have been dignified, but it would have been more graceful than what she'd have to do to take his hand.

Fieran cocked his head, his smile tilting. Then he dropped onto one knee, still holding out a hand near the height of his head. "Perhaps a step would be more helpful than a hand up?"

Pip cocked her head, rolling her eyes. "I suppose. If you insist. You know I could have gotten up there by myself."

"I know." Fieran's grin widened with a hint of mischief. "I've seen how you manage to reach aeroplane engines."

She placed her hand in his, and his long fingers closed over hers in a firm grip keeping her steady as she planted a foot on the top of his leg. She stepped up, grabbed one of the metal bars that held the green canvas top, and pulled herself the rest of the way up and onto the truck's bed.

She walked to the front of the truck bed and took a seat on the bench next to one of the secretaries.

The rest of the girls climbed in, then the young men piled inside, crowding the benches. By the time Fieran and the other half-elf gracefully hopped inside, there was no more room on the benches, and five other men, including a man who was at least part troll, were already standing in the center, glancing around like they weren't sure what to do.

Chelsea popped to her feet, then plunked herself down on the lap of the nearest flyboy. "Now there's another seat."

The flyboy grinned, then settled his hands on her waist. Though he did, at least, keep his hands at a respectful spot that wasn't too high or too low.

"Any of you ladies are welcome to sit on my lap." That rather handsome young man patted his knees, winking at the nurse next to Pip.

The nurse regarded him for a moment, then grimaced. "No, I think I'll stay where I am, thanks." She turned to Fieran, her mouth pursing. "Though if you want a seat, I wouldn't object to sitting on your lap."

The tips of Fieran's ears turned nearly as bright red as his hair. "Uh, no, I'll leave the seats for the ladies. I don't mind standing."

The other half-elf nodded, his ears, too, turning pink.

"Aw, come on!" The rather handsome man flopped against the half-wall of the side of the truck, his head resting against the canvas side. "Why does Fieran always get all the ladies? It's because he's an elf, isn't it? Or because he's—"

A beanpole young man with muddy brown hair punched

the handsome man's arm. "It's because Fieran's respectful, that's why. My mama always said that girls like that."

"Yes, we do." The nurse next to Pip popped to her feet, then sat on the beanpole man's lap. "You don't mind if I sit here, do you?"

He flushed, holding his hands out as if he wasn't sure what to do with them. "Miss, I, uh…no, I reckon not."

"Good." She grinned and rested a hand on his shoulder to keep herself steady.

After a bit more shuffling, one more of the young men found a seat by squishing in. But that still left one human young man, the troll with bulging arms who would have taken up two spots on the bench if he'd sat down, and the two half elves still standing.

The window separating the cab from the back slid open and a young man in a green army uniform swiveled in his seat. "Everyone all set back there?"

"Yep!" several of them chorused all at once.

The truck lurched forward, and Pip was nearly crushed between the secretary on one side and the nurse squished on her other side.

The human young man still standing nearly toppled over and had to catch himself on the shoulder of another man, earning him a shove. The half-troll planted himself like he was a boulder refusing to move, though he did reach up and grab the bar that arched over their heads to hold the canvas.

Fieran lurched slightly, then swayed with the movement, as did the half-elf beside him. Both of them grabbed the bar as well, though they didn't seem to need it.

As the truck rumbled down the road, heading for Bridgetown, Fieran gestured from Pip to the half-elf standing next to him. "Pip, this is my best friend Merrik. We grew up together. Merrik, this is Pip. She's that mechanic I met the other day."

The half-elf, Merrik, nodded to her, though he didn't speak, his gaze dipping to the floor.

Ah, he must be the shy friend. She got the feeling Fieran was rather used to being the spokesman for both of them.

"Nice to meet you, Merrik." Pip stuck out a hand to shake. Merrik stared at her hand for a moment before he took it and shook.

"This is Donkyn, but everyone calls him Tiny." Fieran gestured to the troll.

Tiny nodded to her, then spoke in a voice that was both a little rough and surprisingly high pitched, given his breadth. He used the trolls' dialect of elvish. "Elontir, Pip."

"Elontiri, Donkyn." She responded in elvish, glad for the excuse for the smoother words to roll off her tongue. She could speak Escarlish just fine, but there was just something about elvish.

Grinning, Fieran pointed at the beanpole young man. "That's Elijah, but he goes by Lije."

Lije waved, though he glanced from her to the nurse sitting on his lap as if he still wasn't sure what to do with his hand once he was done waving.

"The flirtatious one over there is Pretty Face." Fieran indicated the all-too-handsome young man.

Pretty Face grinned and winked at her.

"And this here is Stickyfingers." Fieran nudged the one young man who had been left standing. The young man was only about half a foot taller than her, which made him on the shorter side compared to the other young men. "Stickyfingers is harmless, but don't let him get too close to your valuables."

Stickyfingers gave her a smile, which showed off his

slightly brown and crooked teeth. But the smile itself was genuine. "I don't pickpocket friends."

"That's not as reassuring as you think it is." Lije grimaced, side-eyeing Sticky around the nurse sitting on his lap.

The other young men, nurses, and secretaries took to introducing themselves and each other, and that took most of the drive to Bridgetown.

By the time they rumbled across the stone-paved streets of Bridgetown, those in the truck had started to form groups with various plans for touring the city.

Todd pulled the truck into one of the parking spots along a side street. He opened the window again. "Listen up. I need to have this truck back by 19:00. So if you aren't back here by 18:00, you're going to be left behind in Bridgetown. Got it?"

With a few murmurs and sarcastic replies, everyone piled out of the truck.

As the others drifted off, Pip glanced between the groups of others and where Fieran gathered with Merrick, Lije, Tiny, Stickyfingers, and Pretty Face. Should she stick with one of the groups that had some of the other nurses and secretaries? She had gotten to know the other girls, but she wouldn't call herself friends with them yet. She stood out, as the only non-human and the only mechanic.

But she couldn't exactly call Fieran a friend either. Did she really want to be the only girl in a group of guys?

Probably, as long as that handsome one, Pretty Face, didn't get too annoying. Nor Stickyfingers make a try for her money. Then again, if they did, that was what her head-bashing wrench was for.

Fieran gestured to her, flashing that genuine, friendly smile. "Pip, are you coming?"

With one last glance at the group where Chelsea had looped her arms with those of two of the flyboys, Pip hurried to join Fieran. "Where are we going?"

"We were just deciding that." Fieran waved as he spoke, including the full group. "Any place in Bridgetown you've always wanted to see?"

"The Outpost Museum." The words popped out before she'd even thought them through.

Fieran stiffened, the smile dropping from his face. Merrik gave a soft snort, turning slightly away.

"Yes, I've always wanted to see that museum!" Lije's eyes widened.

"A museum?" Pretty Face's lip curled. "We're on leave for the first time, and we're going to spend our day in a museum?"

"Maybe girls would like you more if the space in your head behind that pretty face wasn't so empty." Pip raised her eyebrows at Pretty Face. Teasing him came rather naturally, like he was just another one of her fellow mechanics at the western rail terminal or at the hangar.

"Ooh, ouch!" Stickyfingers bumped Pretty Face's shoulder.

"Good one." Lije grinned at Pip, holding out his hand for her to slap, which she did.

Pretty Face stroked his chin, as if contemplating that. "Perhaps you're right. I need to be more than a pretty face. I should practice a few more cerebral pursuits. Be the complete package of looks and intelligence."

"Sure." Pip drew out the word.

Despite his protests about the museum and comments that were somewhat less than appropriate at times, Pretty Face was here with Fieran's group. He could have gone off with one of the clusters of flyboys and nurses. He could have drifted away into Bridgetown by himself to get into whatever mischief he desired.

Instead, he had stayed here with a group that wasn't about to do anything more sketchy than drink too many sodas.

There was a pause. Then Tiny crossed his large muscular arms. "The Outpost is a culturally and historically significant site. For humans, trolls, and elves. The events there began the Alliance."

Fieran shifted, his ears going even more red as he hunched as if hoping the others wouldn't remember him.

But Stickyfingers turned to him, his eyes widening. "Oh, right. They're your *parents.*"

Right. Pip grimaced. She had forgotten that, for a moment. The reason she'd always wanted to go to the Outpost Museum was that it was the location where Prince Farrendel and Princess Elspeth had been married nearly seventy years ago in the wake of the first treaty forming an alliance between the elves of Tarenhiel and the humans of Escarland. That event started the whole cascade of events that eventually led to Kostaria, Tarenhiel, and Escarland becoming the Alliance Kingdoms.

Even now, the Outpost Museum had an exhibit that featured Princess Elspeth's and Prince Farrendel's wedding attire from the second elven wedding they had in Estyra.

But Pip could understand how seeing his parents' wedding immortalized in a museum might be uncomfortable for Fieran.

"We don't have to go, if you don't want to." Pip had to tip her head back to look at Fieran's face. She edged back a few inches so that she didn't have to crane her neck quite so uncomfortably. "I can go a different time."

Fieran sighed, then shook his head. "No, let's go. I'll be

fine. It isn't like we won't be tripping over monuments to my family members no matter where we go in Bridgetown."

"I think that might be a statue of your uncle King Rharreth over there." Speaking for the first time, Merrik pointed toward the end of the street, where a statue gazed north toward a row of stone buildings.

"You're not helping." Fieran scowled and crossed his arms.

Pip stifled her laugh, even as she joined the others in peering in the direction of the statue, which did indeed appear to be a stately troll warrior regally gazing toward the north.

Yep, she'd definitely made the right call in joining this group. It was like hanging out with a whole gang of brothers. Not that her attraction to Fieran was sisterly, but she could push that aside to be just a friend to all of them.

"And..." A grin played across Merrik's face, banishing that severe look. "Fort Linder is named after the island where your parents met."

Fieran groaned and rubbed his temple. "The island was where both the first and second alliance treaties were signed. I'm sure that's the reason the fort was named Fort Linder. Not my parents' first meeting."

"Uh-huh. Sure it was. It was not like your uncles General Ardon and King Averett were sitting down figuring out the name for the new fort when the old outpost was closed down." Merrik's grin took on the edge of a smirk. "And we both know how sentimental King Averett is."

Pip glanced between Fieran and Merrik. It was so strange to hear them casually joking about such high-ranking generals and kings. But to them, those kings were people they'd actually met, not just a face on a coin or glimpsed at a distance while peering over a fence in Estyra.

Fieran glanced from her to Stickyfingers, Tiny, Pretty Face, and Lije, who gaped at Fieran with various levels of awe. Fieran scowled. "And now you've reminded everyone of just how annoyingly famous all my relatives are. Guys, I'm still me. I'm not uppity or anything."

"How did you manage to turn out so...not spoiled rotten?" Pip shook herself. It wasn't as if she hadn't known exactly who Fieran was related to the moment he'd said his last name when she first met him.

"Well, he is kind of spoiled." Merrik's smirk grew. "Just not spoiled rotten."

Fieran rolled his eyes, then jabbed a finger at Merrik. "Don't say another word."

Merrik grinned back, then turned toward the main road. "Do we want to see this museum or not?"

Pip hurried to fall into step with Fieran. If they were going to see the Outpost Museum, then she wasn't about to miss out.

TWELVE

With Pip trotting along at his side, Fieran trailed after Merrik as they wound their way through the familiar streets of Bridgetown.

Along their walk, Merrik oh-so-helpfully pointed out all the monuments and historical plaques along the way. There was the statue of Uncle Rharreth at the end of the stone buildings, which had been the homes for the troll workers when the Alliance Bridge was built. That workers' camp had developed into the city as it was now. The statue of Uncle Averett at the end of the Alliance Bridge faced a similar statue of Uncle Weylind across the way on Tarenhiel's side of the river.

Of course Merrik would pick this morning as the moment to come out of his shell and show off the humor he hid beneath.

They boarded a trolley and rode that through the streets of Bridgetown until they got off at the stop near the base of a broad, grassy hill. At the top of the hill, a wooden stockade fort overlooked the Hydalla River. A few of the older style historical cannons perched on the corners.

Paths meandered over the grassy hill and along the bank of the river. A few trees had been allowed to grow to form shady spots, creating a place of peace in the bustling city. Several people jogged along the paths, ignoring the museum on the hill.

Pip, her curls bouncing, her eyes sparkling, all but raced up the hill, her gaze focused on the outpost. If not for the utter excitement on her face, Fieran might have dragged his feet as he climbed the winding path upward. But he couldn't dawdle, even knowing the embarrassment to come, when she was so happy to come here.

At the gate, they had to pay for tickets. Fieran kept his head down, holding his breath the whole time that no one would recognize him. The curator would probably dog his steps offering a personalized tour, if anyone realized that he was here.

Thankfully, he was able to purchase a ticket without incident, and he joined the others as they started on the self-guided tour, complete with a pamphlet.

Pip pored through the pamphlet like it held the answers to all of life's mysteries, then pointed. "Let's start here."

As a group, they worked their way along one side of the fort's parade ground. Historical cannons lined the walk, complete with plaques talking about the outpost's history from long before Fieran's parents' wedding.

Finally, Pip led the way inside, nearly skipping like a little girl as they entered.

When they reached the huge assembly room of the old outpost, Pip let out a squeal and raced across the room to where mannequins wore a white dress and a silver tunic and trouser set, spotlights shining down on the clothing. Fieran half expected a chorus of sopranos to burst into song to highlight the moment.

Ugh, this was going to be *embarrassing*.

As the others piled into the room, scattering to the various exhibits, Fieran dragged his feet, though Merrik remained at his side.

For Stickyfingers, Lije, and Pretty Face, all of this was history from long ago. Their parents hadn't even been born when the alliance treaties were signed and the Alliance Bridge built.

While Fieran hadn't yet been alive for those events either, he'd grown up hearing about them from those who had been there. None of this was that far in the past for him.

For much of his life, he'd felt so much more human than elf. But standing there, he truly felt the elf part of his heritage and the long years it gave him. Sure, he wouldn't live as long as a full elf. But five hundred years was still ages longer than the mere ninety or so years the humans in the group might live.

For Pip, too, these events weren't as far in the past as they seemed to a human. He hadn't asked her yet, but as a half-dwarf, half-elf, she might even be a few years older than him, even if maturity-wise they were the same age. Strange thought, that she might have been alive when his parents were getting married. No wonder she had such hero worship for his dacha. She would've been a young, impressionable child when his dacha first attended Hanford University and everyone made such a big deal about it.

Pretty Face, Stickyfingers, and Lije drifted over to the exhibit near Pip, and Fieran braced himself, knowing what they'd see. A huge print of an early photograph hung on the wall and depicted Fieran's dacha and mama posing in the outfits displayed in the exhibit. The photograph had been taken years after the wedding, but his parents didn't appear much older than they had back then, thanks to the heart bond and elven lack of aging.

Pretty Face leaned closer, whistled, then pointed. "Whoo-whee! She is a *dame*."

Fieran groaned and dropped his head into his palm. He'd known coming to the museum was a bad idea, but this was even worse than he'd thought.

Lije smacked Pretty Face upside the back of the head. "That's Fieran's mama!"

"Doesn't make her any less of a dame." Pretty Face opened his mouth, as if he planned to keep talking and really tempt Fieran to give him a zap with his magic. Just a tiny zap. Not enough to hurt. Much.

This time it was Stickyfingers who reached up and gave Pretty Face a smack on the back of the head. "You don't say stuff like that. All women are to be respected, but especially mamas."

All of them from Tiny to Pretty Face turned to Stickyfingers and stared.

Sticky shrugged. "What? I might come from a family of crooks, but my mama raised me right."

There was just something so wrong and yet so right about that statement that Fieran didn't even know how to respond.

"Yes, she did." Lije patted Sticky's back in brotherly camaraderie.

Pretty Face sighed, then gestured at the photograph again. "Fine, fine. I won't say another word about Fieran's mama. But the real question is, how did two people as gorgeous as *that* make something like…*this*?" Pretty Face gestured from the photograph to Fieran.

Fieran finally gave in and gave Pretty Face a punch in the shoulder—probably harder than necessary. At least the focus on himself was better than on his parents. "Are you saying I'm ugly? What would that make you?"

Pretty Face rubbed his shoulder. "I'm not saying you're ugly, exactly. But you have to admit, you should've been the one with the Pretty Face moniker given the way you won the genetic lottery with parents. Instead, well, you're…" Pretty Face waved at him, as if the end of that sentence should be obvious.

And, perhaps, it was. The endless comparisons to his parents that featured in various newspapers and gossip rags told him exactly where he fell short.

"It's my nose." Fieran sighed. There was nothing else for it at this point. "I got my uncle Weylind's nose."

While Uncle Weylind's hawkish nose was tempered by the fine features of the elves, Fieran had also gotten the large nose prominent on the human side of the family. Combined with the hawkishness, it was a blemish on his features that his parents didn't have.

Pretty Face heaved an exaggerated sigh. "It's no fair that you have that nose and still get all the ladies."

Pip wandered over to them, apparently having gotten her fill of admiring his parents' wedding attire. "As we established on the drive over, it's your personality rather than your face that we ladies object to."

"I'm here enriching my mind, aren't I?" Pretty Face placed a hand over his chest as if smoothing a formal necktie.

"Uh-huh. I think your mind needs all the enrichment it can get." Pip rolled her eyes at him. Then her focus caught on something else across the room, and she headed in that direction with the focus of a hunting dog on a scent.

Beside Fieran, Merrik was making little choking noises as he attempted to hold back his laughter.

Time to redirect the attention onto someone else. With a silent apology—and slight glee at the act of revenge for Merrik's teasing earlier—Fieran gestured at another, old-style photograph hanging on the wall a few feet away. As he spoke, he began walking in that direction. "Speaking of parents…"

"Fieran…" Merrik hurried after him, a warning in his tone.

Fieran ignored him. "Merrik's dacha is in this one."

That photograph commemorated the twenty-five-year anniversary of the treaty. As the only elven guard present at the original treaty signing, Uncle Iyrinder had been reluctantly cajoled—well, ordered—to be in the photograph with Fieran's parents, Uncle Weylind, Uncle Averett, and the two diplomats.

Lije, Stickyfingers, and Pretty Face bumped into each other as they hurried to claim spots in front of that photograph.

Pretty Face groaned. "That's it. I'm resigned to third most handsome. There is no way I can compete with elves."

"Hey, look at this!" Lije had wandered over to where Tiny was looking at the exhibit about the building of the Alliance Bridge. "Fieran, is that…"

Fieran joined him, then sighed and nodded. "Yeah. My mama was pregnant with me when the bridge was built."

"Really? The bridge was built ages ago!" Pretty Face hurried over, then gaped, first at the photograph, then at Fieran. "How old are you?"

"Sixty-eight." Fieran winced. "But that's only about twenty-one to twenty-three in human years."

"Human years. Can you hear how weird that sounds? It's like you're a dog or something. Except that you age opposite of dogs." Pretty Face shook his head. "Sixty-eight. You're downright ancient."

Sixty-eight wasn't even that old for humans, but Fieran didn't bother to argue the point.

"My da is in this photograph." Tiny waved to another large plaque a few feet away. A note of deep pride colored Tiny's tone. "He helped build the Alliance Bridge."

Fieran stayed where he was, savoring the relief of having the attention finally taken off him. Not that he minded being the center of attention, but not when it involved his parents, his looks, or the slower aging he experienced as a half-elf.

Merrik wandered off by himself, reading the various plaques and likely taking a moment of quiet away from people. It wouldn't surprise Fieran if Merrik disappeared into one of the side hallways and continued the tour by himself just for a bit of solitude.

While Lije, Pretty Face, Stickyfingers, and Tiny bumbled about the room, pointing out all the photographs they could find of someone related to Fieran—and there were a lot— Fieran joined Pip before the exhibit featuring his Uncle Edmund's and Aunt Jalissa's wedding attire, along with photographs of their rather pageantry-filled wedding on the middle of the newly constructed Alliance Bridge.

Pip briefly glanced away from the exhibit to give him a smile. "Thank you for being willing to come here and put up with all of that." She jabbed a finger at the others.

"It's all right. I'm used to that kind of thing." Fieran shrugged, glancing away from the exhibit. These photographs were nothing he hadn't already seen many times over the years. Standing next to Pip, he became even more aware of how tiny she was. The top of her head didn't even come up to his shoulder.

"I can't imagine how strange it must be. All these people

are so famous and everyone hero-worships them. Even me." Pip's smile turned slightly lopsided. "And yet, they're your family."

"Despite all of them being so famous, they're still a really great family." Fieran's throat got a little rough as he glanced at a photograph of his parents hanging on the wall nearby. "I'm proud to be a part of it."

Pip reached out a hand, but she stopped short, as if she wasn't sure if they had enough of a friendship for that kind of response. "I can see that. It's one reason your dacha—and your macha, really—have been such heroes to me. They might be famous, but they still seem like such normal people, you know? They didn't let fame go to their heads like some people would."

Like many of Fieran's cousins and distant cousins on Uncle Averett's branch of the family, but Fieran didn't say that out loud. Those cousins were higher up in line for the Escarlish throne than he was, and he had enough sense not to denigrate them in public, especially while he wore an Escarlish Army uniform.

"No, they didn't. And they tried their best to make sure me and my siblings didn't get too spoiled either." Fieran stuffed his hands into his pockets, then nudged her with an elbow, keeping his tone light. "I'll have to introduce you to my dacha when I get the chance."

Pip's face whitened. "You wouldn't! I wouldn't know what to say! I think I'd pass out."

"Trust me. My dacha will be more scared of you than you will be of him." Fieran grinned, already picturing it.

THIRTEEN

Fieran could barely keep himself from bouncing on his toes as he stood in the line just outside of the aeroplane hangar. He wore the fur-lined leather cap, coat, and boots needed to stay warm in the air, even though he was roasting in the warmth of the mild spring day. A set of goggles rested on his forehead, waiting to be tugged over his eyes.

Three flyers had been wheeled outside and now waited, one beside the other, to the side of the airstrip. These flyers were two-seater biplanes, which could be controlled from either seat.

He was going to fly today. Finally.

The bubbling, buzzing sensation filled him so completely that he didn't even realize that magic sparked around his fingertips until Merrik nudged him.

Fieran clenched his fists, snuffing out his magic. He worked to stuff his magic down, clamping his control even tighter. He hadn't realized how much those morning practice sessions with his dacha helped keep his magic steady. After so many weeks of not using his magic, the about-to-break-out-of-control feeling in his chest just kept getting worse.

Over the past few weeks, Fieran and the other pilots-in-training had sat in the flyers, familiarizing themselves with the gauges and practicing moving the ailerons and elevators —the flaps on the wings and horizontal flaps on the tail— with the stick. They controlled the rudder—a vertical flap on the tail—with a bar at their feet.

After that, they had spun the flyers up and jounced up and down the airfield, occasionally lifting off the ground, then bouncing back down to earth. Sometimes the narrow, spoked wheels would skid on wet grass, and their aeroplane would veer unexpectedly into the tall weeds. Or the wheels would catch on something, and the whole aeroplane would tip forward. Most of the time, the hooked training skids sticking out of the front caught the aeroplanes on their noses before they turned all the way over upside down. One aeroplane had tipped all the way over, crunching the upper wings. The pilot-in-training had survived with nothing worse than a few broken bones that had been healed by Fort Linder's elf healer.

For the past few days, Capt. Arfeld and the other two flight instructors had been going on training flights with each recruit in alphabetical order. While they flew, the rest of the unit had to spend the hours in that tiny room, studying up on aerodynamics and taking quizzes.

While none of the quizzes were hard, Fieran was glad it was finally his turn to take to the sky instead of take another test.

A few of the men in the training squadron had washed out after their practice flights—and practice crashes— deciding that such danger wasn't for them.

Capt. Arfeld nodded to the lieutenant standing by. The

lieutenant stepped in front of them, then read from his clipboard. "Fieran Laesornysh, Elijah Lake, Merrik Loiatir."

The three of them stepped forward and shouted, "Here, sir."

The lieutenant directed each of them to one of the flyers, and Fieran found himself waved toward the flyer where Capt. Arfeld stood.

Capt. Arfeld started to reach out a hand, as if for a handshake, before he must have remembered that he was now a captain in the army's Flying Corps instead of a civilian daredevil pilot. He withdrew his hand, but there was still something more casual in his gaze than that of an officer interacting with someone below him. "Fieran Laesornysh? Son of Prince Farrendel Laesornysh?"

"Yes, sir." Fieran braced himself, not sure what Capt. Arfeld's reaction would be. So far, the drill sergeants had taken particular delight in doing whatever they could to make Fieran's life miserable because of his last name and who he was related to.

But Capt. Arfeld got that light in his eyes, more like Pip than the drill sergeants. "He's a hero to all of us who flew in those experimental early days of flight. We would not have achieved flight without the inventions created by your father and Lance Marion."

Dacha was a hero to a lot of people, it turned out. Fieran just nodded, hoping that Capt. Arfeld wouldn't gesture to the aeroplane and mention the magic powering the flyer even now. Because Fieran was totally going to lie and agree that it was Dacha's power in that flyer. He was already getting too much special attention from his captain without admitting that it was *his* magic currently powering the aeroplane.

Capt. Arfeld turned and grabbed one of the wing

supports, using the toe step to climb easily into the rear seat of the two-seater. As he settled into the seat, he tugged his goggles down over his eyes.

Using the toe step, Fieran climbed up and over the side of the aeroplane. He had to fold his knees nearly to his nose as he wedged himself into the cockpit. He was on the tall end of the height restrictions for pilots. He shifted his legs and managed to get himself crammed into the space as comfortably as possible with his toes tucked into the toe grips on the rudder bar and his knees braced underneath the engine compartment.

The control column of the aeroplane was between his legs while the panel before him held a temperature gauge for the engine compartment. Another gauge measured the magic levels. It should stay in the green. If it jumped into yellow, the magic was burning through the wiring and would eventually send the aeroplane plummeting out of the sky. If that gauge went into red, well, an explosion might be imminent.

Fieran fixed the goggles over his eyes, adjusting the way the strap ran over the points of his ears. How he missed the goggles he had back home, which were comfortably broken in and shaped to his face and head.

Capt. Arfeld walked Fieran through flipping the correct switches and pushing the right button to start the engine while a crew member turned the propeller. Not that Fieran needed much instruction. It was essentially the same as starting the engine of his automobile back home or starting an engine for testing at the AMPC.

The magically powered rotary engine gave a crackling, high-pitched whine as it powered up. The propeller started into motion, then whirred faster and faster until it set up a deep hum. The aeroplane eased forward.

Capt. Arfeld had to shout over the hum of the propeller as he maneuvered the aeroplane to the end of the airfield, telling Fieran what he was doing as he did it. Fieran kept his hands on the stick, feeling the power and control through the column.

Then they reached the end of the airstrip, and one of the ground crew ran over and put chocks in front of the wheels, staying low to avoid the whirling propeller.

Capt. Arfeld opened the power to full, the propeller buzzing loudly, the engine whining at a pitch that made Fieran wish he had a set of elven moss earplugs. They sat there for several long minutes, held back by the wheel chocks as the aeroplane spun up to full power. The other two aeroplanes waited behind and to the side of them, also spinning up.

Finally, Capt. Arfeld waved to the ground crew, and a man dashed forward, grabbed the chocks, and raced out of the way.

The aeroplane rolled forward, faster and faster. The rubber tires on the spoked wheels bounced over the ground, and the whole wooden frame of the flyer shuddered, as if it were about to be shaken apart. Fieran was rattled from side to side in the seat, his head occasionally banging against the minimal leather padding around the lip of the cockpit and behind his head.

Fieran's heart crawled into his throat as the aeroplane hurtled toward the end of the runaway. The grass strip had seemed so long before, but now the end was rushing toward them, the wind of their passing blasting into his face.

The wings wavered, and the whole flyer felt light around Fieran. Then it crashed back to the ground, and every ounce of Fieran's weight pressed into the hard leather of the seat.

Then he was pressed even harder into the seat, as if a

giant hand was pushing on his shoulders. Yet that same hand seemed to catch under the biplane's wings and pull the flyer off the ground. The tires left the ground as the nose tilted toward the sky.

They were flying.

Fieran swallowed back his whoop and concentrated on breathing through the rush of air snatching at his nose and mouth. The air grew increasingly cold even as the earth fell away beneath him in a way that sent his stomach into his toes.

Yet even as his stomach dropped, his heart soared. This was what it meant to be *alive*. The rush of frigid air. The hum of the propeller vibrating through his bones. The freedom of an open sky all around him.

As they leveled off, Capt. Arfeld shouted, "I'm going to turn control over to you."

Fieran gripped the control column, his heart hammering instead of soaring. Through the stick, he could feel the strange firmness of the air beneath the wings, as if the air was solid rather than immaterial.

"Ease the biplane into a gentle turn. Remember, it will turn slower and tug upward when turning to the left but turn sharper and downward to the right." Capt. Arfeld shouted his instructions from the rear seat.

Fieran eased the stick over while pressing on the rudder bar with his feet. He'd thought it had been gentle, but the aeroplane was suddenly on its side. Fieran's shoulder rammed against the side of the cockpit, and he hung from the lap belt strapped across his hips.

He tried to correct, and suddenly his nose was going over and up, the aeroplane wanting to tug into a roll.

"Gentle movements. Feel the way the air interacts with your wings." Capt. Arfeld somehow managed to sound completely unruffled. Capt. Arfeld's hand appeared in Fieran's peripheral vision, pointing. "Keep an eye out for the other two flyers. They are coming up behind and under us."

Fieran glanced in that direction, leaning over the side of the aeroplane to see a second aeroplane to the side and beneath him, barely visible around the lower wing of Fieran's biplane.

That was something to get used to. When driving his automobile, he only had to worry about a level plane of directions. But here in the sky, all directions were possible. Even above him and below him.

His magic jumped around his fingertips again, as if to protect him in his vulnerable position in a wooden flyer alone in the unprotected sky.

Fieran squashed his magic until he almost felt like he was smothering, his breath hitching. He couldn't unleash his magic here. Not only would he risk incinerating his own flyer if his magic got out of control, but he could overset the magical power cell and cause an explosion.

After several moments of wrestling with the flyer, the wings tipping first one way, then the other, Fieran finally managed to level off again, his heart racing, his hands shaking on the control column.

"Not too bad, but let's try that turn again." Capt. Arfeld's shout somehow remained utterly calm.

Capt. Arfeld talked Fieran through a variety of turns and gentle maneuvers. No spins or corkscrews for this first flight. Even a simple turn felt dangerous enough.

The longer Fieran flew, the more accustomed he became to the way the aeroplane handled. He had the growing urge to throw the flyer into a roll or a sharp banking turn, just to truly test the biplane's—and his own—limits.

But he didn't. He followed orders like a good recruit and stuffed down both his magic and his soaring excitement.

All too soon, Capt. Arfeld directed him to turn around, and they headed back toward the aerodrome. As they lined up for a landing, dropping lower, Capt. Arfeld took over the aeroplane once again, though he continued to talk Fieran through the process.

They swooped lower and lower, the ground rushing up to meet them. Then the wheels touched down with a jolt, and the biplane went from a graceful bird in the sky to a jolting, shuddering contraption lumbering over the ground, the wings wobbling as if about to tip one way or the other.

The tail dropped, and the tail skid dug into the earth, slowing the flyer. As they slowed, Capt. Arfeld turned the aeroplane, finally halting it to one side of the airfield near the hangar.

The ground crew rushed to meet them as Capt. Arfeld turned off the engine, though the propeller continued to spin in ever slowing circles for several more minutes.

Even as Fieran uncramped his legs and tried to pry himself out of the cockpit, another biplane came in for a landing. It touched down, jouncing back into the air to fly another few yards before falling back to the ground and staying there this time.

Fieran finally managed to unwedge himself from the cockpit. He shakily found the toe grip and lowered himself onto solid ground. As the other aeroplane parked nearby, Fieran pulled off the goggles and drew in a deep breath, not sure if the adrenaline coursing through him was from fear or the excitement of flight.

When Merrik climbed out of the other flyer, Fieran met his gaze, unable to hide his grin any longer.

Merrik grinned back unreservedly as he so rarely did.

The flight must have been as freeing for him as it had been for Fieran.

As Lije's aeroplane landed, skidding a bit on the grass, Fieran joined Merrik as they stepped out of the way of the ground crews.

Fieran's face hurt from his wide grin, and he had to clench his fists to hold back his magic from dancing around his fingers. "That was even better than I imagined."

Merrik turned his face to the sky for a moment, as if feeling again the breeze of flight on his face. "I did not think I would enjoy it, but…I do not know how I went my whole life without flight."

Fieran's grin faded as Merrik's words registered. "You didn't think you'd even like flying? And you still enlisted with me anyway?"

Merrik shrugged, not meeting Fieran's gaze. "I could not let you enlist by yourself. We have always watched each other's back, and I was not going to stop now."

"Linshi." Fieran found the elvish word for *thank you* coming out instead of Escarlish. There was just something extra meaningful in the elvish, especially for Merrik.

Lije bailed out of his aeroplane and strode toward them with a huge grin on his face and an extra bounce to his step. "That was epic."

Fieran slapped him on the back, then the three of them strode toward the hangar.

As they stepped into the shadow of the hangar, Pip met them, though her gaze skipped over Merrik and Lije to land on Fieran. "I see you brought my flyers back in one piece."

"Your flyers?" Fieran's grin returned as he fell into step beside Pip. "I thought they were the army's flyers."

"Well, I'm the one keeping them functioning and in the air." Pip gestured at the hangar, grinning back. Her curls were tied back in a high ponytail while her green coveralls weren't yet stained with grease. "Me and the other mechanics, anyway."

"Efforts I greatly appreciate." Fieran didn't want to think about falling out of the sky. Right now, he just wanted to ride the high of the flight.

This was what he'd been dreaming about for years. Flying.

He couldn't wait to do it again.

PIP PERCHED on the stool at the long, stainless-steel countertop in the soda parlor in Bridgetown and sipped her root beer float. The remnants of her chicken sandwich remained on the plate in front of her. It had been so huge she hadn't been able to eat all of it.

"You going to eat that?" Tiny reached past Fieran and pointed at her plate.

"Nope. Go for it." She slid her plate down to Tiny. The half-troll grinned his thanks, then picked up the remnants of her sandwich and dug in.

All around them, the soda parlor bustled with troll children getting sodas and elf families tying their bicycles up outside and coming in for a soda and sandwich to complete their day out in Bridgetown. A few people of all ages—trolls, humans, and elves—came in by themselves and got a soda, sandwich, or a piece of candy.

Even living at the far western edge of Tarenhiel where they interacted with the humans of Afristan and the dwarven kingdoms across the plains, Pip had never experienced a city like Bridgetown where trolls, humans, and elves mingled so freely.

She wasn't even as short compared to many of the humans. She'd seen a few humans on the streets of Bridgetown who were shorter than her. Always an exciting moment for her when she was anywhere other than visiting her dwarf grandparents. There, she was one of the tallest people around.

Next to her, Fieran held up his bottle of raspberry soda. "A toast. To our first flights. May there be many more to come."

Tiny, Stickyfingers, Pretty Face, and Lije all held up their glasses or bottles and clinked them.

Pip clinked her root beer float with Fieran's soda. "And may all those flights land safely again on the ground."

Perhaps it was her dwarf half, but she couldn't quite understand the lure of the sky that drew these flyboys. She'd much rather keep her feet planted on solid earth.

"And to the mechanics who keep our flyers running." Lije leaned forward to grin at Pip, even as he held up his soda bottle again.

The others echoed the toast, clinking their glasses again.

Fieran finished the last of his soda, then pushed his empty plate and glass away from him. He glanced at her. "Are you ready?"

Pip took one last sip of her root beer float. Her stomach was so full her skin ached from being stretched so tight and her lungs felt like they were crowded. She couldn't possibly finish off the last of her float.

She pushed it away from her, then swiveled on her stool. She couldn't touch the step bar, so she gripped the edge of the countertop and slid off the stool, taking the impact with her knees as her feet hit the ground.

Fieran held open the soda parlor's door for her, and she

nodded to him as she stepped through onto the busy sidewalk.

A few automobiles with shining fenders buzzed past on the stone street. Black, intricate lantern poles lined the street, the blue elven lights burning bright as dusk fell over Bridgetown.

Pip glanced both ways, then darted across the street, Fieran easily keeping up with her.

Across the street, a small park filled with trees, brick pathways, and a fountain that tinkled with the splash of water provided a sanctuary amid the bustle of Bridgetown. Parks and squares like this were dotted all through Bridgetown, showing the influence of the elves as this city was built.

Merrik sat at the base of one of the trees, both hands flat against the grass and moss, a hint of his green elven magic twining around his fingers.

"Enjoying your time communing with the trees?" Fieran nudged Merrik's boot with a foot.

"Yes. You should try it sometime. You might be less reckless." Merrik's mouth twitched with a smile, and he cracked an eye open, peering up at Fieran. "You need to do something. You have been even more jittery than usual."

Pip glanced from Merrik to Fieran. She had noticed that Fieran couldn't help but tap his foot or wiggle on his seat in the soda parlor, but she hadn't thought too much of it. He just seemed like the type of person who was in constant motion.

Fieran gave a little shrug, then glanced at Pip. "My magic doesn't exactly enjoy being reined in for so long. But I'll be fine. I'm not going to self-combust."

"Hmm." Merrik let his eyes fall closed again. "I doubt it."

Pip just shook her head. She'd seen the way her dacha

latched on to trees after spending too much time under-ground or crossing the Afristani plains. Merrik was probably wishing she and Fieran would stop annoying him.

Pip grabbed Fieran's sleeve and tugged him away. As they strolled down one of the paths, Pip glanced around, then lowered her voice so it wouldn't carry. "There's some-thing I've been wanting to ask you."

Fieran's shoulders stiffened, his smile freezing into that polite one that he wore as a mask instead of the genuine one that lit his eyes. "Ask away."

"Your dacha is a prince, and your macha is a princess." Pip peeked up at him. Way up, since he was walking next to her. "Does that mean you're actually *Prince* Fieran?"

Fieran grimaced and sighed. "Technically, yes. But it's a pretty useless title. On the Escarlish side of the family, I'm about three hundredth in line for the throne. Well, maybe not quite that far, but a whole trainload of people would have to die before I ever came close to inheriting the throne. There are fewer people between me and the Tarenhieli throne, but enough that I'd assume the world was ending if I inherited it."

"But you're still a prince." Pip couldn't help the slight smile. Fieran looked so uncomfortable admitting that he was a prince.

"Yes." Fieran side-eyed her. "But don't spread that around. I don't want anyone getting ideas. Beyond even the fact that I won't inherit a throne, my title is only a courtesy title because my grandfathers on both sides of the family were kings. But I won't pass on the title of prince or princess to my children, although my wife could be a princess if she wanted. Though, I suppose, I do have a laundry list of other titles that will get passed down."

Pip snorted, then she couldn't stop her laugh. Fieran

couldn't even hear what that sounded like. Titles were so ordinary to him. He just dismissed the fact that he was a duke or lord or something as if it was nothing special. As if everyone had titles they could just throw away as utterly meaningless.

Fieran halted, turning to her. "What?"

He was so puzzled that Pip had to bend over, bracing her hands on her knees, under the force of her laughter.

When she finally got herself under control, she patted his arm. "Don't worry about it. Just don't ever change."

A noise from the street broke through her laughter as Fieran turned in that direction, his forehead scrunching.

A newsie—a young boy in a slouch cap—hefted a stack of papers in one hand, holding up a single paper in the other hand. "Extra! Extra! Read all about it! Mongavarian ships threaten Kostaria!"

After sharing a glance with her, Fieran hurried in that direction, and Pip followed as fast as she could. The newsie —who was probably about ten—was nearly as tall as she was.

Fieran dug into his pocket, pulled out a handful of coins, and paid for a newspaper, handing the newsie far more coins than necessary and waving off the change. After hurrying a few steps away and putting his back to a nearby haberdashery so that they weren't standing in the flow of the sidewalk, Fieran opened the paper.

Pip crowded in next to him, and Fieran held the news-paper lower, putting it more level with her face instead of forcing her to stand on her tiptoes to see.

The black headlines splashed across the page declared that a fleet of Mongavarian dreadnoughts—along with a few of their airships—had come rather suspiciously close to the cluster of islands off the coast of Kostaria. They hadn't done anything aggressive or crossed into Kostaria's waters.

But their very presence was a provocation and a warning.

The main trade route between Tarenhiel and the elven kingdoms on the far continent—the source of Tarenhiel's silks and fine porcelains—cut through those waters. Not to mention, Dar Goranth—the largest naval base in all three Alliance Kingdoms—occupied a chunk of one of those Kostarian islands. Because Dar Goranth was on one of the outlying islands, it wasn't protected behind the magical Wall that shielded the rest of the Alliance Kingdoms.

By sending their warships into waters nearby, the Mongavarian Empire was flexing its might and thumbing its nose at the Alliance and at Kostaria specifically.

Pip swallowed, the bubbling laughter of a few minutes ago turning to ash in her mouth. As idyllic as this weekend of leave was, she couldn't forget that they were all training for war—a war that seemed increasingly inevitable. "Do you think Mongavaria will strike at Dar Goranth or Fort Defense first?"

For weeks, the newspapers had been filled with pundits debating which military base Mongavaria would strike first.

Fort Defense was the joint military base nestled between the foothills of the Whitehurst Mountains and the Hydalla River on the Escarlish side of the border with Mongavaria. Everyone knew that Fort Defense would become the main headquarters in any war with Mongavaria.

However, Fort Defense was protected by the Wall. Mongavaria could send their airships over to duke it out with the airships stationed at Fort Defense, but they couldn't attack more than that.

Since Dar Goranth wasn't protected by the Wall, Mongavaria could attack from sea, air, and land, if they could get close enough. If they took Dar Goranth, they could cripple the naval power of all three kingdoms and likely enforce a blockade of the coast.

Fieran shrugged, grimacing at the newspaper in his hands. "Perhaps they will attack both. Though both are heavily fortified and prepared for such a sneak attack. Any attack would be costly."

"It doesn't seem like Mongavaria cares." Pip resisted the shudder that traced down her spine.

Cut off from the rest of Tarenhiel as they had been at the western rail terminal, she hadn't known how tense things were with Mongavaria. But here in Bridgetown, the possibility of war was just about the only topic in the papers. People chatted on street corners about a coming war as casually as someone might talk about the weather. Everyone talked as if it was a matter of *when* and *where*, and not *if*.

She'd joined the Mechanics Auxiliaries because she'd been restless. But it seemed that her restlessness would lead her straight into a war sooner or later.

FOURTEEN

Fieran added the last item to his rucksack—in the correct layers—then hefted it to his back.

At the end of their bunk, Lije patted the bars of his mama's soap—she had sent him a fresh batch in their latest mail—and stowed them in his footlocker before closing the lid.

"Keep that soap safe. We're going to need it after we get back." Pretty Face glanced at himself one last time in his mirror before he tucked the mirror into his footlocker.

Across the way, Tiny grinned as he swung his rucksack to his shoulders. "Will you survive a week in the bush without a shower?"

"I don't know how we'll survive when *you* haven't had a shower in a week." Stickyfingers shoved Tiny's arm before he stood and grabbed his own rucksack.

Merrik's mouth curled a little bit, as if he was not looking forward to the lack of showers.

The drill sergeant stepped inside and yelled for them to fall in.

Lije grabbed his rucksack as the rest of them hurried to step into line.

For once, Fieran was correctly turned out, and he didn't get his stuff tossed around or had to do extra PT. He was improving. Slowly.

As they marched from their barracks, Fieran tried not to gape at the cylindrical airship that currently rested just above the airstrip, ropes tying it down to the ground and to the roof of the hangar.

The dirigible had a thin canvas sheeting stretched over metal ribs, forming the massive balloon shape. The canvas was painted a matte gray that didn't shine in the sun with the large green, gray, and red circle emblem of the Alliance emblazoned on either side.

Capt. Arfeld waited at the base of a rope ladder, standing next to a short, squat man in a dark blue uniform with gold braids on his sleeves. He must be the captain of the airship, which would take them from Fort Linder to Fort Charibert on the eastern side of Escarland.

As Fieran and his unit halted before the hangar, lined up in two long rows, Pip and the other mechanics hurried from the hangar, falling into place at the end of the column.

Fieran risked breaking formation long enough to send a small wave at Pip.

She smiled and waved back with a subtle movement of her fingers.

Fieran quickly faced forward again before he made a fool of himself by having to do a hundred push-ups in front of everyone, including an airship filled with naval airmen.

Once they were all there, Capt. Arfeld turned to the captain next to him. "Permission for my men—and woman —to come aboard?"

The other captain nodded, though he swept a sour glance

over the long line of flyboys and mechanics, as if he wasn't happy about being the airship captain assigned with the duty of giving army pilots and mechanics some cross training in an airship. "Permission granted."

With a few barked orders, the sergeant had them lined up single file to climb the rope ladder.

Fieran struggled not to tap his foot as he waited for the others. Despite the training on the obstacle course, some of the men in his unit struggled with the long rope ladder, twisting and swinging as they attempted to ascend.

When it was finally Fieran's turn, he climbed the rope easily. Was he showing off a bit? Maybe. It wasn't like he was the only one with elven agility. Merrik, coming up behind him, also ascended the ladder as if it was nothing. Pip, too, likely wouldn't have any difficulty.

At the top, Fieran was directed by an ensign down a cramped corridor. The wooden floor bounced a bit while the passageway was only about two feet wide, the roof only a few inches above Fieran's head. The occasional round window gave a view of the sky, keeping the corridor from feeling too claustrophobic. On the other side, a few doors led into the officers' quarters. Every few yards, a hatch led to a machine gun emplacement in the surrounding catwalk, a reminder that this was no tourist airship on a luxury cruise.

At the end of the corridor, another ensign pointed the way into a large space, where Fieran's unit was falling into line once again. Tables with benches were bolted to the deck so that they wouldn't shift around when the dirigible was in the air. To one side, a window gave a view into the industrial kitchen.

Fieran took his place next to Lije, ignoring the looks sent their way by the cooks bustling about the kitchens. He leaned closer to Lije. "I think they're resentful they have to cook for this many more people."

"Or they're annoyed they have to cook for a bunch of army boys." Lije kept his voice low in return.

"That's probably it." Fieran shook his head, chuckling under his breath. "I'm still surprised the navy and army managed to cooperate long enough to set up this cross training."

At the moment, the army was in charge of the Flying Corps, which consisted of all kinds of flyers, aeroplanes, and that sort of thing. The navy ran the Naval Air Corps, which oversaw the airships. Various leaders were talking about restructuring to place all airborne units into one Corps, perhaps as its own branch separate from both army and navy. Not surprisingly, neither the army nor the navy were in favor of such a plan.

In the meantime, greater cooperation was being encouraged between the Flying Corps and Naval Air Corps of all three Alliance Kingdoms, especially when it came to making sure pilots could fly any type of airborne craft and the mechanics could fix anything that stopped at an aerodrome.

Merrik halted next to Fieran. When Tiny took his place, he looked a little green beneath his gray skin in a way he hadn't when flying an aeroplane. Stickyfingers peered about as if he was contemplating if he could get away with stealing something while stuck on an airship.

Pip and the mechanics came after the last of the flyboys in Fieran's unit. Fieran met Pip's gaze and tipped his head to her, grinning. This trip would be even better with her along.

Finally, Capt. Arfeld and the navy captain entered the room. The navy captain halted in front of them, hands clasped behind his back as he glared. "You are here merely on the goodwill of the navy. If you so much as set a toe out of line, I will dump you out, with or without a parachute."

"And after he is done with you, you will have to deal with me." Capt. Arfeld swept a sharp glance over them. "Do what you're told and answer to an order from Capt. Nien as you would from me."

The nod Capt. Nien gave Capt. Arfeld held a great measure of respect. Perhaps the only reason this cross training was happening was Capt. Arfeld's hero status as a pioneer of flight.

Any glint of respect vanished as Capt. Nien faced them again, a deep scowl putting grooves in his cheeks. "Stay out of my men's way and stick to your assigned areas."

With that, they were broken into groups, and each group was assigned to an airman to show them around the dirigible.

Fieran glanced over his shoulder as his group of Lije, Merrik, and several others were led in one direction and Pip's group was led in another direction.

The airman led Fieran's group through the maze of tiny tunnel-like passageways, explaining navy terms while they were at it. The floor was the deck. The walls were bulkheads. The lavatory was called the head. They had already been in the mess, and each small group would be assigned a time for breakfast, lunch, and dinner since the mess could only handle feeding so many people at a time.

The pilothouse was at the front of the gondola where broad windows provided views of the sky. The pilothouse was far enough from the magically powered engines at the rear—stern—of the gondola that the navigation station was equipped with a compass, since it wasn't affected by the magi-magnetism. There was even a gyroscope to show the horizon line and keep the airship on an even keel. Too bad the flyers weren't equipped with such luxuries. All they had was the *Do not let it go red or you'll blow up* magical power gauge.

Machine guns bristled all along the sides of the gondola. There were even machine guns pointing downward underneath. The ammunition was stored in an armored room in the center of the gondola.

Racks stood next to all the doors on the sides and the bottom, holding packed parachutes. Fieran exchanged looks with his fellow flyboys at that. Everyone knew that real flyboys went up without the coward's assurance of a parachute.

That, and the aeroplanes' cockpits were too small to fit a pilot and a parachute. Nor was it likely a pilot could even lever himself out of a cockpit and push far enough away from a crashing aeroplane for a parachute to do him any good.

After climbing several sets of ladders, they entered the canvas balloon part of the dirigible. Here, the metal ribs holding up the canvas were visible, along with the additional machine guns that were accessible through zippered cloth doors in the canvas or by climbing the ratlines that stretched over the outside of the dirigible balloon.

Inside, the space between the catwalks was filled with multiple air balloons that held the helium. The helium was divided between many smaller balloons so that even if one of the balloons was torn, the others would keep the airship aloft.

When Fieran pressed his hand to the warm, waxy side of one of the balloons, he could sense the faint tingle of magic emanating from inside. Likely magic from a human magician, boosting the helium's lifting power, keeping it heated, and providing a magical barrier inside the balloon to further prevent helium loss in the event of punctures. What human magicians lacked in volume of power they usually made up in versatility.

The airman paused and showed them a section of catwalk where layer upon layer of what looked like white canvas sacks hung from the metal ribs and rope ratlines. "This is where you'll sleep. You take one of these hammocks and string them like this." He demonstrated unhooking one side of the canvas hammock and tying it tight across the way. "In the event the whistle for call to arms sounds in the night, you'll be responsible for stowing your own hammock and gear so that the catwalk isn't blocked."

Only then did Fieran spot the various hooks where they were supposed to hang their rucksacks from a series of ratlines.

As several of the other groups converged on the sleeping area assigned to them, Fieran hung his rucksack from the hook next to the hammock he claimed. "This isn't too different than sleeping high in the trees in Estyra. Just less of a view."

Merrik grinned and hung his rucksack near a hammock next to Fieran's. "Yes. It is almost like home."

A few yards away, Tiny gripped his stomach, bracing himself against the handrailing of the catwalk. "I don't feel so good."

"Don't hurl in my rucksack!" Stickyfingers shifted his hook and hammock farther away from Tiny.

"Why did you sign up for the Flying Corps if you get airsick?" Pretty Face smoothed his hair, trying to peer at himself in the reflection on the railing.

"I don't get airsick in a flyer." Tiny leaned farther over the railing, giving a slight groan, his voice strained. "There's a reason I didn't join the navy."

Fieran paused to better take in the slight sway of the catwalk beneath their feet. He'd barely noticed it earlier since it was so slight, just a gentle rocking not that much different from the swaying of a tree in the breeze. The larger trees in Tarenhiel, like Ellonahshinel where his family's home was located, were so protected with magic that it took a hundred years' gale to make the branches so much as twitch. But some of the smaller trees were left to sway in the wind.

The airman smirked and crossed his arms. "The swaying will only grow worse once we're in the air."

Tiny groaned and made a gagging sound.

The airman's smirk turned into a grimace. "I had better show you to sick bay before you hurl all over something I'll have to scrub later. If anyone else is feeling queasy, you'd better come too."

As the airman led Tiny and three others away, Fieran turned to those who were left. "Anyone else feeling motion sick? Because you'd better take the bottom hammocks."

"Yeah. Elves and those with strong stomachs on top." Pretty Face gave a shudder.

A few of the other flyboys exchanged looks, then rearranged a few of the rucksacks, moving the ones belonging to those who had followed the airman to the bottom.

Fieran peered upward at the various catwalks, rope ladders, and ratlines that led upward between the helium gas bags. He thought he could see a spot where there was a hatch to the very top of the airship.

Merrik heaved a sigh. "You want to go up there."

"When else will we have the chance to sneak away unsupervised?" Fieran debated for one more second before he headed for the nearest rope ladder. "You don't have to come with me."

Even as he spoke, Merrik was already dogging his heels. He might not be as reckless as Fieran, but he was still enough of an elf to want to seek out the highest point.

The various airmen climbing about within the dirigible sent them annoyed glances, then ignored them.

Fieran led the way through the maze of catwalks and ladders, working his way upward. His grin grew with each level they ascended.

Finally, he reached a metal hatch, set in a broad, flat metal roof attached to the I-beam keel that provided stabilization for all the metal ribs that curved from this keel down to the top of the gondola. He turned the wheel to undog the hatch, then levered it open.

As he climbed out, a cold breeze smacked into his face. He sucked in a deep breath as he planted his feet on the walk on the very top of the dirigible.

This walk had no handrails. Just a metal pathway that traversed the spine of the airship.

Someone else might have had a sense of fear, strolling along that tiny walkway so very high off the ground. But this was no different than walking along one of the elven branch pathways, which sometimes were as skinny as a foot or two wide with sheer drops on either side.

Merrik climbed up beside him and shut the hatch behind them. The two of them stood there, taking in the view.

Below, Fort Linder spread out in a grid of both wood and cement buildings. The three flags of Escarland, Tarenhiel, and Kostaria flapped above the central green, which was formed by the infirmary, officers' quarters, communications center, and various other command headquarters.

They couldn't even see the aeroplane hangar directly

below them due to the bulk of the airship. Only the far end of the airstrip was visible, a dusty line between waving grass, pointing toward the Hydalla River rippling and shimmering to the north.

In the distance to the west, Bridgetown's skyline broke the horizon, bordered by the Hydalla River, though Calafaren couldn't be seen among the dense foliage of Tarenhiel.

But it was the Alliance Bridge that drew the eye, arching over the Hydalla River and gleaming in the morning sunlight.

"Was this worth risking extra PT?" Fieran faced into the breeze as it raked through the short strands of his hair.

"Maybe. Depends on the PT." Merrik grimaced and gestured at the airship below their feet. "We are in the navy's hands now. They might have us swab the deck."

"I don't care."

"You will if Tiny hurled all over the deck we are swabbing."

"True." Fieran couldn't resist any longer. He just couldn't stay still in a place like this, with the open sky all around him and nothing but a small walk beneath him. Something about this place just called to his elven blood, despite the fact that it was all human-made metal and mechanics. He ran lightly along the walk, then threw himself into a front flip. He landed lightly in a crouch before he was up again.

Behind him, Merrik matched his movements, not even sighing or rolling his eyes. He, too, must have been itching to let his elven side loose after having to hold back for so long to fit into the Escarlish army's strictures.

Fieran held out his hands as if he held his swords, moving as if fighting an invisible foe. He spun and ducked and flipped, landing lightly on his feet on the narrow walk.

Beneath his feet, the airship lurched. Shouts came from

below, too vague to make out the words, but the intent was clear as the ropes were loosed. The airship shot upward quickly, rising toward the sky.

Fieran laughed at the movement beneath him, not pausing in his invisible sword fighting. He released the tight clamp he'd held on his magic for weeks. It burst around him for a moment, wild and crackling, seeking to devour anything it touched.

Then he squashed down on it again, letting only a trickle of it twine around his fingers and arms.

Still, just that much of a release eased the tightness in his chest and the jitters he'd been suppressing for weeks.

Merrik, too, let his magic glow green around his fingers, despite the lack of nearby plants. He was moving through sword fighting stances of his own, as the airship below them ascended into the heavens.

Fieran gave one last flip, and Merrik mirrored his movements. Both of them landed in a crouch facing each other, imaginary swords in front of them. Both of them were breathing hard, though only a hint of sweat slicked Merrik's forehead. When Fieran broke his stance to swipe at his own forehead, his sleeve didn't even get damp.

Straightening, Fieran let out a long exhale and mimed sheathing swords across his back. "I needed that."

Merrik, too, straightened. "I know. Trust me, I did not want to risk your magic breaking loose while we were stuck on this rather incinerable airship. I would rather risk the extra PT."

"Even if it's swabbing the deck after Tiny has lost his breakfast all over it?"

"Even then."

Pip took in the thrumming magical engines that filled the engineering space at the stern of the airship's gondola. Her fingers itched to dive in and explore all the nooks and crannies of this engineering marvel.

Banks of magical power cells lined one wall, waiting to be swapped out for depleted ones. Each of the two engines had four power cells—two on each side—for a total of eight magical power cells in use at any given time. Each engine turned a massive shaft, which whirled the even more ginormous propeller—or airscrew—on the stern. The two propellers could be controlled independently, making the airship as nimble as possible through the air.

The head engineer swept a glance over each of them, his gaze passing Pip, then flicking back to her, as if he couldn't quite believe a female had been assigned to his crew. "You will be assisting here in the mechanical spaces of the airship in shifts of four. Beyond the engines, the mechanics also maintain all the other mechanical spaces throughout the airship."

She couldn't wait to scramble all over this airship. *This* was the reason she'd joined the Mechanics Auxiliaries. She'd wanted to see and experience things she wouldn't have if she'd stayed tucked away at the far western side of Tarenhiel.

A series of bells sounded, and the men in the engine room jumped as if to obey a set of orders.

The deck below Pip's feet jolted. Then she had the sense of rising through the air, even though the world around her remained static.

They were lifting off. She resisted the urge to grab something to steady herself. Instead, she kept her knees loose, telling herself that she was half elf. Stuff like this should be perfectly normal for her.

As the airmen didn't appear to be paying any attention to the army mechanics unwillingly foisted on them, she walked across the space and peered out the round porthole window set into the rear of the gondola. The blades of the propeller flashed past, but between the blur she could make out the ground vanishing below.

Her stomach dropped, though she wasn't afraid. Not exactly. It was as if she was at war with herself. Part of her—her elven half—thrilled at the height. Her other half—the dwarven part of her—couldn't help a twinge of discomfort at seeing the safety of the ground disappearing so far below.

A whistle came from the door before someone called out, "Officer on deck."

All the airmen in the engine room spun on their heels and saluted the blue-coated officer who stepped through the doorway.

The officer saluted in return, then glanced around the room, his gaze falling on Pip. He strode across the room toward her. "Mechanic Pippak Detmuk-Inawenys?"

"That's me." She was rather impressed that he was able to say her name without stumbling over it. Perhaps he'd been practicing it in his mind the whole walk from the pilot-house to the engine room.

"As you are..." The officer—a young man who couldn't have been much more than eighteen or nineteen in human years—trailed off, his neck growing red.

"Female?" She guessed that was probably the reason for the awkwardness.

"Yes." The officer straightened his shoulders, regaining his professional mien. "You've been assigned a room near the officers' quarters. You've also been authorized to use the officers' head. I'll show you where to find those, if you'll follow me."

The officer spun on his heel, then strode off at a long-legged brisk pace.

Pip trotted to keep up, but she wasn't about to ask him to slow down.

By the time they reached the bow of the gondola, she was panting from jogging the whole way, though she tried to keep her panting quiet so that it wasn't so obvious that she was out of breath.

Her room was basically a closet with barely enough space to stand next to the hammock that gently swung with the motion of the airship around them.

The officers' head was at the end of that same walkway, complete with a locking door, which Pip appreciated.

While she was given special treatment when it came to her room and lavatory facilities, she wasn't invited to the captain's table for supper that night. For which she was grateful. She didn't want to be singled out quite *that* much. Even better, when she stepped into the mess that evening, she found Fieran, Merrik, and Lije sitting at a table. Apparently she had been assigned the same food times as their group.

She claimed her tray, went through the line where a cook placed some kind of savory beef with gravy and vegetables on her plate, and joined Fieran and Merrik at their table, squeezing into the seat beside Fieran that the others had made for her by sliding over.

Loud snickering and a few murmurs came from a nearby table of naval airmen, along with a few sneers in the flyboys' direction. As Pip took her first bite, the tension curled between the tables so tightly that her muscles stiffened.

"If you actually wanted to fight Mongavarians, you should have joined the navy." One of the airmen at a nearby table waggled a fork, his buddies snickering. "We don't sit on our rears just taking pictures and looking at the enemy. We'll actually fight the war."

Across the table from Pip, one of the flyboys clenched his fists. Another gripped the table, his body tensing as if he was going to stand.

Pip let a hint of her magic flow into her fingers, though she wasn't sure what she planned to do with her magical shield. Perhaps shield herself in the event of a fistfight so she didn't get squashed like a bug. Or perhaps prevent a fight from even starting by forming a barrier between the two combatants.

Fieran reached out and snagged the flyboy's arm, holding him in place. "Ignore them. It isn't worth starting a brawl that will just fuel the army-navy rivalry."

"Even if they deserve it," Lije muttered under his breath, his hands clenched on his fork.

Another naval airman grumbled, though he spoke plenty loud enough for them to hear, "General Julien's Follies."

Fieran's jaw flexed at the mocking mention of his uncle. Merrik turned slightly, as if to better place himself to guard Fieran's back in the event of a brawl.

While Pip hadn't heard the phrase "General Julien's Follies" until she'd come to Fort Linder, the sentiment was one spoken on the streets of Bridgetown and reported in the papers. Even a few men in the regular army units stationed at Fort Linder muttered it when they saw the flyboys.

It was a common opinion that General Julien Ardon's push for flyers was a foolish one. The accepted belief was that the war would be fought with airships, and flyers would be nothing more than scouts, too small and useless to actually take down an airship by themselves. Many in the army didn't even think it was worth arming the aeroplanes.

After seeing an airship up close, Pip wasn't sure she

disagreed with them, exactly. What could a flyer—even an armed one—do against such a well-fortified behemoth? Only a pilot like Fieran with a great deal of destructive magic could take down an airship on his own. The rest of the flyer squadron would be like gnats buzzing around a grizzly bear. Annoying, but easily swatted from the air.

Still, she gripped Fieran's sleeve. "It isn't worth starting something."

Not that she would stop him if he tried. Like Merrik, she'd stand at his side if Fieran chose to fight over turning the other cheek.

Fieran sighed, shook his head, and turned his back to the hecklers.

"Shut up." An airman at another table glared at the table of jeerers before he glanced over at Fieran, giving him a slight nod.

Well, at least not all the naval airmen here wanted to play into the rivalry.

As the scoffing airmen turned back to their food with a few grumbles, Pip relaxed, letting her magic drain away back into her chest.

Fieran released the other flyboy's arm, and they all dug into their food like the tension of a moment earlier hadn't happened.

"How are the engineering spaces?" Fieran wolfed down his food between his words as if he worried that someone had mixed up their food with what was supposed to be served to the officers.

She'd heard the rumors that the navy ate far better than the army. This airship was certainly trying to prove that was true. Perhaps the navy cooks were pulling out all the stops, showing off for the army flyboys in their midst.

"I could have spent all day admiring the engines. They

are marvels." Pip blew on her bite of roast beef before popping it in her mouth. The savory taste burst across her tongue. She hadn't eaten anything this good outside of the weekends in Bridgetown since leaving home. "What about you? Did you learn how to fly this thing yet?"

"Not yet." Fieran shrugged. "Hopefully tomorrow. But Merrik and I sneaked up to the top of the dirigible for a while. That was beyond amazing."

Merrik glanced around, then poked Fieran. "Do not say that so loud. No one has given us swabbing duties yet, and I do not want that to change."

Fieran just smirked at his friend. "If they haven't punished us by now, I doubt they will."

Merrik rolled his eyes and turned back to his food.

Still, Fieran lowered his voice as he faced Pip. "They have us bunking in hammocks among the gas balloons above the gondola. But I didn't see your things stowed up there."

"No. I've been assigned a tiny cabin in the officers' quarters." Pip shrugged, her shoulder brushing Fieran's arm with the movement. "It's cramped even for me. I'd almost rather have a hammock up there with the rest of you. Almost."

"Considering Tiny nearly hurled his breakfast all over our hammocks, you'll probably be grateful you don't have a hammock with the rest of us." Lije gave a shudder. "I don't have enough of my mama's soap along to salvage something like that."

Pip gave a shudder of her own. Tight as it was, she'd take her cubby of a room over risking an airsick flyboy vomiting over her during the night.

FIFTEEN

Pip stood on the metal catwalk that ringed the top of the gondola. Standing at the bow, the breeze of the airship's passing toyed with her curls and smacked cold against her face. Stars twinkled in the depths of the nighttime sky that spread out high overhead, partially blocked by the balloon of the dirigible. Below, clusters of lights marked out Escarlish villages amid the darkness of empty farm fields. The distant whistle of a train echoed on the breeze, but it was the only sound that could reach her from the land below.

Behind her came the thrum of the propellers, clank of footsteps on various catwalks, and the buzz of indistinct voices from the dirigible. Despite the noise, her spot at the railing was strangely peaceful, drifting between land and sky.

Bootsteps clanked on the catwalk behind her, but not with the heaviness she'd heard from the airmen. She stayed where she was, not surprised when Fieran leaned against the railing next to her. Only an elf—or half-elf—could manage to walk that quietly on an echoing metal walk while wearing army boots.

"A peaceful night." Fieran breathed in deeply. A hint of his magic sparked over his fingers and jumped to the railing. He glanced down, then clenched his fists to snuff out his magic.

"Yes, it is." Pip gestured to his hands. "Less peaceful if you lose control of your magic. That's getting worse."

"I'll be fine." Fieran shrugged, though another spark of magic jumped from his fingers to the rail. "I'd sneak away to the top of the balloon again to let loose, but I've already risked that once. I think someone would notice a blue glow lighting up the night. Besides, I don't want to risk accidentally incinerating something critical. The balloon looks sturdy, but it wouldn't take much of my magic to damage it enough to take it down."

"Thanks for that mental image." Pip gave an exaggerated shudder. "Just when I was enjoying this airship cruise, you had to go and remind me how easy it would be to crash."

"Don't worry. This airship is heavily armed and magically protected. Nothing short of my magic is going to take it down." Fieran nudged her with a shoulder. "And I have my magic under tight control. No incinerating things tonight."

"We could still crash from a hundred other reasons." Pip found herself gripping the railing just thinking about it. She was doing a decent job of suppressing the longing for the ground, but talking about it was causing that panicky feeling in her throat again.

"That's why you mechanics are here to make sure those hundred reasons don't happen." Fieran's tone was light, but his grin faded as he turned to her, his face visible in the golden light filtering up from the gondola below. "How about a change in topic? I have a question I've been wanting to ask you."

"Go ahead. Shoot." Pip gripped the railing and closed her eyes, concentrating on the cool breeze sweeping across her face.

"What's with the hyphenated last name?" Fieran's voice was low, regaining that hint of a chuckle. "Not that I'm criticizing or anything. My own name is a mouthful."

"I've been wondering about your last name too." Pip peeled her eyes open, focusing on Fieran rather than the ground far, *far* below. "Laesornysh is quite the last name to inherit. I'm a bit surprised your parents didn't settle on something else."

Years ago, elves hadn't had family names like the humans of Escarland and trolls of Kostaria did. They earned titles instead, which held great meaning among the elves when they were bestowed.

Thanks to the alliances, King Weylind had decreed that elves also take last names to create a standard across all three of the Alliance Kingdoms. Of course, they could still earn titles on top of their last names, but it would be an additional third name and not used like a family name.

Pip's dacha's title *Inawenys* meant *Negotiator of Iron*, bestowed for his role in negotiating the current trade agreement between Tarenhiel and her muka's kingdom of dwarves. That title had become a part of Pip's last name thanks to King Weylind's decree.

Fieran rested more fully against the rail and sucked in a deep breath, as if preparing for a long explanation. "Since Mama is a princess of Escarland and Dacha is a prince of Tarenhiel, they could have picked the royal last name of either kingdom. Instead, they decided to leave the royal names for my cousins on both sides and take a new family name."

"I guess that makes sense." Pip tried not to let her bubbling squeal loose at the casual mention of Prince Farrendel and Princess Elspeth. She *would* concentrate on this conversation and not get sidetracked with hero worship. "With how long you will live compared to your royal Escarlish cousins, it would be awkward if you had the same last name as those in line for the throne."

"Exactly." Fieran smiled at her, as if pleased that she'd understood so quickly. "My uncles did the same thing for the same reason. Uncle Edmund uses his elven title for their last name, and Uncle Julien took Aunt Vriska's troll family name, even though neither of them technically needed to drop the Escarlish royal last name for something else."

"So you ended up Laesornysh." Pip gave a slight nod, the elven warrior name rolling off her tongue.

"Yes. I don't mind carrying Dacha's title. It's just..." Fieran sighed and gave a weary roll of his shoulders. "It would have been nice to inherit a last name that didn't carry such weight. It is a title given to a worthy warrior, not carried by someone who has yet to prove himself in battle."

Pip rested her hand on Fieran's forearm, his muscles flexing beneath her fingers as he clenched his fists. "Even if the elves can't see it yet, you have every right to your dacha's title, and I know you will be a warrior every bit as brave as he was. And I say that as someone who is rather overawed by his magical-mechanical accomplishments."

"Thanks." Fieran dropped his gaze from hers, his shoulders hunched. But the melancholy lasted only a moment before he straightened, his smile returning. "The other annoying part about the last name of Laesornysh is the Escarlish find it hard to pronounce. I'm just thankful my

mama managed to talk my dacha out of naming me Fierendel. Can you imagine going around with the name of
Fierendel Laesornysh? People already accidentally call me
by my dacha's name as it is."

"I could see how that would get annoying." Pip laughed,
shaking her head. As she, too, was half elf, he didn't have to
explain the full connotation. Fierendel would have been the
proper elven form of his name, meaning *One with the Fiery
Red Hair*. "Elves have a hard time with the dwarven Pippak,
so I usually go by Pippa or just Pip since it's easier, despite
the elves' horror at shortening a name like that and
butchering the meaning."

"Elves can be quite stuffy about nicknames." Fieran gave
a more relaxed shrug this time. "At least *Red* is what the drill
sergeants call me anyway. Little do they know that my name
is literally *Red Hair* in elvish."

Pip nudged him by leaning into him with a shoulder.
"*Red* fits you so well."

"Doesn't it?" He swiped a hand over the short strands of
his red hair. "Probably even more so if I wore my hair in the
long elven style. But much to my dacha's chagrin, I preferred
to keep my hair short even before joining the army. I didn't
inherit the mystical and magical properties of elven hair."

"I didn't get my dacha's hair either, though my hair
doesn't frizz as much as most curly hair." Pip rubbed a hand
over her chin. "Nor did I inherit the mythical and magical
properties of beard hair. And as much as I love my muka,
I'm elven enough that I can't be too sad about that."

Fieran tipped his head back as he gave a full-throated
chuckle, the kind of laugh that made everyone around him
want to laugh along. "I can't imagine you with a beard." He
paused and glanced at her. "But you didn't answer my original question. What's up with the hyphenated last name?"

"You distracted me with all your talk of magical hair." Pip rolled her eyes right back at him. "A dwarf's last name refers to their clan, which is one large, extended family. But it's more than just a statement of familial relationship. A clan lives in one mountain, which is named after the clan, and the clan head acts as something of a mayor. Groups of clans form the next tier of government, and so on and so forth all the way up to the dwarf king."

"That's neat. So your mama is from Mount Detmuk?"

"Yes. My great-great-uncle is the clan head." Pip rolled her shoulders in another shrug. "I don't really know him. But Clan Detmuk does have a decent amount of influence since Mount Detmuk serves as one of the main railroad terminals between the dwarven mountains and Tarenhiel."

"Was that how your parents met?" Fieran glanced at her before facing the night once again, peering outward as if taking in the view of village lights crawling past below.

"Yes." Pip smiled, remembering the looks on her parents' faces whenever they talked about falling in love. "My dacha traveled to Mount Detmuk to negotiate a renewal of the various treaties and trade agreements, and he and my muka fell in love."

"Sounds like your parents should have legends told about them." Fieran's smile turned lopsided, his face both highlighted and shadowed by the lights from the gondola. "I'm sure my parents wouldn't mind sharing the spotlight."

"Everyone knows elf-dwarf romances aren't as widely celebrated as elf-human ones." Pip shook her head and nudged Fieran again. "Besides, my parents got married before yours in the time when Tarenhiel was more insular. My parents' marriage was far more frowned upon back then."

"I'm glad my parents helped make things better for your

parents." Fieran's smile faded again to that soft, sincere expression of his that darkened his brilliant blue eyes.

"Well, somewhat. My dacha's parents still make snide remarks when we make a rare trip to visit them." Pip rubbed a hand over her jaw again, her chest aching slightly. "They routinely inspect me to make sure I haven't sprouted any beard hairs yet. I don't even want a beard, and it still makes me feel prickly. My machasheni barely even acknowledges my muka."

"I'm sorry. That's hard." Fieran leaned his elbows on the railing, which put his head level with hers, even though he was bent over. "I never knew either of my grandfathers. They were both dead long before I was born. As was my machasheni on my dacha's side. But my grandmother on my mother's side experienced a long life for a human, and I had the chance to get to know her before she died. I also have my dacha's machasheni, who fills that role for all of us. But neither my grandmother nor great-grandmother ever showed any scorn to either my dacha or mama. What about your dwarven grandparents?"

"They're better about it than my elven grandparents, though they still occasionally hassle my dacha for his lack of beard." Pip leaned against the rail, though she propped herself up on her hands rather than her elbows like Fieran. She didn't want to bend over and make herself any shorter than she already was. "We don't get to see them often, though, because it's a long trip, and it isn't easy to get someone to cover our duties at the western rail terminal."

"I can see that." Fieran gestured out at the dark landscape spreading below them. "My parents split their time between Tarenhiel and Escarland while I was growing up, so I was able to know both sides of my family well. Even now, Dacha and Mama still travel back and forth frequently. I don't always go with them, but I know I always have a home in both places."

"That's nice that you were able to experience both sides of your heritage growing up like that." Pip swallowed the lump in her throat. "That's actually the reason for my hyphenated surname. Since my parents lived exclusively in Tarenhiel with only occasional visits to Mount Detmuk, my parents didn't want us to lose all sense of connection to our dwarven side. So they hyphenated my muka's clan name with dacha's elven title. Perhaps we could have used only our dwarven name when visiting Mount Detmuk and only Dacha's name in Tarenhiel. But that always felt like denying half of ourselves, you know?"

"Yeah, I understand that." Fieran stared straight ahead, a weight to his words. "There can be such a pressure to be one thing or another. To be all elf or all human. People don't really know what to do with someone who doesn't fit into their little boxes."

Time to bring back a little bit of levity. Pip leaned into him again, nudging him with her shoulder. "I fit into quite little boxes."

He laughed, nudging her in return. "True. I wedge myself into aeroplane cockpits that are quite small, especially for my long legs. But there are some boxes I don't want to wedge myself into, even if it means I need to work extra hard to forge my own way."

"I think we're making a good start there." Pip waved at the night sky and dark land below them, dotted with pinpricks of life.

"Nothing wider than the open sky." Fieran grinned, his straight white teeth gleaming in the faint light from behind and beneath them.

"Exactly." As they lapsed into silence, Pip breathed in the

comfortable peace of standing there with him. Despite her earlier awkwardness around him because of his dacha, Fieran was one of those strangely comfortable guys to be around, as long as a girl didn't read too much into his smiles.

FIERAN STOOD along the rear bulkhead of the pilothouse with the rest of his small group. An airman walked all of them through the steps of flying an airship, even as they stayed out of the way.

Unlike a flyer, which was simply a matter of the rudder and the stick with only a handful of gauges, an airship flew through the precise working of speeds for the two engines, flaps along the sides, dumping ballast or moving ballast between the tanks, and venting air. Watching it all, Fieran could see why the dirigibles were called air*ships*. This truly ran more like a ship in a sea of air rather than the aeroplane he was learning to fly.

Through the broad windows at the front of the pilothouse, the setting sun highlighted the far distant smudge that was the Whitehurst Mountains. Almost directly in front and below them, Fort Charibert stood in the center of a section of forest that covered this part of Escarland.

Unlike Fort Linder, Fort Charibert had been an army fort for hundreds of years. It sprawled in all directions, strangely higgledy-piggledy despite the army orderliness of the rows of barracks made from a variety of materials, including wood, cement, brick, and stone. The fort's age showed in the shabbiness of many of the buildings.

The airship eased lower as the captain gave orders to shift ballast forward and vent the hot air trapped in some of the balloons. This air was regular air, not helium. These balloons were vented on descent rather than venting any of the harder-to-procure helium.

Gracefully, the airship drifted downward, then leveled off twenty feet above the ground. Orders were given, and airmen hurried to toss ropes off the bow and stern.

Fieran braced himself, and he barely swayed when the airship jerked to a halt, caught on the ropes the ground crew must have secured to something sturdy. Beside him, one of his fellow flyboys stumbled.

As the airship steadied at the end of its ropes, Fieran sighed and turned to Merrik. "I guess our little airship cruise is at an end."

Merrik elbowed him. "Not so loud. If someone hears you, our reprieve from PT will also be at an end."

Lije heaved his own sigh, though he spoke under his breath. "I'm going to miss navy food."

"Me too." Fieran had gained a whole two pounds in the past two days. It wasn't going to be easy going back to bland, tasteless, formless army food. Worse, they were headed out for a week in the woods where they would be living on hardtack and tinned food.

At least Pip wouldn't endure the week in the woods. She and the other mechanics would be spending a week in the airship hangar here at Fort Charibert, continuing their training.

After being ordered to collect their rucksacks, Fieran joined the others in the airship's mess. All too soon, the drill sergeants yelled them off the airship, and Fieran descended the ladder with his rucksack on his back. At the bottom, he assembled into line with Lije on one side, Merrik and Pretty Face in the row behind them.

Instead of being shown into nice, drafty barracks for the

night, they immediately marched through the fort and into the surrounding woods.

They hiked along sandy trails, winding through a forest of scrubby pines, maples, and straggling oaks. At this time of spring, the first red buds sprouted at the ends of the branches, still a few weeks away from bursting into leaves. The night's chill fell around them, so cold that Fieran could see his breath puffing before his face.

Finally, the lieutenant called a halt, and they were instructed to dig foxholes in the dirt at the base of the trees for shelters for the night.

While Lije stood guard, Fieran pulled out his collapsible shovel and set to work digging what would be a two-man foxhole for himself and Lije. The sandy soil wasn't that hard-packed, but there were so many roots that it was hard digging.

A few feet away, Merrik dug the foxhole while Pretty Face stood guard, their foxhole positioned to coordinate lines of fire.

Fieran scraped away the two-to-three-inch-deep hole to lie in, trying to decide the best way to chop through the roots to dig the standing trench in front of his foxhole.

A faint green glow spread through the area around where he, Lije, Pretty Face, and Merrik had been assigned their foxholes. The roots that had been blocking Fieran's way wiggled back into the ground on either side of his foxhole, leaving nothing but dirt in his way.

Fieran took a moment to nod at Merrik before he went back to work. The roots curved around the spot in a wall, making the foxhole almost cozy.

For years, Fieran's family had camped out in the forested parkland of Treehaven several times throughout the summer. Sleeping out in the woods beneath the stars wasn't entirely unfamiliar to him, despite his privileged upbringing. But the whole *dig his own foxhole and sleep with a gun tucked in next to him* was new.

"Aaah!"

Fieran woke up to a scream. He bolted upright, reaching for his rifle.

A few yards away, Stickyfingers was hopping up and down on one foot, holding a boot in one hand. "Snake!"

"What kind?" Lije scrambled out of their foxhole, then dove after the snake. He came up with a long, wiggling black snake that was about three feet long. "Ooh, this one is good eating."

"I'm not eating that thing!" Stickyfingers lurched away from Lije as quickly as he could while hopping on one foot. "It was in my boot!"

"Come on, Sticky! Don't be a coward." Pretty Face smoothed a hand over his hair, though he kept his face turned away from Lije and the snake.

Fieran shook out his boots before he pulled them on. "I've never had snake before. What does it taste like?"

"Chicken, more or less." Lije hiked a few yards into the forest outside of their camp, pinned the snake to a rock, then cut off its head in a quick strike with his army knife. He tossed the snake's head into the brush and hung the body up by the tail to let the blood drain.

Tiny gathered wood while Fieran lit the kindling, coaxing the small fire they were allowed to light into life.

Stickyfingers prepared the coffee pot, and Merrik fetched the water that they would boil to give their salted meat some life. There was nothing much they could do about the army ration hardtack. Pretty Face took his time groaning and rolling out of his bedroll, grumbling the whole way.

By the time the water was boiling, Lije had gutted and skinned the snake, and he dropped the fresh meat into the pot with their pieces of salt pork.

Once the meat was cooked, they divided up the fresh snake meat. Even Stickyfingers claimed a piece, despite his earlier protests. By the time they shared with a few of the others in the unit, they only got a bite or two of snake meat each.

Fieran chewed his bites, taking the time to savor them. As Lije had said, it tasted like slightly gamier chicken. Not bad, really. Better than more salted meat and hardtack.

Perhaps life out in the bush wasn't so bad after all.

SIXTEEN

Fieran waited to one side of the long lines of massive guns that faced into the bomb range at Fort Charibert. All morning, the various guns had been booming as an army artillery unit aimed at various items set out in the bomb range. But about half an hour ago, the guns had fallen silent.

A single machine gun—similar to the type installed on the airships—stood at the far end, and it was the only weapon Fieran's unit was going to be rotating through certifying on today.

Fieran adjusted the army-issue earplugs that were stuffed into his ears. They were, at least, similar to the elven ones he was used to wearing at AMPC, though this mass-produced version was clearly of inferior quality.

There was a stir at the far end of the row of guns. Then a cluster of generals and high-ranking officers came into view, causing everyone in their vicinity to snap to attention and salute.

As Fieran saluted, he resisted the urge to groan. Among those generals was his uncle Julien, his thick red-brown beard and hair lacking any gray, though a few lines etched around his eyes.

Next to Uncle Julien strode Dacha in his elven leather and metal armor, his twin swords sheathed across his back.

Uncle Julien and the other generals saluted the recruits. Uncle Julien, at least, didn't search out Fieran in the crowd, though he must have been aware that Fieran was there. The less attention Fieran had drawn to him, the better, and Uncle Julien would know that, having once been a prince undergoing basic training himself.

"Fieran Laesornysh, step forward."

So much for not drawing attention. Fieran gritted his teeth on his groan and stepped forward out of line, keeping his gaze just over the lieutenant's head rather than look at Dacha or Uncle Julien.

"You have been placed on special assignment under General Laesornysh."

Now everyone standing there—not just his unit—knew he was being given special treatment because of his dacha. If the sergeants didn't make his life miserable once they were no longer under the gaze of Fieran's powerful father and uncle, then the others in his unit—those he wasn't friends with—would see to it that he received a bit of mild hazing.

Dacha nodded to Fieran, then strode past the machine gun, heading out into the bomb range.

Fieran followed, resisting the urge to glance over his shoulder at his unit.

His dacha strolled into the bomb range, avoiding craters in the dirt, until they reached a spot marked with a green flag. Once there, his dacha turned, facing him.

This far from the others, they didn't have to be General Laesornysh and a lowly recruit. A brief smile twitched across

Dacha's hard face as he swept a glance over Fieran. "Elontiri, sason. You are well?"

"Yes. Army life agrees with me." Fieran resisted the urge to hug his dacha. The others would see that, even from so far away. He was already going to get enough teasing for having his dacha pull him aside in front of everyone.

Dacha stepped forward, as if he was going to give Fieran a hug anyway, before a slight breeze kicked up and he halted, his nose wrinkling in that way it did when Dacha was disgusted by something.

The breeze curled around Fieran, and he got a whiff of his own body odor. He sniffed his armpit, then grinned at his dacha. "You don't have to say it. We've been out in the field for a week. I'm a little ripe."

His dacha made a non-committal noise, as if he didn't want to agree and say his son stank but he also didn't want to lie.

"Probably best if we avoid hugging." Fieran tilted his head to indicate the unit he'd left behind. "Besides, getting singled out like this won't help my standing with the guys."

"I am sorry for that, but you need this training far more than you need that." Any hint of a smile faded from Dacha's face as his eyes hardened. "Because of your magic, sason, you cannot simply be one of the lowly recruits. You will always be called upon to step forward and do more."

If only Dacha's words weren't so true. Fieran might have spent the past six weeks pretending he was nothing more than a normal recruit, suppressing his magic and ignoring much of the training his dacha had given him over the years.

But no matter how much Fieran wanted to pretend otherwise, he wasn't normal. He might grit his teeth at special treatment, but he couldn't hide from the fact that he *was* special. He had special written all the way down to his bones, and he couldn't escape that.

He also couldn't escape the burden of having to live up to the destiny placed upon him thanks to his magic and parentage.

Fieran nodded, then met his dacha's gaze. "I understand. So what's this extra training?"

Dacha faced the line of artillery guns pointed at them. "How to use your magic in battle."

Fieran swallowed and nodded.

Dacha had taught them how to incinerate bullets with their magic, but they stood off to the side while Mama fired at a target. It had felt more like a game, trying to incinerate the bullet before it hit the earthen berm. At the time, Fieran had realized only in the vaguest sense that the training was a precaution in case some crackpot assassin tried to shoot Fieran or his siblings.

But this felt far more real, standing there beside his dacha on the bomb range and staring down that intimidating line of guns, their barrels black and ominous. Despite his magic, Fieran shifted at the sheer vulnerability of standing there without so much as a helmet for protection.

Dacha reached into his pocket and pulled out two sets of the elven moss earplugs, handing one set to Fieran. "This will be loud."

Fieran took the earplugs and swapped out his cheap, army-issue ones for the better earplugs from his dacha. Beside him, Dacha tucked his earplugs into his ears, then motioned, probably to someone watching by the line of guns, to indicate that they were ready.

Dacha crouched, then unleashed his magic, the crackling blue bolts bursting around him, filling the air with the power of the ancient kings.

With a deep breath, Fieran crouched. He'd had his magic clamped so tightly in his chest for so long that it took a heartbeat longer than it should have to release his control.

When he wrenched away the tight feeling in his chest and freed his magic, it lashed around him, surging out of his control.

Dacha glanced at him, his eyebrows lifting. Dacha's magic kept Fieran's from getting anywhere close to hurting him or lashing too far out of control, the two magics sparking against each other wherever they touched.

Fieran grimaced, hearing Dacha's reproof without him having to say it out loud. Fieran should have known better than to keep his magic tightly repressed for so long, even if he'd had little choice in doing so.

The magic of the ancient kings never responded well to being restricted. Dacha had always told them growing up that they should regularly practice with their magic for their own physical, mental, and magical health.

After letting his magic rage for another heartbeat, Fieran reined it in as best he could, directing his magic to twine around him in a protective barrier.

With a boom that shivered through the ground, the farthest of the artillery guns belched smoke. Moments later, the ground shook as an explosion kicked up a spray of dirt behind them.

Fieran flinched, unable to suppress the instinctual reaction. Even after six weeks of army training, this was a step beyond anything he'd experienced. Those guns were aimed well above his and Dacha's heads, but it still felt precarious, facing down that menacing line of guns.

Dacha, of course, didn't flinch, his eyes flinty, his jaw hard. In that moment, he was more the legendary warrior Laesornysh than Fieran's dacha.

This was what it meant to be Laesornysh. How many times had Dacha walked onto a battlefield just like this, except the guns he faced were truly aimed at him? He'd done it alone, no one else capable of standing with him.

More of the guns boomed. The machine guns at the end —including the one manned by Fieran's unit—spat a line of lead into the air.

The bullets whined disconcertingly close over Fieran's head, and he ducked again. He barely bit back one of the crude words he'd learned in the past few weeks. He wasn't about to speak that kind of language in front of his dacha.

Dacha lifted his hands, though he kept his magic tight around him. "Expand the shield of your magic, sason, and incinerate the machine gun bullets."

Fieran unleashed more of his magic, creating a wall of magic in front of him and Dacha. The machine gun bullets punched through the magic, traveling so fast with such quantity that a stream of them got through.

Biting back a few more crude words, Fieran adjusted his magic, spreading it so that his magic formed a wall a good ten inches deep. This time, the bullets were sparking lights as he incinerated them.

"Now the artillery shells." Dacha remained poised as another gun boomed. Instead of letting the shell fall behind them, Dacha lashed out with his magic. Somehow, he seemed to catch the projectile with his magic, redirecting it and slamming it into the ground off to the side. The earth beneath Fieran's feet lurched with the explosion.

Dacha caught the next shell the same way, meeting Fieran's gaze rather than look at the shell as he slammed it too into the ground with an explosion of gunpowder and magic. "You can catch the shells with your magic, then change the trajectory to direct it to explode in the location of your choice."

Fieran nodded. The magically powered engines functioned because of the properties of magi-magnetism the magic of the ancient kings had. But right now, his dacha was teaching him to use his magic to turn an enemy's shells against them.

He spread his magic higher, not trusting himself to be able to snag one of the shells as easily as Dacha had.

Another gun boomed, and Fieran felt the shell as it flew into his magic. He wrapped his magic around it, but he couldn't get his magic moving around the shell quickly enough before the shell hit the ground, exploding on impact.

Fieran tried again, this time reacting more quickly and shifting the shell from its trajectory enough to slam it straight down on one of the old boats placed on the bomb range as a target.

"Yes!" He pumped his fist.

"Well done, sason." Dacha nodded, then tilted his head. "You have neglected the machine guns."

Some of the bullets from the machine guns were once again whizzing through Fieran's thinning magical barrier without being fully incinerated.

Fieran grimaced and strengthened the shield, even as he fumbled to grab the next artillery shell with his magic.

He had plenty of magic. That wasn't the problem. But it was harder than it looked to split his focus to both shield himself from the machine gun fire while re-directing the shells.

In a real battle, he would've been dead if he'd let his shield slip. But those standing behind him would be dead if he let shells through.

The rhythm of the booming guns changed, firing the shells even faster.

Fieran drew on his magic and let it surge from him in a way he'd never done before, not even in those morning practice sessions. There was nothing anywhere close to him that he had to worry about destroying.

The more magic he unleashed, the freer he felt. A laugh built in his chest at the heady, reckless feeling filling him. He'd never been this...whole. As if he'd been living with a part of him locked in a box.

Right now, he didn't have to hold back. No making himself less than he was.

For several more minutes, he caught and exploded numerous artillery shells, growing more confident with the practice until it was almost easy to just grab a shell from the sky.

At last, Dacha motioned to him, then shouted, holding his gaze, "There is one last thing I need to teach you. Send your magic behind us."

Fieran spread his magic into the straggling brush of the range behind them. As his magic coiled over the ground and around the scrub brush, he could get a vague sense of what the magic was touching. Dirt. Grass. Trees. He couldn't sense anything with the accuracy of someone with plant magic, but he could sense enough that he could have wiped the ground clean of plant life while leaving the dirt unmarred.

Then his magic encountered something else, just out of sight.

Bodies.

He yanked his magic back. "There are bodies out there!"

"Pig carcasses, yes." Dacha stated it flat and matter of fact, as if it was perfectly normal for dead pigs to be laid out in the bomb range.

Fieran reached out with his magic once again, letting it curl around the bodies. He wasn't a healer, so he couldn't sense more than the difference between tree and flesh. Yet there was still an impression of death that carried through his magic rather than the sensation of life that he could feel when he curled his magic around something alive.

Dacha's magic joined his, wrapping around one of the pig carcasses. Dacha's shouted words held a steely edge. "The army has taught you to kill, Fieran, but now I need to teach you to kill with your magic."

Fieran couldn't suppress the shiver that ran down his back, both at his dacha's words and the fact that he'd used Fieran's name rather than the warmer endearment of *sason*.

Perhaps it seemed harsh, forcing Fieran to practice this.

But Fieran understood the heart behind this gesture, even as he quailed at it. Dacha had been sent into war far too young. The first time he'd wrapped his magic around a body, it had been to kill a living enemy. He would not let Fieran walk into battle so unprepared.

Dacha held Fieran's gaze, his eyes so very hard and unflinching, as he clenched his fist. In the far distance, Dacha's magic incinerated the pig, leaving nothing but ashes behind.

Fieran drew in a steadying breath. Then he wrapped his magic around the carcasses, squeezed his eyes shut, and poured more power into the magic. He could feel his magic eating through muscle and blood and bone, and he let himself imagine that it was an enemy. That he was killing.

His stomach lurched, his breath hitching, but he didn't relent until the dead pigs were nothing but ashes, quickly eaten away into nothing by his magic.

Fieran released that part of his magic, exhaling in a

whoosh. He opened his eyes, his breaths coming hard and fast, as if that had been physically taxing.

Dacha motioned again, and the artillery and machine guns fell silent. Dacha straightened, cutting off his magic so that it fizzled out into sparks in the air.

Fieran clamped down on his own magic, straightening from his crouch as his magic dissipated. In the stillness, he took the moss earplugs out of his ears, his heart still beating, sweat slicking his shirt to his back, as if he'd been through a grueling PT session instead of magic practice.

When Fieran could finally bring himself to meet Dacha's gaze again, Dacha's eyes searched his face, the hardness easing with that undercurrent of fatherly worry. His voice was low, regretful and a touch weary, yet carrying a note of pride. "Well done, sason."

"Linshi, Dacha." This time, Fieran didn't hold back. He reached out and clasped Dacha's shoulders in an elven style hug.

Dacha gripped his shoulders in return, nodding. Then his nose wrinkled, as if he smelled something foul, and he withdrew his hand. "You are still in great need of a shower, sason."

Fieran grinned, sniffing at himself. "If you're going to get me special treatment, perhaps you could get me a hot shower?"

"Do not tempt me." Dacha's mouth tipped with a hint of a smile. "I am a general, but you chose the Escarlish Army. I am not your general."

"I didn't think that one through." Fieran heaved an exaggerated sigh.

Then, together, the two of them strode toward that line of guns.

As they reached the others, Dacha gave Fieran one last nod before he strode away to rejoin the gathered generals.

Fieran turned and faced his unit, bracing himself.

About half the unit was openly gaping at him. Even Pretty Face, Lije, and Stickyfingers had their mouths hanging open, their eyes wide and awestruck. Tiny had his arms crossed. When Fieran met his gaze, Tiny gave him a nod of respect.

Only Merrik didn't appear completely overawed by what he'd just witnessed. He, after all, had grown up seeing the magic of the ancient kings all the time. Perhaps he had never personally witnessed Fieran and his dacha wield their magic quite like that, but he was not unfamiliar with their power.

Fieran gestured at himself. "I'm still me, guys. Don't look at me like that."

Pretty Face whooshed out an exhale, his gaze darting from Fieran to something—or someone—beyond him. Pretty Face spoke in a lowered tone, his shoulders slightly hunched. "I'm going to be beyond respectful of Fieran's mama."

Lije slapped Pretty Face's back. "As you always should have been, even without the threat of incineration."

Fieran shrugged as he sauntered closer. "It isn't my dacha you have to worry about. Thanks to their heart bond, Mama can use Dacha's magic. So all that incineration and exploding stuff? Yeah, my mother can do that too."

Pretty Face gave a little shudder. "Your whole family is downright terrifying."

Stickyfingers shook himself, then grinned as he slapped Fieran's back. "I'm glad you're on our side, Red."

EXHAUSTED, Fieran climbed down from the truck that had carried them from the train station in Bridgetown to Fort Linder. Darkness had long since fallen on the fort, and after traveling all day, his body ached to collapse on his hard bunk and sleep for the few hours that remained until reveille. He stank of body odor after a week without a shower.

He dragged his feet as he marched next to Lije, his rucksack heavy on his shoulders.

The first few people in their column opened the door to the barracks, then halted. The drill sergeant barked at them to keep moving.

As Fieran shuffled inside, he nearly halted in the doorway before the sergeant's yelling forced him to keep moving.

The barracks in front of him looked like a whirlwind had gone through. All the wooden bunks were tipped over, the blankets and mattresses strewn about. The foot lockers were all out of place, and what appeared to be the contents of at least one footlocker joined the chaos. Items of clothing were tossed over everything, including a pair of skivvies hanging from the back door's handle, while cream-colored flakes of something smelling faintly of oatmeal and honey had been ground into the floor, the walls, and even their blankets and mattresses.

The drill sergeant stalked into the center of the barracks. "One of your fellow knuckleheads left his footlocker unlocked. You have four minutes." With that, he stalked out once again.

For a moment, everyone froze, staring at the disaster that was their barracks.

Then they all leapt into motion, still avoiding the center sergeant's zone.

Fieran dropped his rucksack near where his footlocker was supposed to be. He and Lije righted their bunk, then scrambled to help the others right bunks and place mattresses in place.

Fieran located his footlocker and heaved it back into place at the end of his bunk. Everything inside would be all tossed around, no longer arranged properly. But he didn't have time to rearrange it. Nor put the items from his rucksack away.

Lije spat a slightly naughty word, then tipped his footlocker back into place. The top was open, the green-painted wooden box entirely empty.

There was no time for recriminations or teasing. Fieran scrambled around the room, grabbing Lije's things and tossing them at him. Several others hurled items toward Lije.

Several people rushed outside, then returned with buckets of water. They sloshed the water over the floor while others took mops and scrubbed at the cream flakes, creating a flurry of suds. A few people doused the blankets, trying to wash them off.

Lije's mama's goatmilk soap. The drill sergeant must have taken the bars and ground them into the cement walls and floor until the bars were all gone. Worse, Lije had just gotten a fresh care package right before they'd left so the sergeant had plenty of soap to spread all over the barracks.

The more they sloshed water and scrubbed with the mops, the more soap suds billowed and foamed.

Fieran slipped on the wet, soapy floor, catching himself on a nearby bunk. Across the way, Tiny slipped and fell on his rear on the floor. The puddle around him froze into a slick of ice, as if he'd briefly lost control of his magic.

The drill sergeant swept back inside, barking at them to get into formation and chewing them out for not having the barracks cleaned, even though it had been an impossible task in four minutes.

Fieran slid into place before his bunk, standing at attention with Lije on one side, Pretty Face on the other. Merrik stood on the other side of Pretty Face.

The sergeant gave the order, and they all dropped to the floor for push-ups.

As Fieran lowered himself toward the ground, his palms slid on the soapy floor, and he had to slide them back into place before the drill sergeant yelled at him for doing push-ups incorrectly.

When he reached the bottom of the push-up with his nose nearly touching a section of foam, his nostrils and eyes burned with the lye. He'd never known the scent of oatmeal and honey could be an overwhelming stench until then.

Up he pushed. Out his hands slid. Down he went in his push-up. Out his hands slid again. His muscles burned from the extra exertion. Each time he slid his hands back and forth, he created more soapy foam, just making the floor even slicker than it already was. His hand bumped into Lije's, then into Pretty Face's on the other side.

Across the way, Sticky's hands completely slid out, and he ate it, smashing face-first into the concrete, the billowing suds doing nothing to cushion his fall. Another recruit—Stevens—also biffed it, landing with a splat.

Fieran's shirt trailed into the suds, growing heavier and sloppier the more water and suds it soaked up.

The sergeant gave the order, and they all had to roll on their backs and perform kicks, holding their legs out and clenching their abdominal muscles.

As Fieran kicked, he slid on the ground, inching ever closer to the sergeant's zone with each kick. He planted his hands on the floor, trying to hold himself in place as best he could before he crossed the line and ended up with even more PT.

Water soaked through his shirt to slick across his back. The back of his head rubbed in the soap, wetting his hair, while his eyes stung from the lye so much that he was blinking away tears.

By the time the sergeant ordered them to switch to sit-ups, the back of his shirt was gloppy and wet. As Fieran sat up, his shirt stuck to the floor for a moment before peeling away with a slurping sound. He had a moment when he was upright, and he caught a glimpse of the others, just as wet and covered in soap suds as he was. Then he flopped back to the floor with a splat.

Schloop. He sat up again. Splat. He lay back down. Schloop. Splat. Schloop. Splat. The entire barracks room echoed with the noise of dozens of men slurping and splatting in the suds.

When Fieran caught Stickyfingers' eye across the way, it was all he could do to swallow back his laugh. With the sergeant there, he couldn't chuckle. He couldn't even smile.

But this whole situation was so ridiculous. Their entire unit was doing PT in a sea of suds, their clothing making funny noises as they slurped and splatted. By this point, the entire floor was nothing but several inches of foaming bubbles and suds. Their blankets, rucksacks, and anything left on the floor was just as soaked and sudsy as they were.

After two hours of PT, the sergeant finally let them halt and marched from the room. But he only went as far as his room tucked in the front of the barracks, separated from them by a cement wall and a door.

Fieran rolled upright to sit in a puddle of soap suds. A drip of soapy water ran into his eye, causing his eye to burn. He fumbled for a dry part of his shirt. He couldn't find one, so he had to settle for squeezing that eye shut and hoping the burn went away.

Pretty Face swiped a hand through the mountains of soapsuds coating the floor. "Well, Lije, we all got a taste of your mama's soap."

Across the way, Stickyfingers grimaced and spat onto the floor. "Literally. I'm not sure I'll ever get the taste out of my mouth or the smell out of my nose."

Lije grimaced as he shook suds off his fingers. "This wasn't how I planned to share."

"At least we all got a good wash out of it." Fieran planted a hand on a nearby footlocker to steady himself as he slipped and slurped to his feet.

Merrik peeled himself out of a cloud of bubbles so thick he looked like a kid enjoying a bubble bath. Grimacing, he ran his hands down his legs to squeegee some of the soap off his army fatigues before he gestured at the mess before them. "Do you think you could clean this up with your magic?"

"Maybe?" Fieran took in the room. Incinerating the water and soap suds from the floor and walls shouldn't be too much trouble. "Everyone, stand on your footlockers for a moment. I'd like to try something."

Once everyone jumped onto the footlockers—creating sudsy puddles and footprints on their lids—Fieran pressed a hand to the floor. After all the practice with his dacha, his magic crackled from him in a surging, yet controllable tide as he swept it over the floor, then up the walls, letting it consume the soap suds and water.

Almost instantly, the entire room steamed up as if they stood in a sauna. Fieran scoured away the last of the soap suds as best he could before he clamped down on his magic once again.

Pretty Face waved at the clouds of water vapor. "Why didn't you just do that in the first place? Could have saved us a lot of trouble."

"It would have taken far more finesse to try to get all of the soap out of the cement, ground into it as it was." Fieran plucked at his shirt, the sticky, wet warmth of the fabric clinging to him in a way that was even more uncomfortable in the now hot and humid room. "I got as much as I could. We're still going to have a lot of cleaning to do."

Lije sighed, stepped off his footlocker, and reached for the nearest mop.

With one person standing with his ear pressed to the door dividing them from the sergeant's room, keeping watch in case the sergeant came back, the rest of them hurried to grab more buckets and mops, scrubbing the floor and the walls, trying to rinse with enough water to wash away the soap.

Fieran held the back of Lije's belt while Lije leaned way over the line and used the mop to squeegee the soap suds from the center sergeant's zone. Even now, alone as they were, none of them dared cross the line into that area of the barracks.

It took four hours, but they finally had all the soap cleaned up and the barracks set to rights, and Fieran could finally collapse into the damp and soap-smelling sheets and blanket on his bed for a few hours' sleep.

CHAPTER
SEVENTEEN

Shading her eyes, Pip paused in the open door of the hangar and watched as a flyer rattled down the runway after landing, coming to a halt in a cloud of dust. Four other flyers circled in the sky above, following the aeroplane piloted by Capt. Arfeld. Occasionally, Pip caught a glimpse of the orange flag, which Capt. Arfeld used to signal to the other flyers up there with him.

Fieran halted next to her, rocking back and forth from toes to heel in that way he did when he couldn't stand still.

Flicking a glance at him, she smiled. "Wishing you were up there?"

"Yes." Fieran heaved a sigh. "At least I'll be in the next group going up. I'd hate to have to wait all the way until last."

"I still can't understand the appeal of flinging yourself into the sky in a flying contraption." Pip dropped a hand to her tool belt. "I'd rather fix the aeroplanes than fly them."

"I'd rather fly them." Fieran chuckled. But as he tipped his head to the sky again, the chuckle died in his chest. He stiffened. "He needs to pull up."

Pip refocused on the aeroplanes in the sky. The latest one was attempting to land, but he was coming in too fast and too steep when he should have been leveling out for a gentle landing.

Her stomach clenched, her breath catching. *Pull up. Pull up.*

"Pull up." Fieran whispered an echo of her mental chant.

The aeroplane attempted to pull up, but it was too late. The flyer tipped to the side, its wing striking the ground. The whole aeroplane flipped and tumbled, even as the wings shredded on impact. The wreckage settled in a cloud of dust, the figure of the pilot limp inside the cockpit.

"*No.*" Fieran raced forward, his magic twining over his fingertips.

Pip wasn't sure what he planned to do, but she sprinted after him, calling up her own magic.

The ground crew dashed after her, quickly passing her with their longer legs.

Fieran reached the flyer first, clambering over the wreckage to reach the pilot.

Pip was still a few yards away when Fieran's head hung, his shoulders slumping, telling her all she needed to know. She slowed to a walk, her feet leaden as she crossed the remaining space to the downed aeroplane.

The ground crew shoved Fieran out of the way, swarming around the dead flyboy. One of them glanced over his shoulder, then pointed at the front of the flyer. "Pippak, secure the magical power cell. The last thing we need is that exploding."

She nodded. At least the order gave her something to do. She headed for the crumpled nose of the aeroplane, keeping her head down to avoid seeing the pilot's body. At the nose, the hatch was so mangled that she had to use her magic to pry it apart.

Once she had the hatch open, she inspected the engine. The magical power cell still glowed faintly blue, and it didn't appear to be cracked.

There was no reason to waste time with a wrench, especially since they wouldn't reuse these parts without a thorough overhaul first. She pressed her hand to the plate and bolts that held the magical power cell in place and poured her magic into the steel. The steel melted into her hand, flowing as if it were water instead of metal. With her other hand, she twisted the magical power cell to loosen it before pulling it free.

Fieran joined her, his jaw hard, all traces of humor vanished from his eyes.

She inspected the magical power cell before she held it out to him. "I don't think this is damaged, but do you see anything concerning?"

Fieran took the magical power cell and turned it over in his hands several times. The magic inside leapt at his touch. Was that his magic inside the power cell? After a moment, he handed it back to her. "It isn't damaged."

His gaze trailed back to where the ground crew was working. Left unsaid was the fact that the aeroplane's pilot hadn't been so lucky.

Pip rested a hand on his arm. "Did you know him well?"

"He's Stevens." Fieran shook his head, his gaze falling back to her. "He has—had—the top bunk across the way. Next to Stickyfingers. He..." His voice trailed off, rough and strained.

Pip remained next to him, not sure what else to say. Perhaps there were no words for something like this.

FIERAN LIFTED THE BLACK, wide end of the telephone and held it to his ear, the cord trailing to the large wooden box where the telephone's receiver was mounted.

The operator's cool, professional tone rang in his ear. "Operator. Where are you calling?"

"Treehaven House, Greenton, Escarland." Fieran wasn't sure if Dacha had returned to Escarland or if the family was currently in Estyra to celebrate Dacha's birthday a few days ago. But Escarland was the easiest place to start.

It took several minutes for the operators at all the connecting hubs to plug in the correct wires and the telephone to finally ring through to Treehaven.

"Hello, Treehaven House." Mama's voice rang tinny through the line due to the distance, the crackle nearly obscuring her cheerful tone.

"Hello, Mama." Fieran leaned more heavily against the wall next to the telephone. He quickly added, "Don't call for the others. Just Dacha."

"Fieran? Is everything all right?" Mama's tone changed, though it was hard to absorb the comfort of her voice through the crackling telephone line.

"I'm fine. Merrik is fine." That was all he was allowed to tell her.

Over the past two days, three pilots had crashed. Two had died while one had been injured and currently lay in the base hospital in the care of the elven healer. Acceptable losses, according to the army. In fact, only three crashes so far was considered fewer than expected.

Yet two men in his unit had died, and he couldn't even tell his parents that.

"Sason?" Dacha's voice joined his mama's on the line.

Mama hadn't called him over out loud, so either she'd motioned for him or she'd called him through their heart bond.

Fieran would have given anything for his mama's hug or his dacha's shoulder grip right about then. He switched to elvish, and there was something comforting about the graceful language flowing from his tongue. "I am all right, Dacha. It has just been…a long few days."

There was a pause, and he didn't know how much his parents could guess from his tone or how much of his burdened weariness came through the lines.

"I am sorry, sason." Dacha's voice held far too much understanding. Perhaps he could guess some of what must have happened.

"We're here for you, Fieran. Always." Mama's words were as warm as a hug.

"Linshi." Fieran sucked in a shuddering breath, blinking rapidly, before he forced a cheery note into his voice. "Happy 175th birthday, Dacha. I was sad to miss it, but I hope Adry did a good job picking out the gift."

Fieran had no idea what it was. He'd simply wired her his portion of the money for whatever gift all the siblings decided to buy together. With how long mail took to reach him and the limited number of phone calls he was allowed, taking part in the gift arranging had been impossible.

"She did." Dacha's tone warmed, a sign that whatever the gift had been, he had appreciated it greatly.

Mama launched into a description of the birthday celebrations. They'd stayed at Treehaven this year instead of celebrating in Estyra as usual, and it remained unspoken that the tensions between Escarland and Mongavaria had something to do with it.

Despite the way the stories added to the lump in his

throat as he heard about everything he'd missed, Fieran soaked up the comfort of the words and stories until the nearby sergeant indicated his time was done and he had to hang up.

FIERAN LEANED HEAVILY on the wood countertop in the tavern in Bridgetown. He didn't often drink alcohol, but after this past week, something stronger than soda seemed appropriate. The entire unit—including Murray, who had recovered enough to leave the infirmary—along with Pip and the other mechanics and many members of the ground crew had gathered in the tavern on the leave Capt. Arfeld had given them, filling the room nearly to capacity.

All along the wooden bar, each of the men held a glass filled with beer. But at the center of the bar, two filled glasses of beer remained untouched, a glass for each of their fallen comrades.

Fieran hadn't known those who'd died very well, but that didn't matter. They had been in his unit.

Stickyfingers lifted his glass, his voice rough. "To Baker and Stevens."

"To Baker and Stevens," Fieran echoed as he held up his glass. They didn't clink glasses this time. Simply drank their beer and remembered.

Fieran managed to swallow a few sips of his beer, the bitter taste coating his tongue. He set the mug on the bar, just staring at it for a long moment while those in the unit who'd known Baker and Stevens better shared stories about them.

After several minutes, Merrik nudged Fieran, then pointed down at Fieran's hands.

Fieran glanced down and grimaced. His magic had broken loose with the force of his emotions, twining around his fingers and threatening to start scorching the wooden bar in a moment.

Merrik tipped his head to the door, then pushed to his feet. Fieran followed, clenching his fists and pressing those fists against his body to attempt to suppress his magic.

Stickyfingers, Lije, and Pretty Face didn't even look up as Fieran and Merrik made their way through the crowded tavern. Tiny spotted them, nodded, and ordered another beer for himself.

Pip pushed out of her seat from where she had been wedged against the far wall. She joined Merrik and Fieran just as they stepped outside into the crisp air and twilight gray of the spring evening.

The bustle of Bridgetown closed around them, gratingly loud and far too cheery compared to the moments of mourning Fieran had left behind him.

Up and down the street, a few decorations formed from the various flags and colors of the Alliance Kingdoms were already going up in preparation for the Alliance Day festivities in a few weeks. The parade in Bridgetown was always nearly as flamboyant as the one in Aldon, though if his unit was given leave to attend, Fieran would be inundated with teasing at the celebrations for a national holiday to commemorate the first treaty signing—and his parents' anniversary.

Next to him, Pip rubbed at her fingers, grimacing. "I'm such a lightweight that my fingers are already tingling after just those few sips."

"Aren't dwarves supposed to be able to consume prodigious amounts of alcohol?" Fieran had to work to put a light note into his voice, but the humor helped soothe the roil inside him.

"Maybe. But I'm only half dwarf, and apparently my elf side is a family of lightweights." Pip gave a slight shrug before her gaze dropped to Fieran's hands. "Are you all right? Your magic is crackling loose again."

"I was just taking him somewhere quiet before he combusts." Merrik waved at the busy street. "Perhaps we should make our way across the bridge to Calafaren? We'll have enough time to get there and back before the truck leaves to return to Fort Linder."

Fieran nodded. While he normally didn't need the peace and quiet of a forest the way Dacha or Merrik did, something deep in his soul craved trees surrounding him after this past week.

They hopped on the trolley at the nearest stop, finding seats on the hard, wooden benches. They didn't speak as the trolley wound its way through various stops around Bridgetown. Finally, it clanged as it set out across the Alliance Bridge. The bridge's arches glowed with a soft blue light, both from the elven lights strung along it and Dacha's magic embedded in the stone. A cool breeze smelling of wet river mud wafted up from the water rippling below them.

On the far side, the trolley pulled into a circle drive at the edge of a field, where various automobiles had been parked, since no automobiles were allowed into Calafaren itself.

At the other side of the field, racks upon racks held bicycles for rent. At this time of early evening, passengers were in the process of returning bicycles or waiting to take the trolley back to Bridgetown.

Beyond the bicycles, the main grassy path of Calafaren led between tall, stately trees that rose into the sky, the first spring leaves still vibrantly green and new. Buildings formed of living wood had been grown both into the base of the trees and into the large, spreading limbs with swinging bridges connecting them.

The various shops and cafés were all unabashedly touristy, from the wares that were declared to be elven this and elven that to the traditional silken garb of tunics and trousers of the elf proprietors.

But Calafaren was the compromise to give Escarlish tourists a way to sate their desire to see and participate in elven culture without flooding all of Tarenhiel with humans. While trips to Estyra were limited and expensive, anyone in Escarland could take a cheap trip across the Alliance Bridge to experience Calafaren.

Fieran, Merrik, and Pip climbed down from the trolley. Instead of heading into Calafaren, Fieran turned and set off into the dark forest. As the trees closed around them, Fieran released a long breath, the peace of the evening settling into his heart.

Tree frogs blasted their evening song, almost deafening with the numbers gathered along the banks of the river. Somewhere in the distance, an owl hooted, long and low.

Merrik halted, resting a hand on the trunk of an especially large tree. "I will stay here if you want to go on a little farther."

"Don't want me disturbing the peace?" Like Merrik, Fieran kept his voice low, almost reverent, in the softness of the night.

"You will anyway, but I would appreciate *some* peace and quiet." Merrik huffed as he sat with his back to the tree. He pressed his hands to one of the roots, and his green magic flooded from his fingers into the tree and the grass around him.

Perhaps Merrik, too, needed a moment to release his stifled magic.

Fieran set out into the forest once again, following the river. Something in his chest eased still further when Pip fell into step with him rather than staying with Merrik.

He walked for another minute or two, long enough that the glow of green had faded, before he halted at a spot where the high bank overlooked the Hydalla River. A bend in the river hid Bridgetown from view, leaving the night dark, the stars winking far overhead.

Fieran unleashed his magic, letting it burst into bolts around his hands, spilling from him onto the ground around him. The tightness in his chest eased.

He turned to Pip, bracing himself for her reaction.

PIP GAPED as Fieran's magic crackled around him, the power of it thrumming deep inside her chest even as her hair prickled. The blue of his magic lit his face and sparked deep in his eyes as he turned toward her.

She'd known the magic of the ancient kings was powerful. After all, she dealt with the magical power cells every day.

But to see Fieran wield it was something else entirely. He embodied the legends she'd grown up hearing.

"Your magic is…awe-inspiring." She couldn't think of anything else to call it.

He shifted, his magic surging around him in blue, crackling bolts. "My dacha is more powerful than I am."

"By, what, one point on the Marion Scale? No one else is even close." Pip shivered, at the cool breeze tickling her neck or the sight of a warrior wielding the magic of the ancient kings, she wasn't sure.

Fieran gave a slight shrug, before he dropped into a fighting crouch. "You said you could make shields with your magic? You might want one."

Oh, right. This was likely going to get deadly here in a few seconds.

Drawing upon her magic, she let it burst out of her in a hard, iron-like magic shield in a bubble around her. It shimmered a faint blue-silver in the light of his magic.

Fieran's eyebrows rose. "You must rate rather high on the Marion Scale yourself."

She smirked at him in return, waggling her eyebrows right back. "Don't you know you never ask a lady her age, her weight, or her rating on the Marion Scale?"

Fieran laughed, more of his magic pouring from him. "Apparently my parents neglected that part of my education. My mother rather relishes telling people in Escarland that she's ninety years old, just to see the looks on their faces, and my sisters aren't shy about announcing their Marion Scale rating."

It felt good to laugh after so much mourning that week. They would honor those who had been lost, but life had to go on too.

"I can see that." Pip flexed her fingers, then sat down on the grass, holding the shield underneath her as well so that the damp from the ground wouldn't seep into her clothes. "My magic is a 13.4 on the Marion Scale, so that's nothing to be ashamed of."

"Not at all." Fieran tipped his head to her, a nod of respect.

As she settled in more comfortably, Fieran held out his hands, as if he were holding a pair of swords. He spun on his toes, swiping his hands as if slicing with a pair of swords. His magic scythed the air instead, a crackling, consuming arc of power. As he spun and flipped, the amount of power grew around him, flooding the nearby forest. A few of the smaller plants shriveled and turned to ash, but the larger trees remained unharmed.

A stray bolt of his magic lashed out, and Pip poured more of her magic into her shield, bracing herself. As strong as she was, she wasn't anywhere near as powerful as he was. Her shield would likely disintegrate under the force of his magic.

His magic struck her shield. Instead of clashing with her magic, the bolt skittered over her shield like lightning running over an iron rod.

Fieran's eyes widened, and he yanked his magic back, stuffing it back under control in a blink. "Are you all right?"

"I'm fine. That didn't hurt." Pip reached out a hand, pressing it to her shield. It didn't seem weakened at all. Instead, it felt stronger, as if his magic was threading through hers. "It seems that since your magic is similar to electricity and mine is similar to iron—as similar as raw magic can be to either of those things—my magic conducts yours rather than being consumed by it."

"I've never seen anything like this." Fieran held out a hand toward her, though his magic remained a mere simmer around his fingers. "May I test it again?"

"Go ahead." Pip pressed both hands to her magical shield and steeled herself.

Fieran released a larger blast of his magic toward her shield. Once again, his magic curled and sparked over hers, threading her shield with crackling bolts of his power.

One of the threads sparked against her fingers, and she yelped, yanking her hands back.

"Pip?" Fieran took a step forward, his magic winking out once again.

"I'm fine." Pip shook her fingers. "I just shouldn't touch my shield while it's supercharged with your magic."

"Sorry."

"Not your fault." Pip removed the shield beneath her so she was sitting on the ground and no longer touching any part of the shield. A wet rear end was worth it to further test the way their magic interacted. "This is fascinating. Here, I'd like to try something else."

She took a moment to craft what she wanted in her mind before she unleashed another layer of her magic, creating a second shield, this one arching over both her and Fieran. Safe beneath her shield, that left Fieran pinned beneath two shields. "I don't know how much of your magic I'll be able to keep contained, but you'll be able to unleash more without having to worry about it this way."

Fieran grinned, holding out his hands in a sword stance once again. Magic burst from him, choking the forest between her two shields until she could barely make out Fieran through the crackling storm of magic contained beneath her shield.

She gritted her teeth, her magic feeling almost hot and slippery. It didn't hurt, exactly. His magic skittered over hers rather than fighting. But the more magic he unleashed, the more she had to struggle to hold on to her grip on her magic.

Yet she was doing it. She was containing the magic of the ancient kings. She'd never heard of anyone doing something like this before.

Then again, she'd never heard of an elf with iron magic like hers. Even the dwarves with iron magic couldn't create this shield of raw magic like she could because they wielded their magic differently.

Finally, Fieran halted, and his magic burst into sparks all around him, the sparks drifting down around him like embers on a breeze. He turned to face her, breathing hard, his hands down at his sides as if still holding imaginary swords.

In that moment, bathed in starlight and magic as he was, he had the look of an ancient elven warrior, despite his lack of long hair and swords. Perhaps it was something in his eyes, that wild warrior light sparking in those brilliant blue depths. Maybe it was the graceful, dangerous way he moved, different than the easy, almost careless stride he normally had.

Whatever mild attraction she'd had to him that first moment she'd met him had only deepened over the past months, and this certainly wasn't helping.

But Fieran treated her as just a friend, and she wasn't going to make things awkward in the group by crossing any lines.

Besides, as soon as they both finished their training, they would be at the mercy of the army. Who knew where they'd be sent, and the odds were low that they'd be stationed at the same base again. In only a few weeks, they'd go their separate ways.

Fieran dropped his hands, some of the warrior look to him fading. "We probably should head back."

Pip swallowed and dropped her shields. She pushed shakily to her feet. "Yes."

Time to collect her thoughts, collect Merrik, and return to Fort Linder and the coming war.

CHAPTER

EIGHTEEN

Standing before the hangar, Fieran pulled on the leather cap, then his goggles.

Pip shifted as she stood next to him, glancing from him to the aeroplanes lined up.

As excited as he was to fly again, his stomach knotted to the point he was nauseous. This first solo flight was the most dangerous flight for any recruit, as proven by the accidents last week.

"I'm going to be all right." Fieran adjusted the goggles so that they didn't pinch the tips of his ears.

"I know. Just..." Pip dropped her gaze, then gestured at the nearby flyer. "Bring my flyer back in one piece."

"Of course." Fieran forced a grin. He couldn't let the accidents shake him.

He strode to the flyer he'd been assigned, climbed up using the toe step, and folded himself into the cockpit.

He went through the checklist, switching on the power, checking the magic power level gauge, and feeling the vibration of the propeller thrum through the aeroplane's frame and down into his bones. On the ground, the flyer was a hunk of wood, canvas, and metal, and it seemed nigh impossible that such a vehicle could hurl itself into the sky.

Before him on the airfield, Lije in his flyer tore across the grass, the biplane ungainly until it lifted into the sky, a bird set free to soar.

Fieran's heart hammered in his throat as he maneuvered his aeroplane from its spot off to the side to the end of the airstrip, where the ground crew placed chocks in front of his wheels. He sat there for several minutes, letting the engine and the propeller fully spin up.

Shading his eyes, the flight master peered into the sky at Lije's retreating biplane. Then, he waved to Fieran, stepping out of the way as he did so. The ground crew dashed forward and yanked out the wheel chocks. Immediately, his flyer rolled forward, seeming of its own accord.

Fieran's heart worked its way up into his throat as he faced down the end of the airstrip, his aeroplane hurtling forward faster and faster. One wrong move on his part, and he'd end up a flaming ball of wreckage at the end of that grassy field.

Despite the hammering of his heart, his hands on the control column remained steady, his toes tucked into the holds on the rudder bar. He'd only had a few hours' flight time in the two-seater with an instructor, but already the movements were familiar. Similar to driving his automobile, and yet different enough that he'd never mistake this craft for something designed to remain on the ground.

There was that brief weightless feeling as the flyer tried to lift off the ground before the wheels crashed back again. Fieran gripped the stick, timing his moment through every bump and shudder around him, as if he were sensing the flyer's wings and the powers of lift and thrust at work around him. It was almost like the way he could sense the world around him with his magic or the sensitivity of a warrior's hair that his dacha had tried to explain to him.

Now. He pulled back on the stick, and the nose turned upward right at the moment when the wheels left the dirt, the biplane carried upward by a wind that was hard as solid ground.

As the flyer hurtled higher into the sky, the wind rushed past his face, clawing at his exposed skin. The propeller's hum and the engine's whine formed a steady cadence in his ears. His heart steadied as a peace settled over him. All his fears had been left behind on the ground. Only the calm of the sky remained around him.

He fell into line behind Lije, who was behind two more flyers and the lead flyer piloted by Capt. Arfeld. They circled lazily as they waited for Merrik and two more recruits to pilot their flyers into the sky until they formed a flight of eight aeroplanes.

Once everyone was in the air, Capt. Arfeld waved the orange flag in the coded signals to order them to follow him. He led the way on a patrol west, and they traced the Hydalla River as it glittered and rippled in the early spring sunshine, the river swollen and muddy from the spring rains.

Bridgetown appeared below them, its streets laid out in a grid that appeared even more neat and orderly from the air than it did on the ground. The spring foliage of Tarenhiel's deep forests hid most of Calafaren from view, though bits and pieces of it appeared now and then in the meadows and squares. Between the two, the Alliance Bridge soared majestic and mighty over the Hydalla River, a firm connection between the kingdoms as if in defiance of the river and everything else that had once divided them.

Then they were soaring onward, past farm fields and grand estates that bordered the river. A few riverboats with jaunty red paddlewheels plied the river, skirting around the lumbering barges heaped with goods bound for Escarland from the port cities on Tarenhiel's coast. Or headed down-river laden with grain and Escarlish goods to be shipped by sea to Kostaria's northern shores.

Farther still, the cylinder shape of a dirigible smudged the sky as it headed north over Tarenhiel. Probably laden with another group of rich Escarlish tourists seeking a holiday cruise to see the wonders of Tarenhiel and Kostaria.

Everything looked so peaceful, so prosperous, as if most of Escarland hadn't yet gotten the news that war was coming, despite the doom and gloom filling the newspapers in the wake of Mongavaria's invasion of Groyria earlier that week.

Then again, what should the citizens do with the possibility of war looming over them? Cower in their homes, too scared to live for fear of what tomorrow would bring? Or should they go about living, defying fear?

Besides, it wasn't like the war would ever touch this far into Escarland. With his dacha's Wall keeping Mongavaria firmly on their side of the borders, an invasion wouldn't happen even in the event of war. The only thing Mongavaria could do was send over a few of their airships and drop a handful of soldiers on the other side of the Wall.

As much as the tensions were building, especially now that Mongavaria was marching into Groyria, war was still just as futile for Mongavaria now as it had ever been. They couldn't invade. They couldn't claim new territory. They couldn't hope to weaken the Alliance Kingdoms enough to take them out as a powerful player among the nations on this continent. Their steam and gasoline engines couldn't compete with the magical power of the Alliance Kingdoms.

They didn't have any weapon that could match Dacha's magic.

All in all, if Empress Bella of Mongavaria were wise, she would call the whole thing off.

Which would be a bummer for Fieran. His life would become endless rounds of peaceful patrols along the borders, keeping an eye on Mongavaria even as the empire sought to expand into some other hapless nation's territory, like they were doing now with Groyria.

Though the thought of war didn't send the same sense of anticipation through Fieran it once had. Not after the deaths of Stevens and Baker. War would only cause more death. More of those he knew in his unit might die.

The flight of aeroplanes passed over the ruins of an ancient castle perched on a bluff over the river far below. Perhaps a castle from the early history of Escarland. Maybe it was even older than that, from ancient times when elves ruled an empire that spanned over what was now Kostaria, Tarenhiel, Escarland, the Mongavarian Empire, and beyond, all the way to the foot of the dwarven mountains.

More recent military fortifications perched on either side of the river, their artillery guns pointed downriver in the direction from which a Mongavarian fleet would appear, should they somehow get through the Wall and make it this far upriver.

Finally giving the signal to turn around, Capt. Arfeld led them in a wide arc, and they headed back the way they'd come, flying into the late morning sunlight as they headed east back to Fort Linder.

Fieran pulled down the extra lens on his goggles, painting the world in a tone of amber and changing the shades of colors on the circles painted on the wings of Lije's aeroplane ahead of him.

All too soon, seeming far quicker than their outward journey, they circled the sky above Fort Linder's aerodrome.

Capt. Arfeld pointed with his flag, indicating for one of the other pilots to land first.

Fieran's heart leapt into his throat again, but this time he wasn't thinking about himself. It was Lije's craft he could picture burning in a pile of wreckage. Merrik's.

The two flyers before Lije touched down without incident. Then Lije was lining up his biplane with the airfield, bleeding off speed, his craft growing wobbly in the air.

All Fieran could think about was the statistics he'd read in the paper once. That more of those early pilots died while trying to land than at any other time during flight. Recent days hadn't disproved those articles.

Lije came in, his aeroplane a little too far sideways, the wings on one side coming perilously close to the ground. Then he managed to right the craft just enough that it was the rubber wheels that touched down. The aeroplane swerved, sliding on the short grass into the weeds alongside the runway. As the wheels snagged on the weeds, the flyer tipped forward. It was caught on the skids out the front, standing on its nose for a breathless, aching moment before it crashed back onto its wheels. Not on the airfield but unscathed at least.

After a moment Lije climbed from the flyer and waved at the sky, signaling that he was all right.

Fieran released a long breath, flexing his fingers on the control column as he followed Capt. Arfeld in circles high above. Below, the ground crew gathered around the biplane and pushed it out of the weeds and across the field, back to the hangar.

Once they were well away from the airstrip, Capt. Arfeld

waved the orange signal flag again, pointing to Fieran to order him to land.

Fieran circled one last time, controlling the craft with both his feet on the rudder bar and his hands on the control column, using the loop to descend closer to the ground. When he lined his nose up with the airfield, he had bled off enough speed that the aeroplane felt heavy, less like a nimble warbird and more like a lumbering hunk of machinery.

He tried to keep his senses attuned to the craft and regain that sense of oneness with his aeroplane that he'd had before.

A slight breeze kicked up off the ground, stirring in eddies. It tried to shove his flyer over, and he resisted the urge to overcorrect the other way, instead gently leaning his biplane back the other way. Another gust sent his whole aeroplane into a sudden drop, jerking at the stick in his hand.

Gently now, even as he fought the forces that threatened to both drop his aeroplane too fast to the ground and yet also snatch it back into the sky.

The ground rushed up, closer and closer. Then his wheels touched the dirt, the stick nearly jerking from his hand as the grass seemed intent on wresting control of the biplane from him.

The forces yanking on the biplane lessened as his momentum slowed, the forces of gravity and friction winning over all the others. The tail skid dug into the ground, further stabilizing and slowing the aeroplane.

Fieran slowly turned the flyer as it jounced over the ground, heading for the hangar. Once he was just outside, he cut the engine. The flyer creaked and rolled to a crunching halt.

Fieran released another long breath, not quite sure if he

was bleeding off adrenaline fueled by exhilaration or terror. Perhaps a mix of both.

He'd survived his first solo flight. Only a few more hours in the air, and he'd be able to pass his training as a pilot. Only a few more weeks, and he'd have his wings pinned to his chest.

He levered himself out of the cockpit and shakily climbed out. As his feet touched the ground, he turned just in time to see Merrik land his plane in a perfect touchdown on the grass.

Pip halted next to Fieran, glancing from him to the aeroplane behind him. "I see you brought my flyer back in one piece."

"Yep. Not a scratch on her." Fieran patted the biplane's fuselage, then grinned at Pip, even as the ground crew claimed the biplane to wheel it into the hangar.

Perhaps it wouldn't be so bad if war never came. Maybe Mongavaria would realize the futility of going to war with the Alliance Kingdoms. Or their aged queen would finally stop living on vengeance and vitriol, and her heir wouldn't be as keen to fight the Alliance Kingdoms.

Fieran wouldn't mind if life continued like this for a while. Low-key flirting with Pip. Flights over the countryside. Weekends spent with the guys and Pip in Bridgetown.

That wouldn't be such a bad life, even if it meant he'd live in his dacha's shadow forever.

NINETEEN

A boom jolted Pip awake, even as her bunk shook so violently that she might have fallen off if she'd been on the top bunk.

One of the other girls gave a shriek as another thunderous boom tore through the night. A window shattered, the glass smashing into the cement and scattering in a tide of sharp, glittering edges. Mak's miniature wooden train tumbled from the shutters to land on the cement floor with a sharp rap.

"What's that? Did the munitions bunker explode?" Across the barracks, one of the secretaries was sitting up, brushing hair out of her face.

Two more explosions erupted, even as shouting poured through the broken window. A bugle call cut through the din, one Pip had only heard during drills to teach all of them on base the meaning of the bugle calls.

Red alert. The signal of an attack.

A darker shadow passed over the window, black and sinister where there should be open sky, lit only by Fort

Linder's one searchlight. The moon hadn't yet risen, a thick cloud cover creating a black, starless night.

For a moment, they all froze, too uncomprehending of the shadow, the bugle call. They'd all been living on this army base for weeks—months, in some cases—yet the possibility of war was just a figment of newspapers and hypothetical conversations.

Another boom tore through the night. The pressure of it pounded into Pip's chest so forcefully that she struggled to breathe for a moment. Her ears rang, even as something thunked against the outer cement wall of the barracks.

All she wanted to do was curl into a ball under the flimsy protection of her bunk, wishing with everything in her that she'd never come and instead remained safe at the western rail terminal, oblivious and sheltered.

But Pip forced herself to her feet. She called up her magic and pushed it outward, forming a protective shield around the small huddle of wide-eyed women.

Would her magic be enough? She was strong. Thirteen on the Marion Scale. But would that magical strength be enough in the face of whatever was causing those explosions?

Chelsea—the talkative, flirtatious nurse—clapped her hands together. "All right, ladies. This is what we've trained for. Hurry and get dressed. We need to get to our stations. There will be wounded to care for, orders to take in dictation, telephone calls to get out so that the rest of the kingdom knows what is happening."

Her words galvanized the others, as if being given direction broke the paralysis fear and uncertainty had on them.

Pip leapt to tug on her coveralls, throwing on clothes as quickly as she could while still holding that shield over their heads. The cement floor vibrated beneath their feet as the explosions blended one into the other, almost constant.

As she stuffed her feet into her boots, the laces tucked inside rather than taking the time to tie them, she faced Chelsea. "I'm holding a shield of magic over us at the moment. But…"

Chelsea nodded, a light of understanding in her eyes. "You need to get to the hangar. Get our flyers into the air. We'll be all right."

The words were an empty promise. As soon as they ran into the night, going their separate ways, there was no guarantee that any of them would be all right.

Pip still hesitated, her stomach twisting at the thought of leaving this group of women unprotected. How could she walk away, knowing they would be utterly vulnerable the moment she did?

Chelsea gave her a small push toward the door. "Go."

Pip turned and raced for the door, shrinking her shield so that it protected just herself.

As soon as she opened the door, she was nearly shoved back inside under the wave of noise and smoke and shouts that hurled at her through the night.

Silhouetted in the beam of the searchlight, the black shapes of six airships glided overhead. A brief flare of light came from one, then a faint whistling sound. Seconds later, a flash of orange erupted on the far side of Fort Linder near the river fortifications. The ground, the air, everything shook and heaved under the blast.

Bombs. Those airships were dropping bombs, likely rolling them out of an open cargo door.

As tempted as she was to try to extend her shield farther than just her own head, Pip held the shield in close as she sprinted through the fort, dodging around piles of rubble and other people also racing for their stations. She needed to save her magical strength to shield the hangar, assuming the Mongavarians—she could only assume those were Mongavarian airships overhead—hadn't hit it already.

FIERAN BOLTED UPRIGHT at the blast pummeling his ears and chest. He gripped the bedframe as the bunk swayed beneath him. His magic sparked along his fingers, sizzling against his blanket until he yanked his magic back into his chest.

Voices came from the others in the barracks, even as another explosion nearly tumbled Fieran out of the bunk. He swung down, landing on his feet between the bunks, even as he reached for his gun. He already wore a set of fatigues, as army life didn't exactly lend itself to lounging around in pajamas, even for sleep. One never knew when a drill sergeant would wake the unit in the middle of the night for a surprise inspection or ruck march.

Or someone would set off bombs in the middle of the night.

Merrik dropped down next to him, poised and ready, looking to him as if he expected Fieran to give the orders.

Another explosion tore through the night, so close the pressure wave battered the building, popping against Fieran's ears.

Across the room, one of the recruits curled on the floor, whimpering, arms over his head. Others stood around in various states of shock, terror, or a strange sort of calm as they laced up their boots and reached for their guns.

Tiny and Stickyfingers appeared at Fieran's side, joining him and Merrik. Lije and Pretty Face both rolled off their bunks, stuffing their feet into their boots and grabbing their rifles. All of them, from Merrik to Pretty Face, turned to Fieran.

"We need to get to the flyers." Fieran sprinted for the rear door of the barracks, not having to look back to sense the others following at his heels.

As he opened the door, a blast of air hit him with the tang of gunpowder and the acrid scent of burned wood and melted metal. A bugle call rose into the night, piping out the red alert, even as Fieran jumped the stairs, landing lightly on the dirt.

Behind him, the other door to the barracks room banged open, and the drill sergeant barked orders.

Fieran didn't stop. Neither did the others following him. The sergeant was, after all, shouting the others into getting their butts off the floor and into the night to do what they had been trained to do. Fieran was just a little ahead of things there.

Another whistling sound, then a detonation roared into the night, staggering Fieran with the force of the blast that stole his breath for a moment.

Six dark shapes drifted overhead, almost lazy and ethereal in the wash of the searchlight. A brief flare of light opened on the bottom of one, square and orange against the darkness, before it slammed shut again. Seconds later, an explosion erupted, quaking the ground beneath Fieran's boots and ringing loud and painful in Fieran's ears, his hearing more sensitive from his elven heritage.

For a moment, all he could do was stand there, taking in the jets of flame burning against the night, sending up clouds of black smoke. Shouts rose into the darkness. Black shapes of men scurried between the buildings. The crews manning the three-inch guns that guarded the river scrambled to both swivel and crank the guns to their highest elevation to attempt to shoot upward at the attacking airships.

Over the central square of the base, the three flags of Tarenhiel, Escarland, and Kostaria flapped in the light breeze, silhouetted by the fires and wreathed with smoke.

The other flyboys from his barracks streamed around him and his small group, racing toward the hangar at the far side of Fort Linder.

"Fieran." Merrik was suddenly there in front of him, gripping his shoulders hard enough to hurt and giving him a solid shake. "You are a Laesornysh. You have your dacha's magic. Stop gawking and do what your dacha trained you to do."

Right. Fieran sucked in a lungful of smoke and gunpowder, searching for a single moment of calm amid the burning, tearing world all around him. Then he unleashed that tight, mental grip on his magic.

It blazed from his fingers and burst into the sky above him. He let the magic pour from him in a torrent, extending it in a brilliant, crackling dome that covered the entire base.

Something struck the magic from overhead, and he snatched it on instinct, nearly losing his magic grip on it as he felt its size. This bomb was so much larger than any of the artillery shells he and Dacha had practiced with at Fort Charibert.

Fieran growled, hurled his magic at the sky, and heaved the bomb over and away, changing its trajectory enough that it slammed into the open fields that surrounded Fort Linder. It exploded in a spray of dirt and shrapnel that were consumed in the hunger of Fieran's power.

Merrik tugged Fieran's arm, and together they sprinted into the night. The sharp raps of running bootsteps echoed behind them as Pretty Face, Tiny, Stickyfingers, and Lije stuck with them.

Fieran tripped on a block of cement that had been blown out of the wall of the nearest building, and he would have fallen if Merrik hadn't gripped his arm and hauled him onward.

Splitting his focus between his magic and his body's movements was all so much harder in real life than in morning practices with his Dacha. With the airships chucking bombs down onto him, it was all he could do to pay attention to his feet so he didn't take a tumble on the rubble blocking their way.

Another bomb plummeted into his magic, nearly slipping through before he managed to get enough of a grip on it to send it hurtling safely into the ground away from the fort.

Fieran skidded to a brief halt and hurled a spear of his magic upward as far as he could, reaching higher and higher into the sky.

As with his dacha's wall, the magic fizzled out before it reached the airships. While Fieran could—theoretically—stretch his magic for miles with the earth to ground him, he couldn't extend his magic far enough into the empty sky to swat at the attacking airships.

With a growl, Fieran added that magic to his overall shield and kept running.

The hangar was just ahead, huge and hulking in the firelit night. The doors gaped open like black mouths, only a few pinpricks of light showing inside rather than the blaze of the overhead lights.

As they neared, Fieran tasted another, metallic magic filling the air. A few stray bolts of his magic sizzled down from the sky to dance along the shield that arched over the hangar, its edges stopping just below the roof.

"Pip!" Fieran raced inside the hangar, then skidded as he nearly ran face-first into the wheel struts of the flyer the ground crew was wheeling toward the doors.

As the ground crew flung a few curses his way, Fieran scrambled out of the way, then cast about in the near darkness.

Utter chaos reigned. Lit only by the elven lights the mechanics used for shining into dark corners of aeroplane engines, ground crews wheeled the aeroplanes toward the hangar doors, even while others raced about, getting in their way. The men in Fieran's squadron stood about, as if not sure what to do or where to go. A few raced about, each doing their own thing.

In the center of the hangar, Capt. Arfeld cast about, gesturing vaguely with his hands, as if he wasn't any more sure what to do than his men.

This was the weakness of the current Escarlish military, despite their training, their modern weapons, and the structure Uncle Julien had formed in the past seventy years. While the armies of both Kostaria and Tarenhiel had a core of warriors who had fought in the previous wars, no one in the Escarlish military outside of Uncle Julien—thanks to his bond with his longer-lived troll wife Aunt Vriska—had any experience with war. No one at Fort Linder, from the lowliest private to the commanding general, had ever seen combat.

All the training in the world couldn't prepare for the shock of an attack like this.

Merrik and the others clustered around Fieran, waiting for orders.

"Fieran?" Pip appeared at his elbow, her hands spread

and laced with her silver magic as she held her shield over the hangar. "What should we do?"

Fieran drew his shoulders straight, trying to think with the part of his brain that wasn't occupied with holding up his own shield over the fort. "I'm protecting the fort at the moment. Drop your shield and save your magic."

Pip nodded, and the metallic taste of her magic winked out. Fieran couldn't see it, but he could sense the tug of it on his magic disappear.

Another bomb—a smaller one, this time—struck his magic. He felt like his mind was stretching in opposite directions, as he tried to wield his magic with part of his mind while thinking enough to give orders with the rest.

Right now, Fort Linder needed a Laesornysh, and Fieran's dacha wasn't here.

That left only Fieran.

"We need to get in the air." Fieran stared at one of the aeroplanes as it was wheeled past them. What would they need once they were in the sky? How could they take on an airship while in what was essentially an unarmed wooden box with wings, a propeller, and a tail stuck onto it?

"Merrik, Pip, Lije, see what you can do about arming the flyers." Fieran refocused on his friends around him, his stomach churning even as his voice remained almost bizarrely steady. "Pretty Face, start getting the others into aeroplanes. Tiny, grab whatever water you can find to take with you. Stickyfingers, help Tiny."

His friends nodded and scattered.

Fieran lifted his chin and marched toward Capt. Arfeld. Maybe Fieran was about to get himself court-marshaled for insubordination, but someone had to give Capt. Arfeld a good shake.

Fieran halted before the captain and saluted. "Capt. Arfeld, sir."

"Laesornysh." Capt. Arfeld returned his salute with a shaky, sloppy gesture that would have made a true military man cringe. The captain pointed upward. "Is that you?"

"Yes, sir." Fieran braced himself. It was now or never. He might end up in the stockade for this, but the consequences likely wouldn't be too dire, given the protection his high-ranking relatives gave him. "Permission to speak freely, sir?"

Capt. Arfeld's eyes were slightly wide and unfocused. The man had nerves of steel to do what he'd done as a pioneer of aeronautics. But now, facing battle, his lack of military training showed through. "Of course."

"The squadron needs their captain to lead them." Fieran held Capt. Arfeld's eyes, not letting his own panic slip through. "You need to get up there. You've at least flown at night before."

Everyone knew aeroplanes didn't fly at night. Even airships were considered risky to navigate in the dark, and instead often chose to descend into an anchorage for the night rather than risk losing their way. Lacking the instruments and gauges of an airship, aeroplanes were downright dangerous to fly at night. It was pitch black, with nothing to tell up from down. At night, one could fly straight down into the earth and never know it until it was too late. Only a few of the early pilots, like Capt. Arfeld, had flown at night as a stunt.

If only the military and political leadership had listened to Uncle Julien more. Then maybe instead of so much money being poured into building large airships, more energy would have been directed toward designing a flyer capable of taking on an airship. Perhaps someone would have figured out a way to mount a big enough gun or give them gauges to help them fly at night.

After tonight, perhaps the mindset would shift. But it would be too late to save them now.

Yet they had to go up. Never mind the danger. Never mind the fact that their training flyers weren't even armed, unless Pip, Merrik, and Lije could come up with something in the next five minutes. All they could do was take pot shots at the airships with their rifles and pistols.

And they were going to do it anyway. Because their kingdom was under attack, and it was their duty to fight back.

Capt. Arfeld gave himself a shake, his eyes finally sharpening. "What are the limits of your magic? Can you continue to protect the fort once you take off?"

Fieran hesitated, weighing his own capabilities. Despite his training in splitting his attention and magic, flight took too much focus. "No. Once I'm in the air, I won't be able to hold an effective shield over the fort any longer. Pip, one of the mechanics, can create a shield, but I don't know how large her shield is nor how it will hold up under bombardment."

Capt. Arfeld nodded as he absorbed that information. Around them, the chaos of before was slowly being tamed. Pip and Merrik stood next to a flyer, doing something to the side with their magic, while Lije and some of the mechanics hefted guns and ammunition rounds. Pretty Face had organized the other pilots so that each flyer now had a pilot either sitting inside or standing next to it as he hurriedly donned goggles and the leather outer gear.

The captain gestured to the waiting aeroplanes. "Can you shield our flyers as they take off?"

"Yes, sir. At least for most of their run." Fieran paused,

not sure how to word this next part without sounding like he was just as dangerous as the airships dropping bombs. "They won't be able to fly through my magic any more than the bombs can penetrate through. I should be able to tell the difference between our flyers and the airships, but this far away and with this much of my magic unleashed, it would be best if I opened a gap in the magic instead."

"Understood." Capt. Arfeld nodded, his jaw set. "And in the air?"

"I can take down the airships." After spending several days on an Escarlish airship, Fieran had no doubts about that. But…Fieran shifted, something inside him twisting into knots. "I don't know how long it will take. I've never used my magic in the air like that. Always on the ground."

And never in a true battle, though he didn't say that out loud. Would he panic? Would he remember his training once he was in the sky? Would he even be able to focus enough to use his magic while also flying an aeroplane? He didn't even have enough solo hours in the cockpit to be fully certified. None of them did.

Capt. Arfeld nodded, his eyes going unfocused again as he weighed the options.

As much as Fieran had taken charge earlier, he was glad to leave this particular situation in the hands of his commanding officer.

If he went up first, he'd have the best chance of anyone to take down the airships. But it would leave the fort vulnerable until he'd taken all the airships down.

If he went up last and protected the fort as long as possible, Capt. Arfeld and the other pilots would be at greater risk trying to face the airships by themselves.

After an agonizing moment, Capt. Arfeld's chin tipped,

his shoulders straightening. "You'll take off last. Keep things organized down here in the meantime."

"Yes, sir." Fieran let that weight settle on his shoulders. Orders, finally.

Capt. Arfeld had chosen the option that would protect the fort and the civilian contractors like Pip for as long as possible, putting only the pilots at risk.

With a final glance at Fieran, Capt. Arfeld spun on a heel, shouting orders even as he ran to catch up with the flyers waiting outside, their engines and propellers spinning up.

Fieran mentally peeled back the part of his shield by the end of the airstrip, creating an open space for the flyers to take off without being incinerated. Then he hurried to join Merrik and Pip by a flyer. "How is arming going?"

"As well as could be expected." Pip's mouth twisted with her concentration as she melded a piece of metal to a rifle's action, creating a swivel. "It'll be better than trying to take out an airship with a pistol, but not by much."

Merrik folded the flyer's wooden side over the base of her swivel, affixing the gun to the aeroplane's side. As he finished, he flicked a glance at Fieran. "But guns will not be all that necessary, will they?"

"Probably not. I think I can take out the airships. But Capt. Arfeld has ordered me to go up last so I can protect the fort as long as possible." Fieran gestured upward to indicate his magical shield. "So you'll need to keep the airships busy until I join you."

Merrik nodded as he and Pip moved to the next flyer in line. The pilot scrambled into the aeroplane they'd finished, and the ground crew wheeled it out to join the others spinning up at the end of the airfield. An aeroplane roared down the airstrip, taking off into the night sky, its wings lit by Fieran's blue magic.

Stickyfingers tottered out of the gloom of the rest of the hangar, toting a machine gun that must weigh nearly as much as he did. His grin gleamed almost manically in his eyes. "I'm keeping this bad boy for me. Pip, Merrik, think you can install it on one of the two-seaters? Lije will fly it; I'm going to man this puppy." Stickyfingers patted the machine gun lovingly.

"Sure." Pip's magic elongated a part of a rifle's action to attach it to the flyer, even as Merrik melded his magic with hers to keep the mounting in place. As soon as they finished, that waiting pilot climbed in.

As they turned toward the two-seaters waiting at the rear of the line of flyers, a commotion came from outside. Some of the ground crew were shouting and pointing, even as two more flyers roared into the sky. Someone cursed.

Fieran halted, checking his magical senses. His magical shield was holding. Yet, come to think of it, it had been a few minutes since the Mongavarians had tested the magic with a bomb. Were they leaving? Yet that didn't match with the pointing, cursing, and staring of those gathering by the doors.

Fieran dashed a few steps in that direction, then froze as he took in the view outlined by the broad hangar doors.

One of the airships remained almost directly over the airstrip, as if it poised to pounce on the next flyers that dared launch themselves into the sky. A few biplanes danced around the ship's black bulk and, even as they watched, a burst of flames erupted from one of the flyers as it spiraled toward the river.

But the flight crew weren't watching the falling flyer, the dying pilot. They were pointing at the five airships that had drifted farther upriver, coming to a stop directly over Bridgetown and Calafaren.

Fieran's stomach dropped to his toes, even as he pressed a hand to the hangar's wall to steady himself.

Capt. Arfeld had forgotten one important thing when giving his orders. They all had.

Fort Linder wasn't the only nearby target.

TWENTY

Even as Fieran stood there, shaking at the sight, a stream of tiny black specks dribbled out of one of the airships. Explosions flared among the distant, black buildings. One bomb must have struck the Alliance Bridge for it flared with his dacha's bright blue magic. At this distance, Fieran couldn't see if the magic in the stone had been enough to spare the bridge destruction.

The Mongavarian airships were bombing Bridgetown. A town full of innocent civilians. Women. Children.

Fieran sagged against the hangar's wall, chest heaving, head whirling.

Had he caused this? Had the Mongavarian airships decided to move on to a new target once they realized Fort Linder was protected?

Could Fieran stretch his magic that far? He'd never used it at such a distance, but his dacha had done so to create the Wall.

But Dacha had more power than Fieran. Far more experience. By the time he'd been Fieran's age, he'd already fought two wars. Been tortured twice. Used his magic in ways Fieran had never encountered.

Until joining the army, Fieran had never faced anything scarier than his dacha with the light of battle in his eyes.

Fieran raced outside, knelt, and pressed a hand to the ground. At this distance, he needed the firmness of the ground to guide his magic. He dug deep within himself, sinking into the unknown depths of his magic in a way he never had before.

He poured his magic into the ground, pushing it toward the distant city. He could sense the stone, the foundations of homes and buildings. He shoved his magic high into the air over the city. His control stretched thin and slick in his mind. If he'd been holding a wall around the city, anchored into the ground while he stood inside, he could have done it easily enough. But stretching his magic into the sky from that far away left it too untethered.

A bomb sliced through his magic, plummeting into the innocent people below before Fieran had a chance to stop it. More bombs tore straight through his magic, too heavy, too big, for him to snatch away at this distance.

His dacha likely could have done it. Maybe Fieran could have, given more time. More practice.

His shield around Fort Linder faltered, and a chattering filled the air as the airship above unleashed its machine guns at the airfield below, trying to destroy the aeroplanes before they had a chance to take to the sky.

Fieran switched the focus of his magic, consuming the streams of machine gun bullets before they could pierce through his magic and strike the flyers. But doing so just weakened the magic he'd stretched out to Bridgetown, and another stream of bombs poured through his shield as if his magic was gossamer silk instead of the magic of the ancient kings.

Fieran pounded his fists into the dirt and yelled, a hot wetness trickling down his cheek. People were dying, and Fieran was too far away to stop it.

PIP HANDED the roll of machine gun ammunition up to Stickyfingers where he perched in the rear seat of one of the two-seaters, caressing the machine gun as if it were a pet, testing out the crude swivel she'd fashioned. "This is the last of it."

Unless they wanted to try to throw wrenches at the airships, it was the last weapon or ammunition she had left to hand out.

"Thanks." Stickyfingers grinned at her, his gaze only darting away from the machine gun briefly as he stowed the ammunition by his feet.

Lije climbed into the front seat, placing his goggles over his eyes. "Don't shoot me in the back of the head with that thing."

"I won't." Stickyfingers didn't even look up from the machine gun.

While it might have made more sense to place Stickyfingers in the front seat, the wing struts and propeller would have impeded the large machine gun too much.

Instead, Pip had mounted the gun to the left side of the rear seat so Stickyfingers could shoot as Lije paralleled the airship's bulk.

Actually, she'd mounted all of the rifles and guns in similar fashion. They'd be awkward for the pilot to shoot, but if she attached them facing forward, the pilots would have shot their own propellers off, shattering the wood.

Pip stepped back as the ground crew took charge of the two-seater, wheeling it toward the door.

In one of the other two-seaters, Pretty Face adjusted the goggles on his face as Tiny wedged himself into the rear seat, the entire space around him piled with every canteen and bucket they could get their hands on. The water would act as a fuel for Tiny's ice magic. Hopefully the two-seater would still be able to get off the ground, weighed down as it would be.

Only two single-seat biplanes remained, waiting for Merrik and Fieran. She'd scrounged a rifle for Merrik, but Fieran's flyer was entirely weaponless. Then again, it wasn't like Fieran would need a gun.

Merrik glanced around, then he reached out, gripping Pip's arm. "Pip."

"What? What's wrong?" She glanced around. Where was Fieran? He'd been right there a moment ago.

Merrik just pointed ahead of them, toward the growing blue glow that lit the night.

Pip gasped, then broke into a run. Fieran.

Merrik matched her pace, and together they raced across the hangar. As they sprinted outside, Pip jumped at the jolt of power that shocked her even through her rubber-soled boots. A faint blue glow crackled over the ground, brighter and sparking around a figure that knelt on the ground a few yards outside of the hangar.

"He is going to take out the flyers if he is not careful." Merrik waved from Fieran to Pip. "You are the only one with magic strong enough to get close to him right now."

Pip swallowed, taking in the raw power that poured down Fieran's body and into the ground. Most of it seemed to be directed at the distant Bridgetown, a hazy glow surrounding the city. Five of the airships hovered over the city, bombs falling, the city below burning, despite Fieran's magic.

So much magic spilled out of Fieran that it pooled around him in a crackling tide, spreading outward until it threatened to engulf the airstrip and the hangar.

Pip swallowed, her mouth and throat dry. Could her magic withstand the might of the magic of the ancient kings fully unleashed like this? She'd been able to provide a shield when they'd practiced together, but Fieran had been holding back then. No, not just holding back. She could see that now, beholding his true power. He'd been using a mere fraction of his magic, like a faucet only turned on enough to drip. Now his magic was a torrent, a river raging with spring rains and snowmelt.

Calling on her own magic, Pip coated herself with a layer of magic, much like one of the ancient Escarlish knights suited up in armor.

Then she forced herself to take a step forward. The magic in the ground sparked against her magic, both drawn to and repulsed by the iron properties of her magic. Little bolts of blue magic sparked up her legs, but they didn't hurt as they slithered over her shield.

As she drew closer to him, more of his magic fizzled around her, crackling over her shield in dancing blue bolts. They didn't hurt, and the effect might have almost been beautiful, if not for the falling bombs, exploding shells, and the withering crack of gunfire as the airship overhead opened up with machine guns, aiming deadly fire at the darting flyers.

"Fieran." Pip knelt in front of him, a film of her magic coating her skin so thoroughly that he looked a strange shade of blue-gray through the layers of both of their magics flickering over her.

He raised his head, meeting her gaze. Bolts of blue magic flickered across his eyes and danced in the trails that tears had left streaked over his face. "I can't save them. I'm too far away, and I can't save them."

"Then pull your magic back, put your butt in a flyer, and get yourself close enough." Pip reached through the magic and gave him a good hard poke in the chest with her pointer finger. Now wasn't the time for gentleness or soft words. Muka would have given Fieran a good thump on the back of his head if she'd been there.

Fieran blinked, then looked beyond her. His eyes widened, and he yanked back on his magic so fast that it slapped into the two of them with a force hard enough that Pip had to brace a hand against Fieran's chest to keep herself from toppling into him. He grimaced, some of that hard edge disappearing momentarily from his face. "Sorry."

"Don't waste time apologizing now." Pip used his shoulder to leverage herself to her feet.

He stood. With one last look at the distant city, he turned away. That blue glow on the horizon winked out, leaving Bridgetown utterly vulnerable.

As they turned, two more aeroplanes took off, surging into the sky to join the battle. The ground crews wheeled out the last two aeroplanes. Near the door, Merrik gave them a nod before he tugged down his goggles and climbed into one of the flyers.

Fieran glanced from her to the final flyer, waiting for him. "Once I take off, I won't be able to hold the magic over the fort any longer."

Pip straightened to give her small frame every inch of height as the weight of those words settled on her. "I think my shield can at least deflect one of the bombs off to the side. I'm powerful, but I can't hold a shield over the entire fort."

Fieran reached out, as if to clap her on the back, before he glanced at his magic-laced fingers and halted. "Protect the command center unless you're ordered otherwise."

Pip drew in a deep breath as she nodded. Then she gave Fieran a shove. "Go. Just make sure you bring back my flyer in one piece."

Fieran nodded, then jogged toward the hangar. Pip hurried in his wake, even as the rumble of another flyer taking off reverberated from the runway behind her.

There was nothing more Pip could do but watch as Fieran climbed into his flyer, pulling his goggles over his eyes. Then their flyers were bouncing and wobbling as they maneuvered toward the end of the airfield just as one of the two-seaters took off. It must have been the one with Tiny and Pretty Face for it struggled to get into the air, ascending into the sky with almost painful slowness.

Pip stood in the hangar's doorway and lifted her hand. In a wave. In a salute. She didn't know.

First Merrik's biplane, then Fieran's, hurtled down the airstrip. Fieran hadn't even waited for Merrik's flyer to get safely into the air before starting his run, and the two of them rose into the sky one after the other.

As soon as the wheels of Fieran's flyer left the ground, the sizzling crackle of his magic burst into a shower of sparks.

The remaining airship overhead surged forward, almost gleefully. That square door opened up once again, preparing to drop another cargo of bombs onto the now nearly defenseless Fort Linder.

A boom sounded—sharper than the explosions. It had to

be one of their artillery guns, able to fire once again now that Fieran's magic was no longer between them and the airship. But with the airship on the far southwest side of the fort—the opposite side from the gun emplacements by the river—the guns were nearly useless.

Would they hit one of their own flyers darting around the enemy airship? Could the artillery guns even send their shells high enough to hit the airship? She didn't know enough about guns to know for sure.

With a deep breath, Pip cast her shield back into the sky over the hangar once more even as she dashed back inside. She grabbed the sleeve of the nearest man. One of the ground crew. "Spread the word. I'm heading for the center of the fort to protect headquarters. The hangar will be left unprotected."

"Understood. Go." The man waved her off before he raced to the nearest cluster of men, pointing back to her as he spoke.

Pip didn't wait for more. She sprinted across the hangar, then out the far door. Her chest ached at leaving behind the hangar and her fellow mechanics to fend for themselves. But right now, it was more important that the base's command center was protected. If she could extend her power over the infirmary and the communications hub, then all the better.

She resisted the urge to check the sky and search for Fieran. She needed her concentration to dart around rubble. The streets of the army base were clear of people now. Fieran's shield had given them enough reprieve to get organized, manning stations and gun emplacements.

Pip skidded to a halt next to the three flagpoles in the central square of Fort Linder. To one side of her, a long brick building held the officers' quarters. The far end of it was nothing but rubble now, and a fire crew pumped a stream of water onto the fire that crackled amid the wreckage.

In front of her, the headquarters and communications buildings bustled with life, both untouched by bombs and fire. Hopefully all of the underground telephone and telegraph wires that connected Fort Linder with the rest of Escarland hadn't been severed by the bombs.

Behind her, the infirmary stretched in a long, narrow building, thankfully also undamaged. A truck was parked in front of it, and men were carefully unloading a stretcher.

Pip braced herself against the pole at her back, the cool metal soothing. She used the pole as a focal point as she raised a shield once again, stretching it as far as she dared so that it covered the entire central square of Fort Linder.

Overhead, the three flags of the Alliance Kingdoms flapped in the rising breeze, snapping as if in defiance of the airships that dared such an attack.

Pip squinted at the sky through the haze of her magical shield. Black specks of the flyers darted around the airships, only briefly visible in the glow of machine gun fire and the brief brightness when the airship's cargo doors opened to spill more bombs onto Fort Linder. At this distance, the aeroplanes looked like flies trying to harass a wolf. Mildly annoying, yes, but easily swatted aside and ignored.

Another flyer burst into flames, spiraling toward the earth. Where was Fieran? Merrik? The other flyboys she'd gotten to know so well?

The enemy airship drifted closer, dropping bombs as it traveled across the sky over Fort Linder. Explosions tore through the buildings, and from here Pip couldn't see if the aeroplane hangar remained untouched or had been hit.

Then the airship blocked the sky above her, casting a black shadow over her magical shield.

Pip braced herself against the flagpole at her back, pouring more magic into the shield stretched above her head.

The black, tubular shapes of the bombs tumbled down toward her. The first bomb struck her shield, exploding on impact.

She gritted her teeth at the force pounding her magic. Several of the bombs struck without detonating, rolling off and exploding among the buildings she didn't have shielded.

More bombs tumbled through the sky and blasted into her magic.

She cried out, pain stabbing through her skull and into her chest at the force of the explosions she staved off with the power of her magic.

Yet another explosion pounded into her. The enemy must have realized she was holding a shield over the central command of the fort, and they were hitting her with everything they had.

She crumpled to her knees, blackness dancing at the edges of her vision.

TWENTY-ONE

Fieran's flyer lifted into the sky, following Merrik's aeroplane. They pointed their flyers' noses upward, toward the airship hovering above Fort Linder.

Other biplanes darted around the airship, even as the airship's machine guns chattered.

Clawing into the sky took an agonizingly peaceful fifteen minutes. The breeze raked icy through Fieran's hair. He hadn't had the chance to bundle up in the normal leather jacket, fur-lined leather boots, scarf, and cap that he would normally wear to protect himself from the cold air high in the sky. He didn't even have gloves, but he kept his hands from numbing by letting his magic twine around his fingers. At least he had goggles to keep his eyes from tearing up in the wind.

Then Merrik banked to circle the airship, and Fieran followed, shadowing Merrik's movement into a pandemonium of barking machine guns, tearing bullets, a haze of smoke, and whirling aeroplanes.

Fieran called up his magic, but he held it back from fully unleashing. There was so much smoke and chaos he was just as likely to catch one of his fellow pilots in his magic if he sent it at the airship from too far away. He'd have to get closer, using his magic in limited amounts, to prevent hurting one of his own.

As he dove toward the airship, a black shape came out of nowhere around the curve of the dirigible, headed straight for Fieran.

Fieran let out a few crude words and shoved the rudder over with his feet while pushing the stick forward to dive into a right turn. Thanks to the rotary engine, his flyer tumbled sideways even faster than he expected.

A gust of wind took his wings, and then he was spiraling. Everything around was black. Black sky. Black land. Black, black, black.

Was he headed for the ground? The sky? The airship? The jumbled, tugging forces left him with no sense of gravity to tell up from down.

His heart hammered in his throat, his rising bile coating his tongue with a sour taste. His head whirled, all of his senses swimming until he thought he might be sick. Everything in him wanted to just yank on the stick in a blind panic.

Gritting his teeth, he forced his clenching muscles to move. Slowly. Gently. He fought the forces until he regained a margin of control over his flyer, stopping the spin, though he couldn't have said if he was pointed at the sky or at the ground.

Blinking, he forced his eyes to focus. He craned his stiff, aching neck to try to locate something that resembled a light or a landmark.

Over his head, bright orange flames danced among black buildings, a rippling, liquid surface off to his left over his head.

Not over his head. Beneath him. He was flying upside down. Now that he settled back more firmly into his body as his panic receded, he could feel the pain of the lap belt around his hips, the only thing holding him in the cockpit.

This was fine. He was fine.

Trying to calm his thundering heart, Fieran eased on the rudder and control column, trying to turn his craft right side up once again. The aeroplane made only a sluggish attempt to right itself.

Nothing for it. Fieran pushed the control column forward again, putting his aeroplane into a dive, this time curving into a loop so that his flyer slowly righted itself even as it screamed ever closer to the ground.

Fieran braced his feet on the rudder bar and pulled back on the stick, fighting the forces on the ailerons and elevators. His aeroplane finally leveled out right side up, skimming rather disconcertingly close over Fort Linder and punching through the plumes of black smoke.

Ahead and below him, a curving silvery dome of magic arched over Fort Linder's headquarters. While he'd been tumbling through the sky, the airship had drifted, and it now pounded Pip's shield with bombs.

He couldn't have said how he knew, but he could sense her magic wavering, weakening, beneath the bombardment.

Fieran released that burst of magic he'd been holding to so tightly, sending it at her shield. As it had during their practice together, his magic danced over hers, blending together to form an even stronger shield.

The next bomb burst against their combined shield, and this time it held strong.

Fieran sent one more burst of magic at her shield to reinforce it before he gripped the stick with both hands again and pointed his aeroplane's nose toward the confusion in the sky once again.

Aeroplanes darted about in utter disorder around the airship, seemingly doing nothing at all to actually harm the behemoth floating in their sky.

As Fieran swooped back into the bedlam, another flyer came around the curve of the airship's balloon. The pilot didn't seem to see him, and Fieran swerved, this time managing to keep his craft under control as the other flyer darted beneath him, the pilot so focused on firing on the airship that he didn't even glance at Fieran's aeroplane.

As he cleared that flyer, another one appeared out of the smoke. This time a two-seater. Lije remained utterly focused as he flew while Stickyfingers cackled maniacally as he sprayed the side of the airship's balloon with the machine gun. Holes appeared in the canvas skin, but nothing else happened.

The Mongavarian airship was probably constructed with multiple inner balloons beneath the outer dirigible sheathing, those balloons reinforced with magic to prevent air loss, just like the Escarlish airships. It would take more than a few rounds from a machine gun to take the airship down.

Then Lije and Stickyfingers disappeared once more among the smoke and the darkness. Fieran didn't know where Merrik was. Or Capt. Arfeld or anyone else. Each flyer was on his own with no way to communicate with each other, the orange signal flags essentially useless in the murk.

Fieran curved his flyer underneath the airship, his biplane wobbling with the buffeting forces of the air currents tangling as they flowed around the dirigible's bulk. He struggled to keep control of his aeroplane, his entire focus narrowed to just staying in the sky. He didn't have the experience in the air for the maneuvers he was trying to pull off.

He'd have to learn under fire. He didn't have another choice.

A machine gun underneath the airship swung in his direction. He dove and bobbed, trying to avoid the stream of fire.

A buzz whined through the air. A line of pain cut across the side of his arm. When Fieran glanced over, blood welled from a line sliced into his fatigues.

He muttered a rather naughty word and swung his biplane farther over, only to have to swing the other way as another flyer tumbled toward him, spinning out of control, headed for the ground.

This was ridiculous. He was Fieran Laesornysh, son of the legendary Farrendel Laesornysh. Surely he could concentrate enough to both fly his blasted aeroplane and wield his magic at the same time.

If he didn't, his entire squadron would be massacred here in the sky.

Calling on his magic, Fieran let it flow from his finger-tips, coating his biplane with a layer of sparking magic. He extended the layer upward, pouring his magic into the six-inch-deep barrier of magic surrounding himself and his aeroplane, concentrating to make sure that he didn't acci-dentally incinerate the delicate canvas and wood around him.

Merrik's flyer whirled into view around the edge of the airship, his biplane glowing faintly green. He must have reinforced the wooden frame with his magic, protecting himself as much as he could. He lined up with his rifle, aiming for a machine gun emplacement in the side of the dirigible.

Yet Merrik's entire attention appeared so focused on lining up his rifle while keeping his biplane steady that he didn't seem to see that another machine gun farther along the airship's side was swinging toward him, taking aim, seconds away from killing him.

Not on Fieran's watch.

He dove toward the airship, both hands on the stick, squinting to see through the brilliance of his own magic.

Both sets of machine guns swung toward him. Blazing with magic as he was, he made for the bigger, brighter target, even if nothing could touch him.

As the machine guns opened fire, the bullets thwapped into his magic. With barely a thought, he incinerated them, choking the air with the stench of overheated metal.

Flicking out his hand, Fieran sent his magic along the path of the bullets, following the stream of lead back to the machine guns. He wrapped his magic around the guns, then squeezed tight, melting the metal and setting off the gunpowder. The tiny explosions were swallowed up in the fury of his magic.

Fieran swung his flyer to parallel the airship, pouring more of his magic through the air and coating the airship. He glanced over his shoulder, trying to locate any of the other flyers so that he didn't accidentally catch them in the blaze of his power.

Merrik fell in behind Fieran. The two-seater with Lije and Stickyfingers roared up from underneath the airship. At the intensity of Fieran's magic, they nearly stalled as Lije pulled up. After a moment of wobbling in the air, Lije regained control and swerved into line to follow Merrik.

The airship was swinging in a wide turn, drifting over the Hydalla River. Whether to flee for the distant border or turn for another bombing run over the fort, Fieran didn't know. It wouldn't change his duty to take down the airship regardless.

Fieran's magic crawled over the airship, and with that magic, he could sense the canvas, metal, helium, and rope that formed the airship. Bright spots of human magic laced through various parts of the ship, though he couldn't have said what the purpose of the magic was. It didn't matter. His magic would consume it as easily as everything else.

He could also sense the people. All the lives of those swarming over the catwalks and in the gondola. The fear filling them as they watched his magic crawl over their craft.

Something in Fieran went cold, and in that moment, he understood. All of it. All those times his dacha's eyes had gone distant. The way he'd pushed Fieran during training. The practice in killing the pig carcasses.

Most of all, that conversation they'd had the night Fieran enlisted.

He'd always had the sense that, when he killed in war, it would be in self-defense. That it would somehow be more justifiable because the killing was on equal terms, strength for strength, bullet for bullet. He'd kill those who were actively trying to kill him.

But this...this was on a whole different scale. The Mongavarians had no hope of fighting back. He could wipe out every single person on that airship with a twitch of his magic. It was not equal. It was not an honorable battle decided in a test of measure for measure. It wasn't even self-defense, as he was no longer in any danger from the Mongavarian guns.

This was just death. Doing what he had to do to defend his squadron and his kingdom. Killing on a scale the world had not seen since his dacha had fought in the wars between the trolls and the elves.

With one last bracing breath to steel himself, Fieran mentally squeezed his magic tight, devouring the hard sides of the dirigible, the air bags, the catwalks, everything in mere minutes, leaving only tatters of flaming canvas and twisted shards of metal to tumble, burning and groaning, toward the darkness of the waters far below.

He left the gondola, though he wasn't sure if the people within would survive the crash into the water or if he was condemning them to a fate of falling to their deaths if they did not get to their parachutes in time. Assuming the Mongavarian airships came equipped with parachutes.

But right now, there was no time to spare a thought for mercy or regrets. Only logic and cold-hearted duty.

TWENTY-TWO

Pip blinked rapidly to stave off the blackness at the edges of her vision. Her magic burned inside her, as if strained to the breaking point. She was on her knees, though she couldn't remember getting there.

Above her, her shield strained, and she sucked in a painful breath, squeezing her eyes shut. She couldn't withstand another direct hit like that.

Something bright and sizzling burst across her senses. She forced her eyes open as Fieran's magic blasted over hers, a crackling tide shoring up her shield.

Pip gripped the flagpole and struggled back to her feet. She braced herself with her back to the pole, using the metal to strengthen her, even as a second burst of Fieran's magic spread over her shield. Gritting her teeth, she unleashed more of her magic, letting their two powers blend together.

Through the blur of crackling blue and shimmering silver, the black specks of the flyers darted around the huge airship, seeming more an annoyance than a deterrence.

At least the airship seemed too distracted to drop more bombs.

Using the respite, Pip gathered herself, her gasps coming hard in her chest.

Something bright and blue flared across the sky, streaking toward the airship. Moments later, a brilliant burst of blue spread against the darkness over the airship, bathing the night in light.

Fieran. Pip might have breathed his name out loud, though she couldn't have been sure.

One of the infantry men who had been racing toward the headquarters halted, gaping upward. More men halted, gathering into a crowd as they stared upward. Someone nearby murmured, "Laesornysh," loudly enough for the name to carry on the breeze.

The blue magic flared even brighter, and it took Pip a moment of squinting to make out what was happening. The magic almost seemed to be eating the airship, incinerating it to ash before their eyes.

The sheer power he demonstrated was almost enough to make her quake, even knowing him as well as she did. Even knowing he was on her side.

This was the magic of the ancient kings fully unleashed.

The Mongavarians had no idea what power they were up against.

Cheers broke out all around her. Doors slammed open as those inside headquarters and the infirmary stepped out to see what was going on.

The black shape of the airship's gondola plummeted from the sky, looking like it would land in the river beside Fort Linder. A few smaller black shapes jumped from the gondola, their white parachutes opening against the sky a moment later.

Pip propped herself up against the flagpole, finally daring to exhale a long, relieved breath. High above her, the three flags stirred in the breeze, undamaged and undaunted.

Someone—likely a high-ranking commander of some kind—barked orders, organizing a special detail of men to round up the Mongavarians before they could escape into the night. He also called for volunteers to head into Bridgetown, even while that city remained under attack, to provide aid.

Pip pushed away from the flagpole and hurried toward the officer. "Sir, I'd like to go along." She pointed upward. "I'm the one shielding us. But now that Fort Linder is safe for the time being..."

"Go." The officer barely blinked at her offer, despite the fact that she was a tiny girl volunteering to go into a war zone.

This night had changed them all, it seemed.

The next thing she knew, she was being lifted into the back of a truck, packed in with a squad of infantrymen on their way to help the stricken city. A few of the nurses, including Chelsea, also squished inside, clutching boxes overflowing with medical supplies.

Within moments, Pip jounced in the back of a truck as it rumbled at dangerously high speeds over the pitted, bomb-damaged road stretching between Fort Linder and Bridgetown with only the weak beams of the headlights to illuminate the craters before they could plunge into one. Through the canvas flaps at the rear, the headlights from the truck behind them wavered as it mirrored their swerves and dodges.

She struggled to hold the shield over the convoy of trucks as best she could at this speed. As soon as they reached the city, she'd stick with the officer placed in charge, creating a shield over wherever he decided to set up a command post.

Ahead, the city burned. The remaining airships loomed overhead, continuing to drop bombs onto the helpless people below.

A bright ball of blue magic streaked across the sky, headed for Bridgetown and the remaining five airships.

Headed for a reckoning.

AS THE WHITE plumes of unfurling parachutes drifted downward, Fieran pointed his flyer's nose toward the five airships bombarding Bridgetown and Calafaren. There was no need to signal with the orange flag. Merrik and Lije fell in behind him along with a few of the other pilots who had been harassing the airship over Fort Linder, forming an organized force for the first time since this air battle started.

The stretch of open farm fields that they had driven past so often to enjoy weekends in Bridgetown flashed by below, black and empty.

Ahead, the airship nearest them appeared to be sagging, long gashes torn through its outer canvas shell. A two-seater aeroplane flashed into view, Pretty Face in the front seat, Tiny crammed in the second seat.

Even as Fieran roared closer, Tiny poured a stream of water from a canteen, freezing it into a long shard of ice. He hurled the ice downward in a blaze of his magic.

The ice shard tore into the airship below, creating yet another long slash through the dirigible's side.

Might as well help Tiny along, though Tiny looked well on his way to taking down the airship on his own.

Fieran swooped close, tipping his aeroplane on its side so

that his head faced the airship. As the various machine guns opened fire on him, he used the same trick as before to follow the line of bullets back to the airship.

Even as he poured magic into the airship, he spread a trailing shield of magic behind him, protecting Merrik, Lije, Stickyfingers, and the others from enemy fire. Pretty Face dropped his and Tiny's aeroplane into the formation as well.

Lije ducked his flyer below the line of Fieran's magic, and Stickyfingers opened fire at the gondola. Glass shattered. Wood splintered. As soon as a machine gun set in the side of the gondola swung toward the flyer, Lije swerved the aeroplane back into the protection of Fieran's magic.

Fieran poured more of his magic onto the airship. As he swung around the dirigible, he plunged through clouds of smoke billowing up from the burning Bridgetown below. Across the Hydalla River, the trees of Calafaren burned.

When the entire airship crackled with his magic, Fieran drew in a deep breath and unleashed his magic to consume the balloon, gondola, people, everything. While Fort Linder could handle rounding up a few prisoners, the town below couldn't. All he could do now was finish this.

Fieran didn't watch the airship's destruction. Instead, he swung his flyer away, heading for the next one. As he closed in on that airship, more aeroplanes fell into line behind him. He didn't even look to see who it was.

The next two airships sailed nearly side by side with only a fifty-foot-wide space between them.

Fieran led his column of flyers into the gap. Machine guns opened up, but he pinched the control column between his knees and held his hands out to either side, blasting his magic to raze both airships at once. By the time he flew out the other side, both airships were burning hulks.

Fieran's skin burned from so much magic crackling

around him. His eyes watered from peering through the constant blue crackle, a shimmer of blue coating his vision. He'd never used his magic at this strength and to this extent before.

Only two more airships remained. As Fieran turned his flyer in that direction, a wave of lightheadedness crashed over him, his vision blurring. Sucking in a deep breath, he shook his head and refocused. He didn't have time for weakness.

Another aeroplane flashed by, but Fieran ignored it, except to note its location so that he didn't hit it with his magic.

Pushing past the exhaustion and dizziness, Fieran closed on the second to last airship, then blasted his magic outward to coat the airship. He didn't have to brace himself this time. He unleashed his magic, only using the mildest of control to keep it contained where he wanted it. Other than that, he let his magic do what it wished, crackling and consuming with the full fury of the magic of the ancient kings.

As that airship groaned in its death throes, plunging toward the river even as his magic licked over it, Fieran searched for the sixth and final airship.

The dirigible no longer hovered over Calafaren. Sometime during Fieran's destruction of the others, it had turned toward the east, as if to make a run for the safety of Mongavaria.

Fieran pushed his flyer at full power, ignoring the way the gauge jumped dangerously into the yellow. He swooped down on the airship like an eagle on a flopping fish. As he neared, the airship's machine guns opened fire in a valiant but futile attempt to ward him off.

He blasted his magic over the gap, and his magic blazed over the dirigible's skin. Black figures appeared at the doors and windows of the gondolas, and some leapt out, their white parachutes opening moments later.

Fieran's magic ripped through the airship, reducing it to a mangled wreck and sending it, too, plummeting from the sky.

Fieran drew his magic back, though he kept the shield around his aeroplane. A glance around the sky showed that only his squadron remained, buzzing about in the air in a mostly disorganized fashion, except for the ones trailing after Fieran. Far fewer flyers remained in the sky than there should have been, though Fieran didn't take the time to count.

Down below, Bridgetown burned, piles of rubble all that remained of large swathes of the once vibrant city. Across the Hydalla River, the trees of Calafaren sent up clouds of black smoke.

The Alliance Bridge remained, still strong, glowing blue with Dacha's protective magic.

A flash of orange came from an aeroplane in the distance, but Fieran didn't focus on it. If it was orders from Capt. Arfeld, Fieran didn't want to see it. He had his own plans of what he intended to do next, and he wasn't going to let a simple thing like orders stop him.

Instead, Fieran slid his own orange flag out, then he whirled his aeroplane around so that he was flying past Merrik, Lije, Stickyfingers, Pretty Face, and Tiny.

Fieran would have breathed a sigh of relief at seeing all of them alive, but there wasn't time. He started to signal, only for the magic still coating his fingers to incinerate the flag. So much magic still burned through him, and he wasn't sure how to even rein it back in now that he had unleashed it so fully.

He signaled with his hand, his magic a bright slash

through the night, that he was going to land. He pointed at Merrik, telling him to land as well. For the others, he signaled for them to stay on patrol in the air. The six airships had been destroyed, but who knew if Mongavaria would send another wave of airships to attack.

Once he received acknowledgement signal waves from Lije and Pretty Face, Fieran took his aeroplane lower, trying to find a place to land. The road, perhaps. Or one of the open farm fields.

But in the darkness and smoke, he couldn't see anything but blackness surrounding the city. For all he knew, he'd plow his aeroplane right into the side of a farmhouse if he attempted to land.

Or…he pointed his flyer toward the one place that was clear of people and traffic, straight, long enough, and well lit.

The Alliance Bridge beamed blue light into the night like a beacon of hope despite the chaos and death of the night. Even though it must have been a target for the attack, only a few chips and dents scored the stone, not enough to truly damage it.

Fieran lined his aeroplane up, banked lower, and shut off the engine to come in on a glide. He had to lean up as precisely as possible, considering the wall that had been added to protect the lane for bicyclists and pedestrians from the two lanes for trolleys and motorized vehicles.

Keeping his flyer steady as the breezes wafting up from the river buffeted the wings, he touched down at the very end of the bridge. The wheels jounced hard against the firm stones, threatening to skid out and send his wings into the arched walls on either side. The tailskid screeched against the pavement, not doing anything to slow him as he barreled forward.

Fighting the rudder and ailerons, Fieran kept control of his aeroplane by the skin of his teeth. Finally, the upward slope of the bridge slowed him until he came to a creaking halt nearly at the apex of the center span of the bridge.

When he glanced behind him, he found Merrik in his aeroplane rolling to a halt only a few yards behind him. Merrik must have come down behind him, risking both that Fieran would crash and block his way or that Merrik's aeroplane wouldn't stop as fast and crash into him.

Fieran levered himself from the cockpit, climbed onto the lower wing, then leapt to the ground, landing lightly thanks to his elven agility. He jogged a few steps, reaching Merrik just as Merrik straightened from his own jump. Fieran pointed north. "Do what you can to put out the fires in Calafaren. I'll do the same for Bridgetown."

Merrik nodded, then launched into a sprint, racing for the elven city to the north.

Fieran jogged for a few steps before transitioning into a run, heading south toward Bridgetown.

The attack was over, but the battle to save as many lives as possible had just begun.

TWENTY-THREE

Pip crawled beneath the end of a beam where it stuck out of a pile of rubble. The sound of crying came from beneath, and the army medic and four infantrymen with her stood poised at the edge of the rubble, waiting for her to lever the beam out of the way.

Gritting her teeth, Pip poured her magic into a shield over herself, spreading it out beneath the beam and the worst of the rubble. With a yell, she heaved the debris upward.

The infantrymen leapt forward, digging through the rubble until they reached the person pinned beneath. Within a few minutes, they had uncovered another bloody, dust-covered person. A woman this time, tears causing wet streaks through the dust. The medic knelt, assessing the person's injuries before they risked moving her.

Pip didn't look. She didn't want to see more blood and gory injuries.

At least this woman was alive. So far this night, Pip had seen too much, experienced too much.

She'd left home, restless and seeking. But this wasn't the adventure she'd been hoping to find.

Instead, she was trapped in a nightmare of smoke and destruction, blood and ash, death and horrors. Screams and shouts for help echoed into the night as blazing infernos threatened to consume whatever the bombs had missed.

The men loaded the woman onto a stretcher, then eased both her and themselves out of the rubble. Once they were safely out of the way, Pip let the beam fall back to the ground.

Wearily, she crawled out from under the beam, then used it to lever herself to her feet. She didn't even bother brushing off her coveralls.

As two of the infantrymen carried the woman down the road, headed for the one hospital in Bridgetown that had remained unscathed, the medic approached Pip. "Miss Detmuk-Inawenys, perhaps you should rest? You look exhausted."

"I'm fine." Pip couldn't rest. Not until they'd rescued each and every person trapped in the rubble.

But her magic was nearly exhausted. *She* was exhausted.

"I just need a moment." Pip braced herself against the end of the beam, willing away the haze of weariness blurring her vision. Her throat and lungs ached from choking on the acrid smoke. Her eyes burned from the smoke and her unshed tears.

Something sparked nearby. Then a wave of Fieran's blue, crackling magic slithered over the debris and lined each street and building, snuffing out the fires and consuming any smoldering rubble in the vicinity.

"Fieran." She wasn't sure if he was close enough to hear, nor did she have the strength to raise her voice to anything over a weak call.

Moments later, he stepped from the haze and smoke, a tall figure in army green, a few bolts of his magic curling around his hands.

Pip pushed away from the beam and ran to him, not even stopping to think before she hugged him. He was alive, he was here, and she just needed to be held for a moment, safe and secure in this city of destruction, despite the fact that they didn't have that kind of relationship.

His arms came around her, strong and secure. It didn't matter that they were just friends, and he wouldn't mean anything by this beyond comfort on the worst night either of them had experienced.

Before she knew it, she was sobbing, and she didn't even care. She couldn't have even said why. Perhaps the stress. The things she'd seen that night. The sheer relief that both she and Fieran had survived. The fear for the friends who might be alive or dead.

He held her tight, his grip shaky and trembling around her.

She wasn't sure how long she cried as they stood there like that amid the rubble of the city they'd both loved so much.

Finally, she gathered herself, sniffling her tears into silence. Swiping at her face, she pushed away from Fieran, not daring to meet his gaze. "Linshi."

"Tiridari." He returned her elvish *thank you* with a *you're welcome* in the same language, though the meaning was less trite in elvish. He gestured toward the rubble-strewn road ahead of them. "We should keep going."

It was all they could do.

As dawn blushed soft on the eastern horizon, Pip was stumbling with fatigue, both magical and physical. Beside her, Fieran, too, tottered as he put out fire after fire by consuming it with his magic. His freckles stood out even more pronounced as his already pale skin took on a gray pallor.

The morning light revealed just how devastating the damage was to the city. Everything looked so foreign to the Bridgetown she had come to know and love.

Instead of the bustle of a vibrant city, now there were weary people, wandering in mute shock, digging through the rubble, or standing beside still forms laid out on the ground, sobbing for the loss of loved ones.

Several of the monuments and statues she'd laughed over with Fieran were now chipped or missing chunks. The statue of King Rharreth on the corner was now missing its head.

In their favorite park, all the trees were cracked and broken, their trunks flopped over into the streets under the force of the blast. The soda parlor where they'd spent so much time was now a smoking crater, the bricks blackened, the stainless-steel countertop a twisted thing in the debris.

Pip just halted right there in the debris-covered street, too weary to even cry.

Fieran stood next to her, wrapping an arm around her shoulders and tugging her close.

She leaned into him, soaking in his warmth, not caring if both of them reeked of sweat and smoke.

Marching boots echoed off the buildings a moment before a squad of soldiers appeared out of the haze. Their uniforms were far too clean compared to those she'd seen throughout the night, digging through the rubble or patrolling the streets to keep law and order.

Fieran snapped to attention, saluting the lieutenant leading the way.

The lieutenant saluted in return, sweeping a gaze over Fieran and Pip. His eyes were softer, more compassionate, than the hard control she usually saw in the army officers. "Are you from Fort Linder?"

"Yes, sir." Fieran stared over the lieutenant's head.

Pip tried to pretend she wasn't using Fieran as a prop to keep herself upright.

"You've been relieved. Reinforcements have arrived from Fort Freilan." The lieutenant gestured behind him to the clean and bright-eyed soldiers. "Report to the command post on Outpost Museum Hill."

"Yes, sir." Fieran saluted again before spinning on his heel.

Pip nearly toppled over with his sudden movement, and she staggered a step to regain her balance.

Fieran turned back toward her, reaching out a hand as if he wasn't sure how to help.

She waved off his help, forcing her leaden legs to move once again. She might be tired, but she was still perfectly capable of walking the rest of the way to the hill.

Together, she and Fieran trudged through the streets of Bridgetown. Occasionally, they'd come across a block of buildings that stood virtually untouched, only for the next street over to be demolished into nothing but piles of bricks and shattered wood.

Finally, they reached the base of Museum Hill. Her shoulders slumped in relief at seeing that the outpost remained untouched, though a bomb had cratered into one of the surrounding streets. At least something had survived the night.

To one side of the hill, the University Hospital—one of

the two hospitals in Bridgetown—was a blaze of light and hive of activity. Men, women, and children were laid out on the street, waiting for the nurses and the handful of elven healers present to tend to them.

More bustle filled the green before the museum than Pip would have expected. Tents had already been set up while men in army uniforms hustled between them.

To one side of the temporary headquarters, long tables had been set up, providing food to the weary, hungry people of Bridgetown. A smaller set of tables had been set up farther up the hill, where the exhausted, grimy men of Fort Linder were lining up to get food.

Pip dragged her feet in that direction, the steepness of the hill feeling nearly insurmountable in her exhaustion.

"Pip? Fieran?"

She turned at the sound of the voice, her eyes already prickling with tears, her throat choking. Lije stood there, his beanpole frame seeming even skinnier with the way his uniform hung dirty and torn. Ash smeared across his face and into his hair while dried blood coated one leg. A white bandage was tied around his calf.

"You're alive." Pip blinked, then gave him a quick hug. She'd already known that, since Fieran had reassured her as they'd worked throughout the night. But it was different seeing for herself.

"What about a hug for me?" Pretty Face strode up to them, holding out his arms for a hug, though he winced at the movement. A bloodstained bandage was taped to his chin. Despite his joking words, his tone held that weary quality they all had after this night. Dried tracks carved through the dirt on his face, showing that he'd shed a few tears of his own during the night.

"Just this once." Pip gave him a hug as well. He kept the hug short.

As she stepped out of the brief hug, she glanced around. "Where are Tiny, Stickyfingers, and Merrik?"

"Tiny and Stickyfingers are back in the air." Lije gestured upward at the black shapes of the flyers maintaining a patrol over Bridgetown and Fort Linder. "Capt. Arfeld has all of us rotating through patrols."

"Except for me and Merrik. Our magic is more useful on the ground." Fieran gave a tired, rolling shrug of his shoulders. "Is Merrik still in Calafaren?"

"I'd assume so. I haven't seen him." Lije tipped his head along with his own exhausted shrug. "The commander sent a detail over the bridge to offer aid to the elves, if they need it or want it."

Even with the close alliance, the Escarlish soldiers wouldn't be able to operate on Tarenhieli soil without permission. Perhaps Merrik, half-elf that he was, would be able to smooth their way.

"After they moved the flyers you and Merrik parked in the middle of the bridge out of the way." Pretty Face waggled his eyebrows, a strained edge to the humor as if he had to work up the energy to joke. Both the humor and the strain couldn't hide the edge of awe in his voice.

Pip whirled to face Fieran, her own eyebrows shooting up. "You landed on the Alliance Bridge?"

Fieran shrugged, as if landing a flyer on a bridge—a national monument, no less—at night with no brakes and a great risk of skidding out and smashing into the stone walls on either side was no big deal. "It was the only lit, straight, and open spot last night. There was plenty of room."

Not really, but Pip didn't have the energy to banter back. Not this morning.

They were all alive. That was the main thing. All of her flyboys had survived the night.

Pip turned to the east, the morning sunlight warm on her face.

Before, she hadn't truly known what she wanted. She'd joined the Auxiliaries because she was searching for a purpose.

But now she had one. She wasn't the fighter that Fieran and the other flyboys were. Yet she would fight this war in her own way, maintaining the aeroplanes to keep her boys safe in the sky. Last night had burned a steely resolve through her. She would do her part in this war no matter what it took and where she was sent after this.

Hopefully she was sent to the same place as Fieran and the rest of her flyboys.

Her flyboys. No matter what happened in this war, she could face it as long as they were together.

TWENTY-FOUR

Fieran sat with his back to the wooden stockade wall of the Outpost Museum, a bowl of soup in his hands. He stirred the soup, but he couldn't bring himself to eat despite the fact that he hadn't eaten in eighteen hours. Perhaps longer. He wasn't even sure what time it was.

The rays of the morning sun perforated the smoke and shadows of the destroyed city sprawling before him. In the distance, a train whistle pierced the morning. Perhaps reinforcements from the nearest army base to relieve the weary soldiers of Fort Linder. Maybe more elven healers from Tarenhiel to save those who could be saved.

Pip had gone into the Outpost Museum, which had been turned into temporary quarters for the army personnel and the other volunteers to rest after the long night. Hopefully she had managed a few hours of sleep.

Daylight hadn't made the destruction look any better. If anything, light just made everything worse. He could actually see the rubble. See the mangled, dead bodies laid out in the streets and on the stretchers as they were carried to the temporary morgue. See things so seared into his memory that he wasn't sure he would be able to sleep, despite the exhaustion weighing so heavily on him that lifting the spoon to his mouth seemed too much work.

Even his magic was a faint crackle inside his chest, though he wasn't sure if he'd used enough magic to actually deplete his power or if he was simply exhausted from wielding such a quantity of magic. Perhaps a little of both.

It wasn't just the physical and magical exhaustion, though there was that. He'd been up for over thirty-six hours, broken only by those handful of hours between falling asleep and waking just after midnight due to the attack. The rest of the night had been spent expending his magic, killing hundreds of Mongavarians, then digging through rubble to find both the living and the dead.

So many dead.

Women. Children.

His squadron. His brothers. Several had crashed during the night, and most of those had been from pilot error rather than the Mongavarian guns. A few had survived their crashes, but not all of them. Or even most of them.

So many empty bunks. He didn't yet know how many untouched glasses of beer would grace the bar when his squadron had a chance to mourn. It was all he could do to focus on those still alive.

Fieran squeezed his eyes shut. It did little good. He could still see the bloody faces of the dead. Taste the acrid smoke on the breeze. Smell the stench of blood and sulfur that hung over the whole city.

A stir of murmurs rose from the base of the hill. Fieran wearily peeled his eyes open.

His dacha stood among the cluster of officers with Uncle Julien and Aunt Vriska at his side. Dacha's long silver-blond hair hung down his back over his green and brown fighting leathers, his twin swords resting against his back. With the morning sunlight glinting on his armor, he looked like an elven warrior of old stepped from the pages of legends.

Dacha, Uncle Julien, and Aunt Vriska must have arrived on that recent train. Politically, it was a statement of support as top generals of Escarland, Kostaria, and Tarenhiel surveyed the destruction.

Something that had been wound tight in Fieran's chest eased. The burden of protecting Bridgetown and Fort Linder from another attack no longer rested solely on Fieran's shoulders.

Dacha glanced up, meeting Fieran's gaze across the distance. After a low murmur to Uncle Julien, Dacha stepped away, the officers and enlisted men parting for him, giving the famed General Laesornysh space.

Fieran set his bowl aside, not caring if he dumped the soup onto the ground. He shoved to his feet, stumbling down the hill.

He met his Dacha halfway, skidding to a halt, the words already rising out of his choked throat. "I understand now, Dacha. I understand. All of it."

"Fieran, sason." Dacha reached out and clasped one of Fieran's shoulders. With his other hand, he cradled the back of Fieran's head before briefly resting his forehead against Fieran's.

That lump in Fieran's throat grew, and he didn't care who might be standing around witnessing this moment. While elves were not the most touchy-feely culturally, this particular gesture was one of the few more intimate ones, signifying a great relief and comradeship in the face of great tragedy or struggle.

The gesture lasted only a moment, before Dacha stepped back and dropped his hand to clasp Fieran's other shoulder. "Today you are Laesornysh."

As if Fieran needed anything else to shake him today. Dacha didn't merely mean Fieran had earned the legacy he'd inherited. He was naming Fieran with the elven title Laesornysh, giving it to him in his own right.

More than that, elvish was a subtle language, and Fieran could hear the slight change in inflection. While Dacha had been titled *Death* on the Wind because he moved like a whirlwind, tearing into all who stood before him, Fieran was Death *on the Wind*. He was literally a weapon of death carried on the winds.

All Fieran could do was nod, his chest too tight, his throat too strangled, for any other response.

"Come, sason." Dacha steered Fieran back up the hill, away from the clusters of generals talking of war and flyboys struggling for a wink of sleep before going back up on patrol.

Almost before he knew it, Fieran found himself sitting with his back against the outpost again, his dacha beside him. For long moments, they simply sat there in silence, regarding the destruction laid out before them.

After a moment, Dacha's gaze dropped to his hands, some of the hardness to his expression cracking. "It is all right to be strong, Fieran, but it is also all right to talk to someone. If you find yourself struggling after the past night, do not hesitate to reach out to someone. If not me or your macha, then there are counselors available. There is no shame in needing help."

"I know." Fieran shifted, not looking at his dacha. "I'm all right, Dacha."

Right now, he thought he was okay. He wasn't sure how he'd tell if he wasn't.

Strangely, the admonishment to talk just made him *not* want to do so. Even though this was his dacha. Even though Dacha would fully understand.

Fieran's gaze drifted from the blackened rubble to the shriveled remains of one of the airships crashed in the shallows of the Hydalla River, tatters of canvas rising and falling with the rippling eddies.

He'd been prepared to kill when he joined the army. He'd known war would entail death.

Yet even with Dacha's warning, he hadn't been prepared for killing on this scale. For the deep, shattering knowledge that he'd be asked to repeat such killing many more times before this war was over.

"I killed last night. Not just one person. Not just two. But whole airships full." Fieran gripped his knees, not daring to meet his dacha's gaze. Not because he feared he'd see disgust. No. It was the understanding he couldn't handle. "How many do you think I killed last night?"

"Sason." Dacha's voice remained low, dragging out the endearment on a sigh. "Do not go down that branch. It will shatter you under the weight. You are a warrior. Your duty will be death, no matter whether that death is dealt to a few or to many."

Fieran managed another nod, the reality of that sinking deep into his bones in a way he wouldn't have understood before.

"Fieran." Dacha's use of his name brought Fieran's head up. Dacha's gaze held that wealth of understanding, just as Fieran had feared. But there was also a hard layer of respect, the regard of one warrior to another instead of only father and son. "How many would have died in Bridgetown, Calafaren, and Fort Linder last night if you had not acted?"

That answer was easy. Too many. The Mongavarian airships wouldn't have stopped until they had run out of bombs. Without Fieran, there would have been nothing the Flying Corps training squadron could have done to dissuade them. The entire squadron might have been wiped out in the attempt.

"There were children, Dacha." The words came out a whisper past the squeezing in Fieran's throat, and he had to drop his gaze. "There were children in the rubble who were…that I…"

A tear trickled down Fieran's cheek, and he ruthlessly swiped it away. He hadn't cried all night, even when pulling little ones from the rubble.

Others had cried. Grown men who just sat right there in the rubble and sobbed.

Dacha rested a hand on Fieran's shoulder again. "This is why we fight. We are Laesornysh for them."

"Yes." Fieran took in the destroyed city before them, this time resolve hardening inside his chest, steadying him.

This was what he'd signed up for when he enlisted in the army. Not glory. Not legends. But to bring death to the enemy before that enemy brought death to others. It would mean killing. He would bear this burden so that others never had to.

Perhaps that was what he'd been struggling with this morning. Because he didn't regret what he'd done last night, despite the fact he'd killed hundreds of Mongavarian airmen. He couldn't regret it when he looked out over Bridgetown and saw what those same Mongavarian airmen had done to his home.

The only thing Fieran regretted about the previous night was that he hadn't been able to stop the destruction sooner and spare more of Bridgetown's people. The city had been hit harder by the bombing than the fort had been, thanks to Fieran's protection early in the night.

"How could Mongavaria do this?" Fieran clenched his fists, a heat rising in his chest to wipe away the pain of before. "I understand attacking Fort Linder. But Bridgetown? Calafaren? I know they are communications centers. I know they are a link between the Alliance Kingdoms. But it's still just...is this the kind of war Mongavaria intends to fight?"

"Sadly, yes. This city is a symbol." Dacha gestured at the rubble before them, his wave ending at the Alliance Bridge arching over the river. "Bridgetown and Calafaren were born out of the Alliance, and this attack was a strike at its heart. I —and your uncles—suspect the cities, and not Fort Linder, were the true targets of the attack all along."

That was both a relief and a blow. At least Fieran didn't have to harbor guilt that his actions in protecting Fort Linder had caused the Mongavarians to shift their attack to the cities. But it also meant that the attack had never been about crippling Escarland's ability to fight back in the sky. The bombing had been a message.

"Thus the choice in day as well as target." Dacha's tone turned even more weighty.

"The day?" Fieran blinked, his groggy mind unable to think of why this particular day would have any meaning.

Dacha's mouth tipped, though the expression was too grim to be called a smile. "It was seventy years ago today that your macha and I married, and the initial alliance was formed."

Oh. Fieran had forgotten that today was Alliance Day, a

national holiday in all three kingdoms and his parents' anniversary. Today didn't feel much like a holiday.

He opened his mouth, but the words stuck in his throat. It didn't seem right to say happy anything on a day like this. Instead, he managed a croaked, "I'm sorry."

And he meant it. Dacha and Mama should have been celebrating this day, taking Tryndar to the parade in Aldon or quietly relaxing at Treehaven.

Instead, Dacha was here in a destroyed city, carrying his swords and dressed for war, while Mama remained behind in Aldon preparing for that same war.

Dacha just shrugged wearily, staring at the city and the arching bridge beyond. "Seventy years ago, our marriage stopped a war before it had begun. Today, our anniversary starts one."

Fieran had no words for that. Despite the pall of the day, he couldn't let the grimness linger so darkly. "It was just the Mongavarians' bad luck that I happened to be at Fort Linder when they attacked."

"Yes. It seems they were given some bad information when it came to the whereabouts of certain important people." Dacha shook his head, a note to his tone indicating that there was something to those words. "They had intended to assassinate your uncles Averett and Weylind last night as well, but your uncle Edmund thwarted both of those attacks."

Fieran straightened, a chill stabbing through him. "Was anyone hurt?"

"No. The assassins did not come anywhere close." Dacha waved the words away, as if attempted assassinations weren't a big deal. "I do not wish to worry you but to warn you. After what you did here, you will have an even larger target on your back. The Mongavarians know they cannot kill either of us in a simple assassination attempt, but they might grow desperate enough to try."

"I'll be wary." Fieran resisted a shiver. He'd been shot at last night for the first time, but he'd never been in that much danger. His magic was too strong. But someone lying in wait for him was another thing entirely.

Dacha nodded, as if satisfied his warning had been effectively passed along. After a moment, he breathed a soft, weary sigh of his own, a sadness dragging at his otherwise hard expression. His gaze dropped to his hands where a few bolts of his magic appeared, crackling blue in the sunlight. "I did my best to raise you and your siblings to see the possibilities and uses for our magic beyond killing. But I fear, in the end, that war will always remain the primary use of the magic of the ancient kings. That is a burden but perhaps not the thing to be scorned I once thought it to be. Yes, it means killing and death. It can be twisted for empire and greed. But the true purpose of the magic of the ancient kings is protection."

Fieran let a whisper of his own magic twine over his fingers. "Right now, our kingdoms and people need protectors."

If it took every spark of magic Fieran possessed in his whole body, he would make sure no other city suffered the way Bridgetown had suffered the previous night.

Forget whatever foolish ideas of glory and making his own legends he'd entertained before. This was his new mission. Protect Escarland, Tarenhiel, and Kostaria so that no more tragedies like this happened ever again.

He could see his resolve mirrored in his dacha's gaze. Protecting the Alliance Kingdoms wasn't a duty that rested on Fieran's shoulders alone. Dacha, Mama, Adry, and Louise would all do their part in this war.

Dacha gave him a slight nod. "I am proud of you, sason."

"Linshi, Dacha." Great. Now Fieran's throat was closing again.

For a few more minutes, they sat in silence, and Fieran wouldn't have wanted it any other way as he soaked up the comfort of having his dacha at his side in this moment, the darkest morning he'd ever experienced.

Then two figures strode up the hill toward them. One was Merrik with his short chestnut hair looking more red in the morning light and grime smeared over his uniform.

But the other…

Fieran jumped to his feet. "Adry?"

He hadn't thought he'd spoken that loudly, but his sister's head snapped up. She smiled, then broke into a run up the hill. Her hair—a red-blonde that was lighter than Fieran's hair but darker than Dacha's—whipped behind her.

Fieran jogged to join her, though he had to skid to a halt as she flung herself at him in a hug that was nearly a tackle. Not that he minded. He hugged her right back.

"Fieran!" Adry's hug was so tight it nearly hurt. "I'm so glad you're all right." She pulled back, her smile fading as she glanced from him to the destruction. "This is…really bad."

"Yes." Fieran couldn't bring himself to follow her gaze to take in the city yet again. There were a lot of words both of them could use. Terrible. Awful. Tragic. But somehow that simple *bad* seemed the most fitting. In the end, there were no words that could capture what he had witnessed that night. Instead, he kept his focus on Adry. "What are you doing here?"

It seemed strange that Dacha would take Adry along when traveling to something like this. Dacha was protective of all his children, but especially of his daughters.

"I'm on my way to join the Tarenhieli Army Reserves." Adry clenched her fists, her jaw tightening in that mulish way Fieran recognized even as her green eyes flashed. "I might be a girl, but I can't sit on the sidelines any longer. Not after something like this. Escarland might not allow women to join their army, but Tarenhiel does."

"I'm sure Mama and Dacha weren't too happy with that." Fieran glanced over his shoulder.

Uncle Iyrinder had appeared from the crowd—of course he would have come with Dacha, loyal friend and guard that he was—and he and Merrik now talked.

Dacha remained alone, leaning against the Outpost Museum. He'd closed his eyes, and if Fieran's guess was correct, he was likely communicating with Mama through the heart bond as best they could as they could only share emotions and impressions, not words.

"They weren't. But they couldn't really argue that all of us will be needed." Adry sighed and grimaced. "They kind of got their way in the end. I wanted to join Tarenhiel's regular army, but Uncle Weylind wants me in the Reserves so I'll be stationed in Estyra. After this attack, I understand why one of us needs to be in Estyra to make sure it won't be bombed the way Bridgetown was. But it's still frustrating."

Fieran opened his mouth, but his words caught. Before yesterday, he would have told his sister he was sorry that she was being held back like that. But now, all he could feel was relief that she wouldn't be put on the frontlines alongside him and Dacha. Finally, he cleared his throat, settling on, "You've been thinking about this for a long time."

"I have." Adry swung her clenched fists, not looking at Fieran. "But I couldn't do it too soon after you left, and I didn't want to disappoint them, you know?"

"Yeah." Fieran flicked a glance over his shoulder again to

where Dacha was still sitting. Perhaps that was the burden of having a good relationship with parents instead of a bad one. The fear of disappointing them had a different taste, a different hold, when that fear came out of love instead of terror.

"But there's no choice now. Not after this." Adry waved at the rubble in the streets down the hill. "I'm needed in Estyra."

"I can't imagine something like this happening there." Fieran didn't want to imagine the great oak Ellonahshinel reduced to splintered limbs and burning, blackened branches.

He hadn't crossed the Alliance Bridge to see the destruction in Calafaren, but Merrik had come back with that grim, mourning look elves got when trees were hurting. From what Fieran had gathered, Calafaren hadn't been hit as hard as Bridgetown. Smaller and tucked in the trees as it was, Calafaren wasn't as big a target as the sprawling, well-lit city on the southern side of the Hydalla River. But Calafaren had still suffered, especially from the fires that had spread from the few bombs that had fallen on the elven city.

"Mama is going to stay in Aldon for the time being and protect the city. Louise will stay there, too, to fill the magical power cells." Adry gave a little shrug. "And, of course, cousin Rhohen will keep Osmana safe. He wouldn't exactly take it kindly if we offered any help."

"No, he wouldn't." That brought a huff of a chuckle, something Fieran hadn't thought he'd be capable of that morning.

His cousin Rhohen was the half-troll, half-elf son of King Rharreth and Queen Melantha of Kostaria. Even though he was only eight months younger than Fieran, the two of them had gotten along about as well as a perpetually grumpy cat and a far-too-friendly dog, especially once Rhohen came into his magic, a rather rare mix of ice magic and the magic of the ancient kings. Rhohen would clench his fists and threaten to fight someone if any of them implied he needed help protecting Kostaria's capital.

Adry hugged her arms to her stomach, any trace of humor fading from her voice. "We won't be all together until after this war ends, most likely. You left first, and now I'll be in Estyra. Dacha is headed for Fort Defense at the border."

"At least Mama, Louise, Ellie, and Tryndar will be together." Fieran had to cling to that, even as his family scattered in a way it never had before.

Yes, he and Adry had traveled independently between Escarland and Tarenhiel more and more often in the past decade or two. He'd stayed behind in Aldon many times while the rest of his family traveled to Estyra.

But that separation only lasted a month or two at the most, and none of them had been heading into war. They'd still had plenty of family dinners, all gathered around the dinner table, chattering and laughing so boisterously that Dacha needed earplugs to keep from being overwhelmed.

Those family dinners wouldn't happen again until the war was over. They might never be the same again if something happened to Dacha or Fieran or Adry during this war. As the Mongavarians had proved with this new warfare of bombs and flight, no one was truly safe. Mama and the younger siblings would all be in danger in Aldon. Both from bombs and perhaps even assassins, if the Mongavarians decided to target the main source of Escarland's power to fuel aeroplanes, airships, and their entire infrastructure.

"Yes." Adry sighed and dropped her hands back to her sides. "Mama will keep them safe."

"And we'll have to keep ourselves safe." Fieran tipped

his head in Dacha's direction. "We have Dacha's training. We'll be all right."

He had to believe that. They had been born with the magic of the ancient kings. This war had always been theirs to fight.

TWENTY-FIVE

Fieran stood at attention in line with what remained of his squadron at the edge of the main parade ground of Fort Linder, facing the three flagpoles, the flags flapping at half-staff.

All around the parade ground, the various units stationed at Fort Linder also stood at attention, all wearing grim expressions.

Before the infirmary, all the off-duty nurses, secretaries, and other civilian personnel of the base assembled. Pip and the other mechanics stood there, but for once Fieran didn't smile when his gaze briefly met Pip's. She didn't either.

The general in charge of Fort Linder halted beneath the flagpole bearing Escarland's flag, Capt. Arfeld and the other officers beside him. The general unfolded a piece of paper and cleared his throat. "By order of His Majesty King Averett, the following is to be read throughout Escarland. Last night, the Mongavarian Empire executed a cowardly and shameful attack on Fort Linder, Bridgetown, and Calafaren. Many Escarlish and Tarenhieli lives were lost in this sudden and unprovoked attack on our soil."

Standing at attention as he was, Fieran couldn't look around. But he didn't have to sweep a glance over his column to feel all the holes of those missing in the formation.

Beside him, Lije shifted and swallowed. A small, strangled cough came from someone behind them.

"It was only due to the actions of a squadron of Flying Corps pilots-in-training that the attack was halted and all Mongavarian airships were destroyed."

At least Uncle Averett didn't point out Fieran by name. He'd rather the credit be given to the entire squadron. The others had been far more brave than he'd been, hurling themselves at the airships with nothing but miscellaneous weapons and flimsy wood fuselages for protection.

"It is evident by this attack that a state of war now exists between the Mongavarian Empire and the Alliance Kingdoms of Escarland, Tarenhiel, and Kostaria. This morning, His Majesty requested a declaration of war from Parliament, which Parliament unanimously ratified and His Majesty duly signed. Their Majesties King Weylind of Tarenhiel and King Rharreth of Kostaria have issued their own declarations of war against the Empire of Mongavaria on behalf of their kingdoms. As of 14:30 today, we are at war."

The words weren't a surprise, yet Fieran struggled to breathe.

Yet there was also a strange relief that the war was finally here. The pressure of this looming war had been hanging over the Alliance Kingdoms for so many years, weighing especially heavy in the past year and months. At last, they could fight this war rather than living under the ongoing, agonizing trepidation.

Capt. Arfeld stepped forward. "Training Squadron, as of last night, your training is complete."

Fieran's ears buzzed as the others shifted around him. By rights, they should have had another two weeks of training.

But it seemed, now that the Alliance Kingdoms were officially at war, the army was eager to hurry them on their way to make room for the next batch of pilots-in-training.

One by one, Capt. Arfeld called each of them forward and pinned a badge formed of two eagle wings rising out of a shield in the center to their uniforms.

When Fieran's name was called, he stepped forward, his ears still ringing a bit. Yet he stood tall as he faced his commanding officer.

Capt. Arfeld pinned the badge to his uniform and stated, "I commission you Second Lieutenant Fieran Laesornysh in the Escarlish Flying Corps." His voice lowered so only Fieran could hear. "See me after dismissal."

Fieran spun on his heel, then marched back to his place in line. After the darkness of the night, there was something healing in watching Merrik, Lije, Pretty Face, Tiny, Stickyfingers, and the others of the squadron step forward and receive their wings.

As the last of them received their wings and commissions, all the sergeants, corporals, and privates assembled around the square lifted their hands in salutes.

Fieran had to swallow back the lump in his throat at seeing those drill sergeants—the ones who had harassed and harried them all through training—now saluting them with a glimmer almost like respect in their eyes.

After all the weeks of training—the crashes, the losses, the attack during the night—they were now officially pilots.

Fieran knocked on the door to Capt. Arfeld's office and stepped inside when called. He halted before the desk and saluted. "Second Lieutenant Laesornysh reporting as requested, sir."

Capt. Arfeld saluted in return, leaned back in his chair, and regarded Fieran for a long moment before he heaved something like a sigh. "What am I to do with you, Lt. Laesornysh?"

"Sir?" Fieran's stomach twisted. This almost sounded like a lecture would be forthcoming. Or like his famous family was getting involved in some way.

"The night of the attack, you didn't wait for your sergeant's orders. You gave commands when you had no authority to do so. You presumed to tell your commanding officer what he should do. You landed on the Alliance Bridge at great risk to yourself, your aeroplane, your fellow pilot who was crazy enough to follow you, and a rather culturally significant national monument. And..." Capt. Arfeld's weathered face showed no hint of the softening or uncertainty he'd worn during the attack.

Fieran braced himself for whatever the captain would say next, somehow unable to regret what he'd done, even if the litany of his offenses the night before sounded quite insubordinate when put that way.

Had he gained his wings only to promptly lose them? Surely what he'd done wasn't enough to get him dishonorably discharged from the army, especially not with the added protection of his name and relatives, much as he hated to rely on those things.

"And...you saved us all last night." Capt. Arfeld gestured at the chair across the desk from him, next to where Fieran was standing. "Take a seat."

Fieran sat, though he kept his back straight with military

posture instead of relaxing. So...was he being reprimanded? Or commended? He still couldn't quite read the captain's tone or expression. It took everything in him not to bounce his knees.

"In my years as a pilot, I have lost many friends and rivals, all of them my brothers and sisters in innovation. I've known many a good and experienced pilot who has panicked or grown disorientated or made a mistake that led to a crash." Capt. Arfeld's voice lowered. "Last night, I had to order a squadron of inexperienced pilots into battle at night, knowing many of them would panic. Many would crash because of their own mistakes rather than anything the enemy had done."

Perhaps this was where Capt. Arfeld's lack of a military background showed through. He was speaking to Fieran as a fellow pilot and a mentor rather than maintaining military distinctions in rank.

Capt. Arfeld's gaze sharpened. "And one of those inexperienced pilots had magic capable of wiping out not only his entire squadron but also the fort and the cities we were trying to protect, if he should panic in the face of unprecedented war."

Fieran shifted in his seat, unable to maintain his discipline with the weight of those words settling on his shoulders. Sure, he hadn't panicked, but Capt. Arfeld hadn't known how Fieran would react once he took to the sky.

"And yet that same pilot was our only hope of actually fighting back, and all I could do was hope that the training I'd witnessed at Fort Charibert and the lack of panic he showed in defending the fort during the early moments of the attack would hold once he was in the air." Capt. Arfeld's eyes grew distant, almost as if he'd forgotten Fieran was even there. "Worse, I had no experience to lead my men or give them the orders they would need to fight effectively. Before last night, no one had ever fought a battle in the air. There is no training, no textbook, no experience that any of us could bring to that fight."

For the first time, war had taken to the skies. Despite all of Uncle Julien's planning for a war that would likely be fought in the air, given the barrier of the Wall, there had been no way to truly prepare for what fighting in the air would be like.

Despite spending seventy years anticipating this war, in many ways Escarland had still been woefully unprepared, complacent with the safety provided by the Wall.

Especially since many military leaders had gotten so much wrong. They'd assumed the war in the air would be fought by the behemoth airships duking it out in the same manner as the ships on the seas. Flyers were considered only useful for scouting, so no one had put much effort into trying to arm them or make them capable of fighting.

Hopefully military command would take note and put more effort into the aeroplanes. Though knowing the army as Fieran did now, last night's battle would likely convince the leaders more than ever that flyers were incapable of standing up to airships and should remain relegated to scouting and surveillance.

Capt. Arfeld met Fieran's gaze again. "You have great potential, Lt. Laesornysh, even beyond your magic. You have a natural talent for flying, and you have the charisma needed to become a leader. Already last night, your squadron rallied behind you. You have that extra spark that makes people look to you to lead them."

Fieran sat even straighter. Praise, not PT. He wasn't sure how to react to that.

"I tell you this not to make you cocky but to caution

you." Capt. Arfeld's eyes sharpened further. "With that great potential comes a great potential for disaster. If you grow too arrogant, you will flame out in a cataclysmic mistake, leading all those who follow you into catastrophe."

Fieran dropped his gaze. The losses of last night already weighed heavily on him, and he hadn't been the one giving orders—at least, not most of them. "I understand, sir."

"No, you don't. Not yet." Capt. Arfeld's voice roughened, the weight of his gaze falling away from Fieran. "Even without overconfidence, catastrophes can still happen despite your best efforts. There will be times in command when you will have to order your men to their deaths."

Like last night. The memories hung heavy between them.

"I will remain here to continue training pilots. But you and others like you will be the ones who will develop the strategies that will eventually make it into the textbooks. You will surpass me. I only hope you live long enough to see it."

Fieran swallowed. Was this supposed to be a pep talk or a warning? It seemed to be a bit of both. "Yes, sir. Thank you, sir."

"For that reason, I'm promoting you to First Lieutenant." Capt. Arfeld pushed a stack of paperwork across the desk toward Fieran.

The words swam, but Fieran's name jumped out, typed in black ink. Promoted, and he'd only been commissioned for all of twenty minutes. That had to be some kind of record.

"You earned it. You proved you are capable of keeping your head during battle and not wiping out your own men with your magic." Capt. Arfeld sighed and scrubbed a hand over the bristles of scruff on his chin. "If you were anyone but who you are, I'd likely be under great pressure to submit your name for a medal. As it is, everyone from Bridgetown's mayor to the Escarlish palace's press office want to celebrate you with parades and war propaganda tours."

All Fieran wanted to do was fly. If he'd wanted to glad-hand and schmooze people, he could have done that as a prince. No joining the army necessary. "With all due respect, sir, please tell me you've refused their requests."

"I have, as has everyone in the chain of command. You're the best weapon we have in the air. The last thing we need is for you to be sidelined on some propaganda parade." Capt. Arfeld shook his head, then sighed. "But as it is, there are some who will still think this promotion is because of your name and your connections rather than something you earned."

"I understand, sir." Fieran sighed, understanding all too well.

A promotion was more than enough. He didn't need—or want—a medal or parades or celebrations for what he'd done last night. It had simply been duty, and he needed no reward for that.

FIERAN STOOD with his back to the warmed metal side of the hangar, staring at the airfield and the distant smudge that was Bridgetown. Even now a full day and a night after the attack, the taste of ash drifted on the breeze, though smoke no longer rose above the city.

A few tiny blue flowers dotted the new spring grass beneath his boots, a splash of life and cheer amid the bustle of war going on in the hangar behind him.

Soft bootsteps padded on the earth a moment before Merrik joined him, staring over the sunny, grassy field before them. After a long moment, he spoke, his tone so low no one standing near the hangar's door would overhear. "Do you regret it?"

With the long years of friendship stretching between them, Fieran didn't have to ask to know what Merrik meant. He wasn't asking about the events of the attack, or not only about that. But about flying and the army and everything that had happened in the past months since that day Fieran had dragged Merrik away from breakfast, filled to the brim with dreams of the sky.

"No, I don't." Fieran turned to better face Merrik, though Merrik's gaze remained fixed on some distant point on the horizon. "Do you?"

Merrik remained as he was for a long, aching moment before he shook his head. "No."

Fieran released a breath, trying to force out the words he should have said long before now. "Thank you for always guarding my back. Even now."

Merrik made a weary, scoffing noise, even as he shook his head. "Little good that I did. Your back does not need much protecting when you unleash your magic."

"Still, I was glad to have you there regardless." After the attack and the squadron mates they'd lost, Fieran didn't want to take that for granted again.

Merrik just tipped his head in that subtle elven nod before the two of them returned to soaking in the warm rays of the morning sunlight, gathering a last few minutes of peace before they were launched back into a war.

Their new orders had come through first thing that morning. They'd be leaving in a few hours, headed north for Dar Goranth and the icy waters off the coast of Kostaria.

Their destination hadn't been much of a surprise. With Mama at Aldon, Adry at Estyra, and Dacha at Fort Defense, that had left Dar Goranth as the one likely Mongavarian target still undefended by a warrior with the magic of the ancient kings—unless one wanted to count Rhohen, and Fieran wasn't sure his troll cousin would appreciate the way the military leaders were counting him out.

Pip stepped from the hangar, her green coveralls rolled up at the ends of the pant legs to make them short enough and her brown curls stuffed into some kind of messy bun at the top of her head. She glanced around, and Fieran lifted a hand in a small wave to catch her attention.

As her gaze swiveled in his direction, she smiled, and the expression twisted in the pit of his stomach. Something had changed between them in those nightmarish moments standing in the ruined streets of Bridgetown, just holding each other amid a shattered world, although Fieran couldn't have said exactly what it was just yet.

Pip strode over to join him and Merrik in the patch of warm, spring sunshine, claiming the spot on Fieran's other side from Merrik. She reached over and tapped the silver wings pinned to his uniform. "These look good on you."

"Linshi." Fieran glanced first at the wings, then at her. After everything that had happened, he craved levity more than more mourning, especially if they'd be parting in a few hours. His breath hitched at the thought of never seeing her again. Swallowing, he plastered on a grin. "My dacha was in Bridgetown. I thought about waking you to introduce you but…"

As he'd known it would, her face washed pale, her eyes widening, her mouth falling open in hero-struck terror. Her voice squeaked. "It's…okay."

Merrik snorted softly, easing slightly farther away from Pip and Fieran.

"Maybe a different time." Fieran rolled his shoulders in a shrug. He wasn't sure when he'd started to find Pip's hero worship of his dacha humorous rather than embarrassing. He gave her shoulder a gentle poke. "Breathe. My dacha isn't here now."

Pip released a breath in a whoosh, all but slumping against the metal siding behind them. "Fine, fine. Just...give me a warning first, all right? No just showing up with your dacha in tow or shaking me awake and he's just right there. I'm not sure I'd survive."

Fieran chuckled, though his laughter lasted only a moment before the weight in his chest squashed it. "I don't know when I'll have the chance. My squadron is being sent to Dar Goranth."

Pip straightened, a smile brightening her face. "I'm being sent there too."

"Oh. Good. That's...really good." Fieran reached to pat her shoulder, then halted short of touching her. He dropped his hand, clenching it into a fist at his side instead. "Someone in the army must have noticed that we make a good team."

It wasn't exactly what he wanted to say, though what he wanted to say was eluding him at the moment, so it would have to do.

"That we do." Pip grinned, tipping her head back to look up at him. The warmth in her eyes kindled that inexpressible *something* inside his chest.

With a loud tromping of boots and the bang of his shoulder hitting the metal siding, Pretty Face leaned against the hangar next to Pip, though he didn't crowd her. He grinned, the expression pulling tight the new scar tracing across his jaw. "Did you hear that we're being shipped out?"

"Yes. I'm shipping out with you." Pip lightly punched his shoulder in the way she did when she was trying to pretend she was just one of the guys. "You boys aren't getting rid of me that easily."

Pretty Face waved to Tiny and Stickyfingers, who were walking toward them. "Guess what? Our Pip is coming with us to Dar Goranth."

"Yes!" Stickyfingers pumped his fist while Tiny gave Pip a nod.

Lije poked his head around the door of the hangar. "What's going on out here?"

"Pip is coming with us to Dar Goranth." Stickyfingers gestured to her, his gap-toothed grin wide.

"That's great!" Lije stepped forward and held out a hand for her to slap.

Fieran settled more comfortably against the warm metal siding at his back, crossing one leg over the other at the ankles. So much for his quiet moment with Merrik and Pip.

But that was all right. He'd started this adventure with just Merrik at his side, but it felt right to have all of them together for whatever came next.

FREE EBOOK!

Thanks so much for reading *Wings of War!* I hope this beginning of Fieran's story (little danger child that he is) brought a few laughs. If you loved the book, please consider leaving a review on Amazon or Goodreads. Reviews help your fellow readers find books that they will love.

A downloadable map and Fieran's family trees are available on the Extras page of my website.

If you ever find typos in my books, feel free to message me on social media or send me an email through the Contact Me page of my website.

If you want to learn about all my upcoming releases, get great book recommendations, and see a behind-the-scenes glimpse into the writing process, follow my blog at www.taragrayce.com.

Did you know that if you sign up for my newsletter, you'll receive lots of free goodies? You will receive the free novella *Steal a Swordmaiden's Heart*, which is set in the same world as *Stolen Midsummer Bride* and *Bluebeard and the Outlaw*! This novella is a prequel to *Stolen Midsummer Bride*, and tells the story of how King Theseus of the Court of Knowledge won the hand of Hippolyta, Queen of the Swordmaidens.

If you don't wish to sign up for my newsletter, *Steal a Swordmaiden's Heart* is available on Amazon, though it isn't in KU like the rest of the series.

You will also receive the free novella *Torn Curtains*, a fantasy Regency Beauty and the Beast retelling. This one isn't available anywhere else besides my newsletter!

Sign up for my newsletter now

DON'T MISS THE NEXT ADVENTURE!

STALK THE SKY

In a war fought high in the sky over the northern seas, one half-elf defends his legendary legacy.

With the Alliance Kingdoms and the Empire of Mongavaria now at war, half-elf Fieran Laesornysh has been sent to the naval base of Dar Goranth with one mission: protect the strategically important base from attack.

But when he arrives, he discovers there are no aeroplanes for his men, they have been assigned to a squadron of elves, and the elven commander resents Fieran for his lineage. Defending Dar Goranth will be a little difficult if he can't even get off the ground.

With his motley crew of squadron mates at his back and the half-dwarf female mechanic Pip at his side, Fieran must navigate the challenges of his first command and the war both in the sky and within his own squadron.

Stalk the Sky is book 2 in the *War of the Alliance* series, a humorous steampunk fantasy series filled with magical gadgets, elven warriors, and a hint of no-spice romance perfect for fans of Lindsay Buroker and K.M. Shea.

Find the book on Amazon today!

DON'T MISS THE SERIES THAT STARTED IT ALL!

FIERCE HEART

Essie would do anything for her kingdom...even marry an elf prince she just met that morning.

The human kingdom of Escarland and the elven kingdom of Tarenhiel have existed in an uneasy peace after their last wars ended with both kings dead. As tensions rise once again, desperate diplomacy might be the only way to avert war. If only negotiations between elves and humans were that simple.

When a diplomatic meeting goes horribly wrong, Essie, a human princess, finds herself married to the elf prince and warrior Laesornysh. Fitting in to the serene, quiet elf culture might be a little difficult for this talkative princess, but she's determined to make it work.

With impending war and tenuous alliances, it will be up to Essie to unite her two peoples. And maybe get her hands on elven conditioner while she's at it.

Find the Book on Amazon Today!

ALSO BY TARA GRACE

World of Elven Alliance / Alliance Kingdoms

ELVEN ALLIANCE

Fierce Heart

War Bound

Death Wind

Troll Queen

Pretense

Shield Band

Elf Prince

Heart Bond

Elf King

WAR OF THE ALLIANCE

Wings of War

Stalk the Sky

Fly to Fury

Tales of the Fae Realm

COURT OF MIDSUMMER MAYHEM

Stolen Midsummer Bride

Steal a Swordmaiden's Heart

Forest of Scarlet

Wild Fae Primrose

Night of Secrets

A VILLAIN'S EVER AFTER

Bluebeard and the Outlaw

SACRIFICED HEARTS

Mountain of Dragons and Sacrifice

Middle Grade

PRINCESS BY NIGHT

Lost in Averell

ACKNOWLEDGMENTS

Thank you to everyone who picked up this book, whether you are picking up one of my books for the first time or you grabbed this book because you had to know what crazy stuff Farrendel and Essie's children would get up to. Either way, I hope this book didn't disappoint!

A very special BIG thank you to my brother Andy. Thank you first of all for your service. Second, thank you for your service in reading through this book as I wrote it to check my military stuff to make sure it was as accurate as it could be (given this is a steampunk fantasy not set at all in our world). Any mistakes still left are fully mine or are changes I made to fit the world building. Third, thank you for the use of some of your basic training stories here, especially the PT in soap suds story.

Thank you, as always, to my parents who are always so supportive and excited for each of my books! Thank you to my other brothers Ethan and Josh: if readers love how I write brothers in my books, it is because of you three. For my sisters-in-law for everything from book chats to painting days to trips to the zoo to thrift store finds.

A special thank you to my nephew Elijah for loving the book (and loving having a character named after him!) For my nephew Danny: I hope you love the books just as much once you read them! For my nieces Adry and Louise: I hope both of you enjoy seeing your names in a book someday!

Thank you to my friends Bri, Paula, and Jill for all the

encouragement, support, and years of laughter. For my author friends, but especially Molly, Morgan, Addy, Savannah, Hannah, and Sierra. I wouldn't have dared tackle writing Elven Alliance: The Next Generation without your belief that I truly could pull this off!

Thank you once again to Deborah for a copy edit that was as filled with fangirling as it was with edits. Those copy edits always make my day!

www.ingramcontent.com/pod-product-compliance
Lightning Source LLC
Chambersburg PA
CBHW070435170726
48291CB00002B/516